TOYS OF TERROR

Annabelle

She felt scared, icy little rivers running up and down her back, and she remained standing by the chair, looking at the tall papa doll. He was dressed all in black, and he stood with his arms down at his sides, and his face frozen in white, his eyes painted on, and a fine, black mustache painted above the pink, round lips.

She remembered well what Mrs. Archer had said about dolls' not being real, but this doll, standing in front of her, was different. He was real.

He thought she was someone named Annabelle.

There was a movement in the doll house, a sliding of feet, a thump as the mama doll almost fell from the floor of the doll house to the bedroom floor.

Now there were two of them, facing her, standing between her and the door.

There was something about them that she didn't like. The fingers were too long and too pointed. Too sharp.

And they were closing in on her. . . .

TALES OF TERROR AND POSSESSION

MAMA (1247, $3.50)
by Ruby Jean Jensen
Once upon a time there lived a sweet little dolly, but her one beaded glass eye gleamed with mischief and evil. If Dorrie could have read her dolly's thoughts, she would have run for her life — for her dear little dolly only had killing on her mind.

JACK-IN-THE-BOX (1892, $3.95)
by William W. Johnstone
Any other little girl would have cringed in horror at the sight of the clown with the insane eyes. But as Nora's wide eyes mirrored the grotesque wooden face her pink lips were curving into the same malicious smile.

ROCKABYE BABY (1470, $3.50)
by Stephen Gresham
Mr. Macready — such a nice old man — knew all about the children of Granite Heights: their names, houses, even the nights their parents were away. And when he put on his white nurse's uniform and smeared his lips with blood-red lipstick, they were happy to let him through the door — although they always stared a bit at his clear plastic gloves.

TWICE BLESSED (1766, $3.75)
by Patricia Wallace
Side by side, isolated from human contact, Kerri and Galen thrived. Soon their innocent eyes became twin mirrors of evil. And their souls became one — in their dark powers of destruction and death . . .

HOME SWEET HOME (1571, $3.50)
by Ruby Jean Jensen
Two weeks in the mountains would be the perfect vacation for a little boy. But Timmy didn't think so. The other children stared at him with a terror all their own, until Timmy realized there was no escaping the deadly welcome of . . . *Home Sweet Home.*

ANNABELLE

RUBY JEAN JENSEN

ZEBRA BOOKS
KENSINGTON PUBLISHING CORP.

ZEBRA BOOKS

are published by

Kensington Publishing Corp.
475 Park Avenue South
New York, NY 10016

First printing: March 1987

Printed in the United States of America

ANNABELLE

Prologue

Annabelle lived in dread of the days when business took Papa away from home, as it had now. She sought the sanctuary of her large doll house, and lost herself in her doll family, but sometimes a cry from another part of the big house reminded her that she, like her doll, Vesta, also had a brother and a baby sister.

Annabelle's papa had built the doll house especially for her, perhaps because he knew she would need it for refuge from her mother's explosive anger. It was tucked into the corner of her bedroom, a doll house of four rooms, two above and two below, large rooms in which her family of dolls lived comfortably. Only the papa doll, who wore a topcoat and spats like her papa, and of course a stovepipe hat, was too tall to stand up in the house. But when he came in it was his right to sit in his chair by the fireplace and rest, while in this house his wife, the mama of the children, made good things in the kitchen for them all to eat.

Upstairs in the children's bedroom the baby slept in its crib, and the other two children played at the mama's feet in the kitchen. Oh, but it was a happy home, and the ceilings of the lower floor of the doll house were high enough that Annabelle could sit there herself. Of course, she had to move furniture a bit, but the papa didn't mind. He loved her. But most of all the mama loved her. And her brother and sister loved her. Their names were Victor and Vesta, named by Annabelle, the prettiest names she could think of. They might have been twins, because they were of a similar size. Only the clothing they wore, and the length of their hair, separated them in identity, for each of them had fine china faces, with pink cheeks and rosebud lips. They loved Annabelle and accepted her as their sister, and the papa loved her too, and the mama, of course.

On his last trip, her real papa had brought her a beautiful new doll, as tall as Annabelle herself. Too tall for the doll house. Annabelle, unable to find a place for her in the doll family, stood her in the corner between the doll house and the bedroom wall. She, unnamed, was going to be the beautiful visitor. Later, when Annabelle thought of a name suitable for her. She was a very alert, very intelligent doll who was appalled at the crying that came from downstairs. She returned Annabelle's gaze in silence and dignity and with a growing horror in her blue eyes.

In real life, only papa loved her. Mama was . . . well . . . as Papa had said once, "not well."

The cry became a scream that Annabelle could no longer pretend did not exist. It rose from somewhere below, penetrating walls and floors to reach Annabelle at the rear of the second floor. It was her brother, Zachary. There was a hoarseness in his scream, as if he had been crying for a long, long time. The scream was worse than any she had heard before, and she shrank from it and tried harder to pretend it wasn't happening. Their mama often beat Zachary.

8

Annabelle had tried to tell him to keep away, to go outside and play when Papa was gone, but though Zachary was two years older than herself, almost ten years old even, he seemed unable to remember her warning. Sometimes their mama was nice and loving and Zachary enjoyed her hugs so much that he forgot. But now Papa was gone, and Mama had sent the servants away, and Annabelle knew by the look on her face, the set of her mouth and the madness in her eyes, that it was going to be a bad time. And so she went immediately to her bedroom and her doll house as soon as she could be excused from the breakfast table. But Zachary had stayed downstairs, as if he were too charmed by his mother's last hug to see what was in her face today. Oh, Zachary, Zachary, don't scream so loud.

And now the baby, in her crib in the nursery, was adding her cry, and the sounds gathered, and amidst it all came another cry, almost a scream, but this of terrible anger from their mother. The sounds intensified as they came up the stairs, and there too was a terrible bump, bump, as Zachary was being dragged upward from step to step, and then a sliding as they went down the hall to the nursery.

Stop crying, baby sister, stop. Quickly, stop. Before she reaches you.

The mother's scream of anger continued and grew louder as the baby's crying changed from fear to helpless terror. Then there was a loud thump against the floor, a cracking sound that made the floor beneath Annabelle tremble, and abruptly the crying baby was stilled. Only the screams of Zachary continued, and even those ceased suddenly a moment later.

A deadly silence prevailed. Annabelle's ears rang with it. Echoes of the screams of her real-life brother and sister died away.

Annabelle crept quietly into the doll house and huddled back in the corner. "Papa," she whispered, pleading to become one of them. "Mama?" She reached through the doorway into the kitchen to pull the large mama doll toward her, seeking the protection it gave, but her hand grew still on the arm of the doll.

Footsteps were coming down the hall, and sounds of a long skirt sweeping the oak floor.

"Annabelle. Annabelle answer me!"

"Papa," Annabelle whispered, "you'll be sitting by the fire, while Mama is in the kitchen baking sweet potatoes and making cornmeal pudding, and when the witch knocks on the front door you will take your walking stick and go to—"

The footsteps, growing faster and faster, had entered the bedroom, and the maddened voice was calling, "Annabelle, you have hidden from me for the last time! Come out, come out of there!"

The hand reached in to get her, and Annabelle realized there was no door closed against her because there was no front on the house at all. She began to scream in fear, as the baby had, and then in pain as the hand, covered in blood, reached her, tangled in her long hair, and began to pull her from the doll house.

"Papa! Papa!"

Behind her the papa doll stared straight ahead, toward the woman and the little girl.

CHAPTER ONE

Jessica had lived across the meadow from the old abandoned stone mansion all her life, but she was five years old before she actually noticed it, hidden as it was in the midst of its own tangle of woods and vines and encroaching swamp. As if suddenly on this day of her unhappiness it showed itself to her, it was there, one of its towers rising above the trees.

Jessica had been huddling at the corner of the duck pond, a small pool of water located near the pine grove in the back yard. Her hands covered her ears, but still she could hear the voices of her parents. They were mad at each other again, and Jessica had run out of the big house and hidden and they hadn't noticed.

She looked up, tears blurring all that she saw, the shrubs behind the pines, the wire links of the six-foot-high fence that protected the back yard. A couple of cows in the meadow beyond the fence blurred into dark blobs. But suddenly she was noticing something, and as she stared her vision cleared.

There was a castle in the woods on the far side of the meadow. She could see a round room with a caplike roof sticking up almost as high as the tallest tree. She got to her feet, went to the fence, and with her fingers hooked in the links, looked at the house, straining to see through the trees, vines and bushes that surrounded it.

When had the castle come? Had the elves and the fairies built it in the night? Was it a castle built for her? Was there someone living in it who wanted to be with her? It called to her and helped her forget that her mother and daddy were mad at each other. They had even forgotten that it was Sunday morning. She had come downstairs in her new blue Sunday School dress, bringing her hair brush for her mother to brush the tangles out of her long blond hair. But her mother hadn't seen her. With her familiar face all strange and ugly, she had stood there, seeing nothing but Jessica's daddy. They had forgotten Sunday School.

Jessica went back into the lawn and stood looking toward the room where her parents were. Open windows allowed their voices to reach Jessica across the back lawn.

"—you're trying to make another June out of me, Paul, don't you see that?" her mother shouted. "I'm not your first wife. I have a personality of my own. It so happens I want a career, and you've known that for years. Why do you think I went to school? And now—it's an opportunity I can't miss. Why can't I make you see that? I have worked my butt off these past four years getting that degree and I'll be goddamned if I'm going to throw it all into the closet and slam the door on it! What the hell do you think I was doing it for? My health?"

"Why do you need to work? When you married

me, you were content. It was never agreed that you would work, take a job, whatever."

"You said nothing when I wanted to go back to school!"

"I thought it was just a whim."

"You are so old-fashioned, Paul. I never thought the difference in our ages went so deep, Paul, but do you know what you've become? A nineteenth-century husband!"

"What about Jessica? I thought that when you got that degree you wanted you'd stop flitting around for a while and spend some time with your daughter!"

"Jessica is doing fine. What is this? Some more of that 'stay in your place, woman'? Barefoot and pregnant? Jessica's five years old. She's not a baby. I want this job, Paul, and I'm taking this job!"

"Diane, New Orleans is more than a hundred miles away. Do you plan to commute?"

"No, not daily."

"Then when in the hell are we supposed to see you?"

"The weekends, of course."

"The weekends, shit! If that's all you plan to be home, you can just damn well pack your things — all of them — and stay permanently."

"Fine! That's fine with me! I've never liked this country living anyway. Small town bunk. I don't know why I ever let you seduce me into coming here. You'll love it, you said, it's part of an old plantation, a sweet clover meadow right across the backyard fence. Cows. You can hear the birds sing, you said. You didn't say they'd wake me up at the ungodly hour of five A.M. You didn't say anything about how

13

boring a meadow with cows is. And nothing to do. Absolutely nothing to do."

"You could take care of your child."

"So what kind of life is that? Have you ever tried carrying on a conversation with someone who can't read yet?"

"You liked it at first," Paul said in a weaker voice. "You loved it here."

"It was unique, that was all. It didn't take me six months to find out how boring a small town can be. I want out, Paul."

"Oh, so now we hear the truth. You're not only bored with the house, you're bored with me and Jessica. What about Jessica? Doesn't she mean anything at all to you? When she was in diapers you bitched about that, and said you'd have more in common with her when she was older and could talk. Well, she's older. She talks. So what about her? She needs a mother's love and attention."

"I can see her on weekends."

"You can go to hell, Diane. If you leave here today, you can stay. And don't think you'll get Jessica if you ever change your mind."

"Fine! Great. I never said I wanted to take her away from here, did I?"

Jessica ran back to the fence and looked across at the castle hidden among the trees. She had never climbed the back fence before, but now with her mother's voice vibrating in her ears, her head, her heart, with her feelings bursting out of her in a torrent of fresh tears, Jessica hooked her fingers in the strong wires of the chain link fence and began to climb. When she fell into the soft, sweet clover on the other side of the fence she stood up and ran, straight toward the hidden castle that beckoned, like the castles in her favorite stories.

Cows raised their heads and placidly watched her, a small figure in her blue Sunday School dress, fighting her way through the tall grass of the meadow.

Jessica stopped a hundred yards from the fence that enclosed the trees around the castle. She could no longer see the peak of the roof above the trees, but she had glimpses of old gray stone. She went closer to the fence and saw red-lettered signs that were fading to pink tacked to the wood posts. Even though she couldn't read much yet, she knew the letters, and she spelled aloud, "D O N O T E N T E R." And another, on a neighboring post, had N o T r e s p a s s i n g.

Jessica went slowly to the fence and peered in. The yard was full of briars and trees and vines. Long streamers of moss hung down from the heavy limbs of the live oaks and dark green vines climbed their trunks. The sun didn't shine there. The front of the house was shadowed and grey, the stones touched with greenish moss.

Jessica walked along the fence looking for a gate. She paused and listened. It was very quiet here. She listened for voices, and heard none. She wondered how the people who lived here went to town, for there was no road, no driveway. And behind the house the forest began, and the swamp. She could hear the frogs now, in the swamp, a hundred pitches, from fine to low. The tree frogs and the bull frogs, and all the other frogs in between that she didn't know much about. Her big brother, Robert, had told her about the frogs. And Mrs. Archer, the housekeeper, told her about everything else, when she wasn't busy, or wasn't reading. Her mother didn't tell her anything. Her mother was beautiful, with full, black hair all in glossy curls around her face. Sometimes she allowed Jessica into the dressing room while she brushed and styled her hair, while she applied her makeup. But one day when Jessica experimented, and used her mother's mascara and lipstick and all the other powders and rouges and pretty colors that she put on her eyelids, her mother had spanked her. It was the only time in Jessica's life that she had been spanked, and remembering it now brought a new batch of tears. She sobbed against the rusting wire fence that surrounded the old castle.

Her mother didn't want her.

Her mother was leaving, and she'd only come home sometimes. If Daddy would let her.

Suddenly Jessica heard a voice. A sweet, high voice singing. Or was it wailing in sadness? It was hard to tell, for it rose and fell, fading in and out of her grasp. It was so far away, so deep within the castle that she only caught snatches of it. There were no words, just a fine singing, a wailing, like the sounds of a plucked string on a harp. A feeling in the air of song and beckoning, Jessica decided.

Jessica drew in a deep breath and wiped her fists across her eyes to clear away the last vestiges of tears. Someone in the house was singing to her. Perhaps that person was high in the tower, and had seen her cross the meadow.

Jessica began moving along the fence again, looking for a gate. This fence had barbed wire at the top. Three strands. The barbs were triple barbs and very sharp, even though they were rusted. She wouldn't be able to climb this fence. She knew that. And she knew about barbed wire because Mrs. Archer had told her. She had wanted to know one day how the cows knew to stay in the meadow, and Mrs. Archer had said they stayed in because they had to. Their pasture was surrounded by barbed wire. But, she said when Jessica cried, feeling that the cows should have more freedom than that, the cows really wanted to stay there, because they were safe there. If they got out on the highway a car or big truck would kill them. So the barbed wire was a good thing. Jessica supposed that whoever owned the castle didn't want the cows in their yard. At her own house there was no barbed wire, but the fence was tall. And on the sides it was brick. Only at the back was it wire.

She came to the corner of the fence, and found a gate, just around the corner. It was wired shut, but she began to work with the wire, untwisting and untwisting, as the singing from the tower faded and returned. Gnats collected and swarmed around her face and she knocked them away. They flew on, a small cloud, going into the cool shadows of the yard.

The wire came loose, and Jessica carefully hung it over the barbed wire of the fence. The gate moved rustily, its sound raucous as the crows' voices from over the swamp. The singing in the house stopped. It began again as she passed through the gate and paused. A faint path curled into the wilderness of the yard. She pulled the gate shut behind her to keep the cows in the pasture from entering, although none of them was close. They had forgotten her and had gone back to eating clover.

She moved along the path cautiously. Vines grew across it sometimes, obliterating it, so that it was hard to find it again. Streamers of moss had to be pushed aside. A large spiderweb held a fat spider, right over the path, and she got down on her hands and knees in order to crawl under it. She looked back at the spider and felt that it was watching her with its many eyes. Mrs. Archer had told her about a spider's eyes. They were lined around its head like clearance lights on a big truck. Because of spiders, she didn't go into dark places very often.

Suddenly the steps were in front of her, and she looked up. It wasn't really a castle, she saw, not a huge one. It had only one tower, and that was nearly choked by dark green vines. There was one small window in the tower that she could see, but it didn't look sparkling and clean like the windows at her own house.

The rest of the castle might have been disappointing, too, if she had compared it to the castles she had seen pictures of, but she was no longer comparing. There were long galleries across the front and down both sides of the house, but the upper gallery had fallen on the far end of the front. Set deep into the gray stone were narrow windows, all of them shuttered as if the castle were asleep. Some of the shutter slats had rotted away, and darkness peeked out. The big door was back in the shadows of the gray stone, just as the windows were. The ledges of the windows were wide enough to sit on, but the wood that held the windows was rotting, too, like the upper gallery floor, and the shutters.

Jessica began climbing the stone steps. She'd tell

18

her daddy, she thought, that the lady who lived here needed help with her porches and her windows. He could send over the man who came to work at their house. The handyman, Mrs. Archer called him. "Loosely," she had said, "mind you use the word loosely when you call Jake a handyman." So, Jessica remembered to call Jake loosely a handyman.

Jessica crossed the stone porch to the door and stopped suddenly. The shadow of the doorway fell upon her and a chill wind came from somewhere around the house and made her feel cold. She looked up at an iron door knocker, a hideous face staring down at her, its eyes crusted with green moss. It was too high for her to reach even if she dared touch it.

Annabelle.

Jessica drew back, startled. Her sensitive ears had barely separated the word from the other sounds that reached her, the frogs in the swamp, the soft wind, the movement of things growing. She stared at the front door and listened, and heard no more.

The singing had stopped. She heard only the whine of the wind as it came through the cracks of the stone at the corners of the house. A wind that wasn't blowing out in the meadow.

Diane flung clothes from her closet toward the luggage open on the bed, and on the floor beside the bed. The floor was strewn with clothing. Dresses, long and short, skirts, blouses, sweaters, jackets, suits, robes. She caught a glimpse of herself in the full-length mirror in the back of the large, walk-in closet and paused. She looked wild, as if she'd been running through the woods, her hair snagged and

19

tangled by reaching limbs. Her dark eyes snapped their fury. She paused, caught up in her image. Sometimes she could look at herself with the critical detachment of a model, as if she were examining someone else's face. And always, she was surprised by the beauty. Stopped short. Brought to a stare. She could do this, she felt, without vanity. It was a cool and detached admiration that she might have for any beautiful creature, be it human or animal. And then when she attached it to herself, she became emotional. And filled with anxiety. Here she was, twenty-four years old now, and buried, you might say, on the remnants of an old plantation out on the edge of a swamp that reached miles into the background. Her beauty would dry up and she would become old and ugly, and for whom?

She wanted to see and be seen. There was a whole big world out there, and she wanted to live in it. The trips Paul had taken her on had been fun at first, and coming here to live in a home that was very close to being a mansion in its own magnificent setting was something different from her own modest background. But it hadn't taken her long to find out that it was somewhat like looking at a beautiful painting. You could only enjoy it for a certain length of time before you wanted to move on.

She wanted to *live*. Why couldn't anyone understand that? It was so frustrating she wanted to cry. Her mother didn't understand. Their last conversation about it still irritated her ears like a mosquito buzzing there. "I always said I'd never say I told you so," her mother said, in that maddeningly calm and oh-so-right voice of hers. "But when you wanted to marry Paul, I told you that the age difference would matter someday. What he wanted was something different from what you wanted. Oh, I know, you were eighteen, and you thought you were grown. But . . ." Uh-huh. Yeah, sure.

Well, now she knew. Her mother had been right, but that didn't give her a right to be so certain now that she was doing the wrong thing again.

It always came back to Jessica. As if being the mother of Jessica had subtracted from her all other identities.

"I can't do it," she said aloud. "I can't do what they want."

She'd gone to work in one of Paul's offices part-time while she was a senior in high school. She was eager to get out into the world and her grades had been good enough that she was allowed to work half a day and go to school half a day. It was also a kind of training program that some businesses offered to the students. She knew when she saw the big boss that he was twice her age or more, but it didn't matter. He was handsome and rich and exciting. She had come on to him with all her power, and though he had at first acted scared of her, he had finally begun to relent.

The wedding was magnificent, and so was the wedding trip. To Honolulu. But then she had gotten pregnant almost immediately. And sick! Just thinking of how nauseated she was during the whole time made her want to run to the bathroom. The doctor and her mother and her husband had said it would only last a few weeks, but it had lasted the full nine months. By the time the frail little girl was born, both of them were about worn out. Even the baby had been sick for a while afterwards, spitting up milk, crying. A nurse had been brought in to take care of her and had stayed for six months. But even after that something had been lacking, even though the baby had begun to be well and beautiful. Diane thought now that perhaps some kind of attachment had not been made, especially on her part. Maybe she had been too young, yet she saw mothers just as young who adored their babies. Maybe she wasn't meant to be a mother.

She stood in the middle of her bedroom and looked at the mess around her. Did she really want these clothes? With her promised salary, she'd be able to buy almost everything she wanted. A new life asked for new clothes. And how much fun it would be to be back in the city with all the shops and the restaurants.

She had to go. She had to hurry before Paul found some way of stopping her. If she tried to take all her things it would only delay her.

From the floor she picked up a couple of skirts and blouses, one long dress and one short, and threw them into a suitcase. She closed the case and latched it, then tossed makeup into the overnight case. When she went downstairs she chose the front door as her exit because she knew that Paul was probably back in the library where she had left him, or in his study. Pouting. He was such an old-fashioned guy. He had thought that all she wanted or needed was lodging and such for herself and the children she would bear. Like his first wife. She had to get out before he made her into that kind of woman.

She threw her suitcases into her car—Paul had, at

least, given her that when she had gone back to school, and she was grateful. But did she have to pay for it with her life?

She went into the back yard to look for Jessica.

The child had everything a child could want. One wall of her bedroom had floor-to-ceiling shelves with a large collection of dolls and stuffed animals. In the back yard, a large area was allotted to play, with swings, slides and a merry-go-round. And over in one corner of the enclosed rear grounds was a miniature railroad track with its own little engine and passenger cars. The track curled around among the trees, shrubs, and flowers and had been Paul's special gift to Jessica on her third birthday, and of course to Robert, his son by his first marriage, who now was fourteen and seemed as distant as a guest. She had never been close to Robert. She had failed as a stepmother, too, she supposed. But the train was still now, and the playground deserted. Nor was Jessica near the sandbox, her favorite outdoor play area.

Diane went impatiently into the center of it all, as nearly as she could find a center, and began yelling.

"Jessica! *Jessica!*"

She hated to leave without saying good-bye. But on the other hand, she had to hurry. Where on earth had the kid gone?

"JESSICA!"

Jessica picked up acorns that had fallen onto the stone floor of the porch. She squatted on her heels and looked at one that had taken root between two stones and was now a tiny tree with real oak leaves growing on it.

The singing began again, faraway, so finely pitched it was almost inaudible. She raised her head and listened. It came from beyond the front door, clearer, nearer, as if the lady in the house had come down from the tower and was coming to let her in. The harp strings of her voice reminded Jessica of angels. Mrs. Archer said angels sang, in fine, beautiful voices. But this was not really singing, she suddenly realized. It was a calling.

Jessica got up and went to the door. Just as she reached its shadowy recesses and was again feeling intimidated by the ugly metal face of the door knocker, the door opened and swung a few inches inward, and Jessica heard the voice again, more clearly, as fine as the voice of an elf, *Annabelle, we've waited so long for you.*

Timidly, Jessica took a step backwards. She put her fingers to her lips and murmured, "My name is Jessica."

She could see into the dark hall only a short way, and she saw that no one was there. From within the hall came a cold wind that washed softly over her, making goose bumps rise on her arms. She took a hesitant step forward, then another, and then she heard her mother's voice. Faint. Far away over the meadow.

"Jessica! Where are you? Do you want to tell me good-bye or don't you!"

Jessica whirled and began to run, down the steps and along the path. She forgot to go down on her knees to avoid the spiderweb and tore into it, and spent a precious moment fighting it away. She ran on, leaving the gate partly open. The cows in the pasture looked up and then went back to their business of eating. Jessica plowed through the clover, her breath fast and gasping. She tried to call out in answer to her mother, but had no breath for it.

When she reached the fence she climbed carelessly, her fingers hurting from the thin bite of the wires, her toes slipping from the links. At the top she forgot about sharp twists on the wires, and caught one in her dress. It ripped as she went over, a long tear beginning at her waist and going almost to the hem. She dropped to the ground on the other side and paused to exclaim, "Oh!" at her dress, ruined now, forever. But then she heard her mother's car, and she began running again.

She reached the driveway just in time to see the low red sports car drive out onto the highway and shift into another gear as it roared off out of sight. Jessica dropped down where she was, her head between her knees, and sobbed.

Her mother had gone away. She had gone away. Gone away. Jessica's heart felt as if it were dying. She didn't want her mother to go away. "Come back. Come back. Come back," she sobbed, and then something occurred to her that made her heart leap with hope. Maybe it was someone else driving the car. Maybe it was her daddy instead. Once before he had taken it to the garage to have something done.

She ran to a back door of the house, the one that went into the hall and to the library, where her parents had been earlier. She stopped on the threshold. Her daddy was sitting by the desk, staring at the wall, and in front of him there was a decanter, and a glass. He was clicking his fingernails against the glass. His face was dark with anger, and he didn't see her, just as he hadn't seen her earlier when she had come down in her new blue dress ready to go to Sunday School. She turned away.

She went to the front of the house and climbed the stairs, and went down the long hall to the side hall, past Robert's room where his strange, ugly music pounded against his closed walls, and then to her room. She closed the door and sat down against it, and wept into the ripped skirt of her new dress.

CHAPTER TWO

Robert didn't communicate a lot with his family. It was impossible. They were in a world apart from him, a world of finance and fashion, of booze and parties, and fights. Even though he had turned up the volume on his radio, still he had caught gists of a fight going on somewhere below. Echoes, sort of, or vibrations, or frequency waves in the air that irritated him as much as his music irritated his dad. Diane hadn't said much about his music, and he had a hunch that the stuff she danced to wasn't much different. But if he and Diane had anything at all in common it was no more than that. So he hadn't minded hearing her car roar out of the drive. He'd felt a little sorry only when the kid had come running up the stairs and gone to hide in her room. From his window he had seen her with her new dress torn and dirty, come into the driveway and squat down, her head between her knees, her face crumpled and wet with tears when she finally got up and turned it so that he had gotten a full view. He wanted to call out to her, but he didn't.

From his window he saw a lot of things. He had a full view of the driveway on the south side of the house, and if he leaned out he could see the garage, and the breezeway that connected it to the house, as well as the gate into the back yard. On the south there were trees, but if he looked hard he could see the beginnings of Pincwood, the village, through the trees a half-mile away. The church steeple, for one thing. It stuck up above the trees like a spear, or a lance. At night it glowed, lighted from somewhere below, and looked more weird than anything. Mrs. Archer had called it beautiful. Some tastes, yuk. He'd had more than one nightmare about that pale, glowing spear above the black trees.

He flopped down on the bed on his back, his right knee drawn up, and began beating a rhythm on his knee in time with the music, but his thoughts strayed back. Today Diane had left with a couple of suitcases thrown into the back of her Porsche, and six years ago she had come, in the crook of his dad's arm, looking bashful and demure, with him beaming like an old idiot. "This is your new mother," he had said, and Diane had giggled, though she put a hand to her mouth to stop it in a hurry, and Robert knew, even at his brief age of eight, that she was trying to be older than she was. For the first time in his life he had really felt isolated from his dad. Had Dad forgotten that Robert's own mother had lived here in this house? That her picture was on Robert's bedroom wall, and would stay there always? That her face was in the house in a dozen places and in his heart as well? He couldn't put suitable words to it at that time, but it amounted to a terrible betrayal that his dad should bring this young girl and tell Robert that she was his new mother. He had only one mother. He remembered her. He knew she had passed on, as Mrs. Ashley said, a year before, but still she remained, invisible, in the house, all around, everywhere. Diane was an intruder, if she were trying to take the place of his mother. He didn't want her there.

But she had never tried to be his mother, and after a year or so he had accepted her as part of the environment, like the furniture in the house, and the trees outside. Lots of times they passed each other in the hall without even speaking. It was like Diane didn't see him. And as he usually carried his radio, along with an ear plug, she was like a specter slipping by, silent, brief.

What relationship he'd had with his dad deteriorated from the day Diane came. Dad had eyes only for his bride. It didn't matter. Dad hadn't been around a lot, anyway. Business. Robert knew nothing about the family business, except that it had been founded by his great-grandfather, and there were offices in New Orleans as well as in Shreveport and Alexandria. Pop had a couple of small planes parked in a nearby airfield, which he flew to Shreveport or New Orleans. He drove to Alexandria. Someday, Pop had told him one day when he was mad and snorting about the way Robert was wasting his time doing nothing but plugging up his ears with trash, he was going to have to go to work in the family business, and he was going to start at the bottom sweeping floors and dumping wastebaskets. Robert didn't bother to answer. He knew that wasn't true. He might have to do something grubby, but it wouldn't be the janitorial work.

Pop hated to be called Pop. But when Robert grew

up, to age thirteen or so, it seemed mawkish to call the old man *Daddy*. That was Jessica's name for him. And once, back when Robert was small like Jessica, the old man had been Daddy. But now he was Pop, like it or not. However, he did try to remember to address him as Dad when he was forced to address him at all.

It wasn't that he didn't like his old man. It wasn't that at all. In fact, there were only three people in the world whom Robert loved, and one of them was his father, and one his older sister, Brenda. The other was Jessica.

The little kid didn't know it, but she'd probably be better off with her mother gone. Diane had never given her much but tears, anyway. Mrs. Ashley did ten times more for her than Diane had ever done. Robert wondered about the love a person can have for someone who didn't love back. She was like a puppy trotting at the heels of its master, wagging its tail, lolling its tongue, trying to look pleasant when the eyes of the master noticed it. A loving puppy that wasn't loved back. What made love? Robert had loved his mother, but she had loved him in return. She had been tender and gentle and always kind. She hadn't run off and left him and Brenda. She would never have done that. She had died instead.

When his mother was alive there had been beautiful flower gardens on the grounds. She had worked right with the gardener, and her gloves still hung in the garden shed, right by the door. They had green leather thumbs on white cloth gloves, and wrists that splayed out to cover the cuffs of the shirts she had worn. She was still there in her big floppy hat, bent over a bed of colorful flowers, and he could see her sometimes when the rest of the landscape blurred.

When he thought of Brenda he missed her. She was eight years older than he, and had been home only once in the past two years. He never wrote to her, and seldom talked to her on the phone. Though he wanted to talk to her, he never could think of anything to say. They always wound up with a conversation that went something like: What are you doing, Robert? Nothing. How's school? Okay. Gone to any ball games lately? A couple. Do you play? Not much.

How could he feel so uncomfortable with his own sister?

How could he feel so uncomfortable with *everyone*?

There was this girl at school. Gorgeous. Absolutely. She was so pretty that when he looked at her he just couldn't pull his eyes away. And she'd turn around in class sometimes and see him gawking at her, probably with his mouth open, and she'd give a toss of her hair and whirl back with her shoulder shutting out his attempt to get closer to her, as if he were white trash. Her name was Shelly, and on Valentine's Day he'd grabbed the opportunity to give her the prettiest card he could find. But then he'd been afraid to put his name on it. He'd watched her open it, and look and look for a name. After she'd opened all the other cards she had gone back to his, for it was the largest, the most costly, and by far the most beautiful. Then her gaze had flitted over the classroom of boys and girls. But not once had she looked at him. He hadn't mattered to her. She didn't want it to be from him. And meantime, there was

31

dopey Cindy, hanging over his shoulder, smirking, smiling, her eyes as soft as a puppy's, and she'd had the gall to put her name on the mushy card she gave him.

He liked Shelly and Cindy liked him. Love? Yes, sort of, in a different way from the love he had for his sisters and his pop.

What was this thing called love?

He stared at the ceiling, seeing images there, Shelly's beautiful face beside Cindy's dopey one. He no longer heard the music.

A sudden restlessness seized him. He rolled off the bed, snapped off the radio, and was stunned for an instant by the silence that was left behind. Outside the birds sang, and from the swamp came the sounds of frogs, as musical to his ears as any bird ever was. He wondered sometimes if they were related. Of course he knew the birds were said to be a leftover from the dinosaurs, and the frogs were of the order *Salienta*, tailless amphibia. He'd gone through a period of catching frogs and toads and identifying them before he turned them loose again, and he had found dozens of different kinds in his own yard and in the swamp. His favorite was the meadow frog. It was the one most used in laboratories in schools, and he hated what they did with it. He had refused, and was given a D in biology. He never caught the frogs anymore. For one thing he liked to see them free, and for another he had come to the awareness that being caught scared the piss out of them.

He went down the hall to the end door. He pushed it open a few inches, and leaned in, opening it farther. Jessica was lying facedown on her bed. Her room had windows facing both south and west, and both of them were open. A warm breeze crossed the room.

"Jessy?" he said in a half-whisper, testing. She was lying so still, her dirty, torn dress twisted and crumpled beneath her, her small, pretty legs arranged as if she'd been thrown onto the bed, her plump arms spread wide. A sadness struck him, causing him to frown, as if from pain; and another feeling that he'd never had before in his life: foreboding. A feeling that something really bad was going to happen to Jessica.

"Hey, Jess."

He went over to the bed and around to the other side so that he could see her face. She was asleep, her mouth lax and pushed open by the pressure of her cheek against the satin comforter. Blond curls, as soft and fine as angel hair, fell across her forehead and cheek. Robert backed away. Funny, he thought, that her hair was so blond, while Diane's was almost black. And Pop's hair, what he had left, was also dark. And his own hair was dark, too. And so was Brenda's. Jessica was the only blonde in the family. It was almost like she didn't belong.

That feeling hit him again, and he spun away from the bed, from his sister. It was only a feeling, had nothing to do with her, he told himself. The little kid would be better off when she forgot that flighty Diane.

Through the open window he heard murmurs of voices, and looked out. In the driveway toward the front of the house were three bicycles with appropriate riders. Out for a Sunday afternoon. His spirits lifted, as swiftly as a frog leaping from one place to another. He hurriedly tiptoed out of the room and then, with no attempt at keeping quiet, hurried on to the stairway that went down to the hall by the kitchen. Half a minute later he was across the kitchen and utility room and through the outer gate of the breezeway. He ran around the house and stopped at the side of a flowering shrub. The kids on the bikes had come closer, and he could see who they were. Kenny Blevins, Melody Rogers, and—crap! dopey Cindy. They stopped their bikes and greeted him, all smiles.

"Want to go riding?"

Robert shrugged. "Sure." He looked at Cindy, though he cringed inwardly at meeting her eyes directly. Today her hair was in braids, and there was a fringe of bangs curling above her eyebrows. She actually had a pretty nice face, he saw, when beautiful Shelly wasn't around to outshine it. Her eyes were bright and brown, and her eyebrows lifted away on her pale forehead as if she were asking a question. One long, nice leg touched the ground, steadying the bike, while the other was bent, foot resting on a pedal. She really wasn't so bad after all, he saw. Physically. But still . . . she was dopey Cindy, the girl who'd had a crush on him since they met in kindergarten.

"Let me get my bike," he said. "It's in the garage."

They came along with him, their chatters worming away the last vestiges of his feeling of doom.

Paul poured himself another shot of bourbon from the leatherbound decanter that Diane had given him for his birthday. His hand squeezed its neck, harder,

harder, as if it were around *hers*. He felt impotent. Helpless. What was there about a small girl like Diane that could make a man feel so goddamned helpless? It was like trying to make your daughter behave. She wouldn't do what you wanted, and you felt like exerting your strength and your power and forcing them to your will; but all you could do was squeeze the neck of the decanter.

Feeling silly, he released it and shoved it across the desk. It struck the wall with a soft thud and stopped.

He had to admit to himself, no one else, that he wanted to get back at her. He'd bar his house to her, and not let her see their small daughter. He'd tell her okay, girl, you've made your bed, now lie in it. Don't come to me for money, either, because you won't get it. And you won't get Jessica. . . .

If he'd been a weaker man he would have cried. Whose nose was he cutting off? His own, only his own. Diane wouldn't be back asking for any of those things. It was she who had left him, and all he stood for, including the child.

Think of the child, think of the child, he told himself.

She needed a mother. If not a mother, then a woman relative. A mother figure. He didn't have the time to stay around and be both mother and father to her. Sometimes work kept him away for several days, and he had a feeling that it was going to take him away more and more from now on. What did he have at home to come back to every night? If he could be sure that Jessica was being taken care of, there'd be nothing. Robert was old enough now that he didn't need daily supervision.

There was Mrs. Archer, but she was only daytime, six days a week, Sundays off. Of course he could probably hire a full-time governess. He supposed such creatures still existed; but in a way, Diane had been right about him. He was an old-fashioned man with old-fashioned ideas about what a woman, especially a mother, should be. His first wife had been the perfect example. She had tended the home, the flowers, the kids. In fact, it had been an effort to get her away. She hadn't needed the trips, nor the parties that Diane needed.

He still thought of June. She was the warmth of his heart. After her death he had been so lonesome for her that he had filled the emptiness with the first girl who seemed to love him. It was June's love he wanted back, he knew inwardly; it was the warmth and security of June. And he had tried to mold Diane to fit June's place. Impossible. Impossible.

Now his sense of helplessness was replaced by despondency, and for a few minutes he put his head down on his arms and closed his eyes. But that thing about booze that he hated came over him, and he felt his head swimming off into space. He opened his eyes swiftly, got his bearings, stilled his head. And pushed his half-filled glass away.

His gaze fell upon the telephone. Brenda. What was she doing these days? She was twenty-two now, but she hadn't married yet, had never even been engaged or brought home anyone whom she seemed interested in. She'd bummed around the world for the past two years, and her addresses had varied from Amsterdam to Hong Kong to London. Now she was in California, and her number was on page one of the address book that the telephone sat on. She'd gone to school in Paris for a while, studying art, and there had been mentions of continuing the art study elsewhere. The last time he'd heard from her there was an art show in which some of her paintings were displayed, and she'd told him, when he'd asked if she needed more money than her barely-subsistence-level monthly allowance, that she'd been selling enough paintings that she had even bought herself a car.

To Paul it all boiled down to footloose and fancy free. Brenda was available, whether she knew it or not. Jessica needed a relative to see after her, at least until school started in the late summer, and Brenda was the only female relative who would do.

He picked up the phone, checked the number, and punched it out. While a phone at the other end rang and rang, Paul looked at his wristwatch, even though there was a large clock on the mantel that he could have seen without turning his head. Twelve-forty, and a two-hour difference. Or was it three? Whatever, it would still be morning in her apartment. Midmorning. She might still be asleep, or in the shower.

But when she answered she sounded fully awake and slightly breathless, as if she'd been running.

"Get you out of something important?" Paul asked.

"Dad!" she cried, smiles in her voice. "How are you? Robert and Jessica? And Diane?"

"Well," he said, hesitating. "None of us on our deathbed. How are things going with you, puddin'?"

"What is this? You haven't called me that since the last time I sat on your lap, when I was about ten. You must be lonely today, Dad."

"I was thinking of your mother."

There was a lengthy pause, and before Brenda could end it, Paul forced lightness into his voice and inquired, "Had any art displays lately?"

"Nothing of any consequence. I have a couple in a local restaurant; so have several of my friends. Not that we're in competition with each other. Rick, my favorite, is into reality. His paintings are as precise as a photograph. He's turning to nature painting, and they are beautiful. His sell better than the others. Mine are more surrealistic. I like to paint my dreams. I have another friend who does portraits. I was downstairs talking to her just now when the phone rang."

"Are you planning a visit home soon?"

There was another hesitation, and Paul filled it in. "It's been over a year since we've seen you."

"I know. I'm sorry. I do think of all of you often, and I've been wanting to see you, of course. How's Jessica?"

"She's—uh—upstairs, I guess. I've only had a glimpse of her this morning," Paul said, skirting the question and wondering precisely how to word what he wanted of her. "She's going to be going through some emotional problems, if she isn't already. Her mother left this morning."

"For good?"

"Yes. She's taken a job of some sort in New Orleans. She'd been going to school, something to do with fashion in women's clothes and buying. So now she's gone, and Jessica doesn't have a mother, and only Mrs. Archer to guide her. And Mrs. Archer goes home early in the evening, and sometimes it's midnight when I get home. Of course Robert is fourteen now, but he's got a radio in place of a head most of the time. This generation of his is going to be deaf as gourds from the music they listen to all day, and with about as much sense."

"Ah Dad. I had my music, and you had yours, didn't you?"

"Well . . ." Some wild memories hit him unexpectedly, of a young Elvis Presley and his exciting performances. Of rock 'n' roll screaming out from the car radio as he and his friends danced on the grass and the pavement of the street. He smiled and was glad that Brenda couldn't see him. And earlier than that, when he was a young teenager, like Robert, there had been the marvelous swing music of the forties. But he hadn't glued himself to a plug in his ear. He had learned to dance, though, and had gone to the local ballrooms with the rest of the kids. His dislike of present day music returned, and he said, "But that was music. Real music."

"That's probably the very words that Robert will someday be saying to his son. Where is he now? What's he doing?"

"I don't know. Probably in his room plugged in to his radio, or his record player, or tapes, or whatever all that junk is. The thing we're supposed to be discussing here, though, is Jessica being alone this summer. When school starts it will be easier, but still school doesn't last long when the child is only five and in kindergarten. Half a day, isn't it?"

"You might be able to hire someone, Dad," Brenda said softly, perhaps reluctantly. "And isn't Mrs. Archer there all day? And Robert could look after her

39

until you get home."

"No, that isn't good enough. Our children have always been reared by family women. Always. You were, your grandmother was, and her grandmother."

"But there were governesses also."

"Only under the supervision of a family woman."

"Well perhaps, but times are different."

"Not here at Belle Lake, they aren't. Our children come first."

"Of course."

Paul sighed. "We need you, Brenda. Just for the summer, perhaps. You have no other family to hold you away, and the care of Jessica really won't take up much of your time. She's always been used to playing alone, and seems quite capable of entertaining herself. So it's not as though she would be demanding, or your time wouldn't be your own. Especially in the daytime. You could go ahead with your work. I really ask only that you be here for her in the evenings, or see to it that a responsible sitter is called in when you want to go out." He was pleading, he realized, and so he stopped. The problem had been presented to her; now let her make up her mind. He could, he supposed, if he had to, make a point of getting home shortly after Mrs. Archer left for the day. And he could make a point of staying around on Saturdays. Damned nuisance, though. A man needed his freedom from home responsibilities in order to properly attend to business. That was the way it was, and that was the way it should be. It was a woman's place to stay at home and keep the kids and house.

"It would be a week before I could get there," Brenda said, and the reluctance in her voice came through clearly.

Paul frowned at the wall. What was the name of the artist she had mentioned? Who was into nature and realism? Something going on there, he'd bet, that she didn't want to leave.

"I'd like to think it over a couple of days," Brenda said in a stronger voice.

Uh-oh, Paul thought. So much for that. She'd be calling back and saying she just couldn't. What else had he expected? Wasn't she close to Diane's age? That generation of young women who put career above all else?

"Fine," he said in the tone of voice he used for business acquaintances. Carefully unrevealing. But then he remembered whom he was talking to, and the love that would always be reserved exclusively for her. "Take care," he added, before he hung up.

He looked at his watch again. He would like to leave now, go to his apartment in New Orleans, go out to dinner at an anonymous back street restaurant that specialized in good old Creole recipes, go to a show or to the club, see a few friends. To sit here sesemed impossible. But what could he do? Call Mrs. Archer? He had never bothered her on her day off, so perhaps she wouldn't mind this one time. Maybe by next weekend he would give in and hire someone to stay twenty-four hours a day. He opened the address book to Mrs. Archer's place in it, and dialed her number.

She drowsily answered the phone on the second ring. He could almost see her, in her small living room, leaning back in her recliner napping in front of her twenty-five-inch color television. There was probably a black and white western movie on made sometime back in the fifties, or even as far back as the thirties. He had seen her house, a small white frame house with a porch across the front, on a tree-shaded side street down in the village. It was only about one mile away, maybe less, because on a really pleasant day Mrs. Archer walked over.

"Who is this?" she was saying, awake now, and he realized he'd been holding the phone while he visualized her house and her within it.

"Ah—this is Paul, Mrs. Archer."

"Mr. Norris?"

"Yes. I do hate to disturb you, Mrs. Archer, but a problem has come up. You might as well know now that my wife has left me, and Jessica. Jessica's alone. And a business problem has come up also that I simply must attend to. I have to be away for the afternoon and night. I'll try to be back tomorrow evening, so that you can go home as usual, at your usual time, but if you could help Jessica out by being here the rest of today and tonight we would—uh—well, pay you double your usual rate. And be very grateful."

"Oh, well, I suppose I could. When is it you have to leave?"

"I'm going up to pack my bag as soon as I hang up."

"I can be there in thirty minutes or an hour."

"That's fine. I'll just go on. Jessica will be all right until you get here."

Paul hung up, feeling as if a great load had been taken off his shoulders. Pack a bag? He really didn't even have to do that. In the apartment he kept in New

42

Orleans were a few suits and whatever else he needed. He had only to leave.

At the door he hesitated, remembering that he should say something to Robert and Jessica. He turned back toward the front stairs and went in search of them. The silence in the upper hall was overwhelming. No music? Of course Robert might have turned the sound off for some reason and simply put the usual plugs in his ears. The ones he used when he came downstairs with his radio in his hand, knowing his music wasn't allowed out of his own room.

However, Robert's room showed only recent habitation. A wrinkled bedspread, a cluttered floor. But no Robert.

Paul went on back to Jessica's room. The little girl was curled into a knot on the bed, on her side, sound asleep. He thought of waking her, to tell her that she'd be alone in the house for a few minutes, and decided not to. She might sleep half the afternoon if she were left alone. She could easily sleep until Mrs. Archer arrived.

He left without disturbing her.

Jessica woke to stillness, yet a sound had brought her up, startled, to sit listening. Then she heard it again. A car. Down in the driveway. With her heart exploding into hope, she ran to the window. Had her mama come home? Was she just now driving back into the garage?

No. It was her dad's car, the dark blue one. He had backed it out into the turn-around place and was heading away, toward the street beyond the end of the brick wall. She leaned against the screen of her open window, but he didn't look up at her. The car pulled onto the road and disappeared in the direction opposite the village. Toward the airport, where he kept his plane.

Jessica stood by the window, weakened by sleep and disappointment. Across the driveway in a pine tree a red bird sat on the end of a branch and sang. She could see it, a red dot among the green, and hear it, but she was not cheered by it.

She moved, and her dress rustled. She looked down and held the skirt out in her hands looking at the damage she had done. Then, hastily, she began pulling it off. She removed her taffeta slip also, and her white stockings. They too were torn and peppered with burrs and bits of weed. She wadded it all together and put it into the wastebasket. None of it could ever be worn again. Even the skirt of her new white slip had torn. Sometimes Mrs. Archer mended things, but not always. And Jessica didn't want the dress anymore. She didn't want it mended.

From her dresser drawer she pulled cut-off jeans and a knit shirt and put them on. From the closet she got a pair of sandals.

On her way down the hall she paused at Robert's door. It was standing open and she looked in and wrinkled her nose at the mess his room was. Then she went on, Robert forgotten.

The downstairs seemed even more quiet than the upstairs had been. The central hall was dark and cool, and the kitchen bright and open to the air, with its door open and the windows by the breakfast table raised, yet there was something cold and empty about it. The rocking chair by the table in the corner was there all alone, the cushion sagging as if someone had just left it, had hurried out when they heard her coming. Nobody wanted to be with her. That was Mrs. Archer's chair, and its emptiness made the whole kitchen hollow and silent and lonely.

She went back to the small side hall that led to the TV room in the back corner of the house to see if Robert might be there, but he was gone, too. Everybody was gone.

Nobody wanted to be with her.

She wandered desolately out into the back yard, and to the brick wall with the carefully spaced holes in it that formed the outside wall of the breezeway between the house and the garages, and peered through one of the holes at the driveway. It was wide and smooth, and no cars were parked there. Late afternoon shade made the pavement dark. No cars were passing along the road at the end of the driveway.

In the yard behind her the peacocks began to call, their voices loud in the silent air that had been touched only by insects, frogs and birds that she hadn't been conscious of. The shrill call of the peacocks brought her away from the brick wall, and she crossed the back lawn to the pond where the peacocks were strutting and scolding the ducks that swam on the water of the pond. She sat on the grass for a while and watched the ducks. They came closer to her for a special feeding, but she had forgotten to bring food, so she tore off bits of grass and threw it to them. They shoveled it out of the water as if it were manna from the hands of an angel, but Jessica only smiled. She didn't feel like laughing out loud.

She got up and went around the pond and squeezed through the shrubbery on the back side and came to the tall chain link fence that separated her yard from the meadow. She hooked her fingers in the cool wire and put her face against it and stared at the tower of the castle hidden in the trees and vines on the other side of the meadow. She wondered if the lady who lived in the castle could see her. The lady who had called her Annabelle.

Annabelle.

It was a name prettier than her own.

It was a name like flowers and bells and fairy tales.

The lady wanted Annabelle to come see her. She wanted to be with her. Annabelle was someone special.

Long shadows were reaching across the swamp toward the castle, covering the meadow and driving away the golden sun. Shadows suddenly were all around Jessica. If she climbed over the fence again and went to the castle, it would be dark soon after she got there. And Jessica was afraid of the dark.

A voice from the house shouted, "Jessica?"

Mrs. Archer!

What was she doing here on her day off? Jessica whirled away from the fence and ran around the pond toward the open porch at the rear of the kitchen. Mrs. Archer stood there, the kitchen behind her now lighted and its light trailing out behind her from the open door.

"My goodness, child, are you all alone?"

She reached down and took Jessica's hand into her

big, warm palm and led her firmly into the lighted kitchen.

"And out there in the dark! Where's Robert? I'm here to stay all night with you, while your daddy goes away on business. That must have been Robert on the bicycle I passed off down the road pedaling like mad, trying to get home before dark, I reckon. Well, set yourself at the table—*after* you wash your hands, and we'll see if we can find something special for Sunday night supper."

But even as Mrs. Archer talked, Jessica thought she heard the fine, small voice calling, *Annabelle, Annabelle.*

And there was such sadness in the voice that Jessica wanted to cry.

CHAPTER THREE

It was something Brenda wasn't sure she wanted to do, yet she knew she would, for family obligations called her. For two years she'd had no real family ties, but that hadn't eliminated the family. She was grateful for her family, and she knew if ever she needed them they would be there for her. The problem was, Brenda had fallen in love, and so far it was only a secret, sweet, strong feeling in her heart, unrevealed, unsatisfied. Rick thought himself only another of her artist friends, she was sure. She had laid her hand on his shoulder a few times, while she tingled the length of her body, as if her touch had made a live connection with a source of electricity, but if he had felt anything he had kept it carefully hidden. She was afraid if she pulled out now and stayed away the summer, and perhaps longer, he would forget her. More than that, she would probably never see him again. He would drift away from this small coastal town, following his artistic needs, looking for new landscapes, for animals and birds in the wild. She wanted to go with him. She longed to go with him, but he hadn't asked.

There was really no choice. She had to go home. Jessica needed her.

She walked along the beach, only half aware of her surroundings. On the horizon above the water the sun was a ball of incredible light, impossible to look into, the god upon whose face a mortal could not look; a moment more and it would plop out of sight beneath the horizon, and the street lights, pale but growing, would try to take its place. The ocean roared and waned to her left, coming in and drifting away, leaving the sand packed and damp. She turned her steps toward the sidewalk and the street lamps. She passed benches, all of them occupied this time of year. On the sidewalk late skaters swerved around her.

"Hey, Brenda. Wait, I'll walk with you."

Even his voice could cause that jolt of electricity to plow through her. How could there be so much emotion on her part without his being aware of it? There were times when she felt like withdrawing from him in a kind of juvenile embarrassment. She was almost tongue-tied around him sometimes. Certainly she couldn't loosen up the way she could with the men she occasionally dated. Although dates were becoming rare, because she could give them nothing of herself but a few hours of dancing and laughter, it was strange how she couldn't laugh with him as she could with them. With him life became more serious, more intense.

"Are you feeling like being alone?" he asked. "I don't want to interfere."

"Oh no, no."

"You were looking as though you were having some pretty private thoughts."

He was walking slowly, his hands behind his back, but she could feel the intensity of his gaze and the underlying seriousness of his question. He really seemed to be interested in her, and yet—

Suddenly it occurred to her that this might be one way to bring out of him a deeper sign of interest, if he possessed any. If he knew she was leaving, might he not suddenly turn to her, take her into his arms, and tell her he couldn't face life without her? She could then invite him to go with her. One summer at her home might be an interesting change for him, a different environment.

"I had a phone call from my dad this morning," she said. "His wife, Diane, has left, and Dad feels that Jessica, my five-year-old half-sister, needs a relative to stay with her this summer."

They walked in silence. The crowd had drifted away, and only their own steps on the concrete of the sidewalk sounded in the sudden fall of night. They were hollow sounds, magnified.

"How long have we known each other?" Rick said. "Three months? You were already here when I came."

"Yes, three months."

"I've been thinking I knew you very well, Brenda, and now it dawns on me that I know you only as you are now. I hadn't even thought of a family. I don't even know where you're from."

"No, I guess we just never talked about our families and backgrounds, did we? I'm from Louisiana. My mother died seven years ago, and my dad married again a year later. Jessica was born just nine months after that. I also have a brother, Robert. He's fourteen now. Home is a place on the edge of an old plantation. My dad bought a few acres of an old place that had been abandoned, and built our house on it. I lived there all my life until I went away to school. I haven't been home to live since then. And how about you, Rick?"

"Originally from Idaho. But I've been here and there since I was fifteen. My folks died when I was a kid, and I lived with an aunt and uncle in Idaho, on a farm. It was there that I got interested in animals. I don't like what's being done to animals, the way they're exploited. I know there's no easy answer, but I don't have to participate. So I left the farm, and drifted. I've never studied art formally, just the art courses one finds around here and there. No time away at school like the rest of you."

"Which is a great argument for innate talent. You could teach us."

"I wasn't after flattery, Brenda. Just stating a fact of life."

"It wasn't flattery. Just another fact of life, Rick." They laughed.

"Have you ever been to Louisiana?" Brenda asked.

"No, I haven't. Your place is in the country?"

"Yes. A half-mile or so away from a small place that is the typical wide spot in the road. There's a grocery store, a post office. I think there's a feed store, for the local chicken keepers. We used to get feed there someplace for our ducks and peacocks and hens."

The more she talked about it, the more torn she became. She could almost feel the warm, humid air on her face, and hear the calls of the night birds, the whippoorwills, the mockingbirds.

51

"And the frogs! You should hear the frogs. My little brother had a collection once that was unbelievable. He had a cage that he kept them in, in the edge of the pond, and he had them all named. The last time I asked him about them he said he'd turned them all loose."

"Sounds like my kind of guy."

"I haven't seen any of them for almost a year. I was home for a few days before I came on out here."

"When are you leaving?"

She was committed. She wasn't sure exactly when or how that had been determined, but Rick was expecting her to go, and of course duty was calling her. But —

"It's not as though Dad couldn't hire someone to be with Jessica. I'm sure there are college students who would need money and would be happy for the job."

"But he wants a relative. If not the mother, then the sister."

It was a statement, not a question. Had she told him that was the way Dad felt, or was it something he himself felt?

"I need time to get my things together," she said, lamely. "I'll call him tonight and tell him I'm coming. Maybe he can manage for a couple of weeks until I can get organized. Mrs. Archer still works for him, though she must be in her sixties by now. Close to retirement, I'd guess. She's been our housekeeper as long as I can remember. Mama depended on her a lot. She was a kind of mother-figure for my own mother, I think. *Her* mother had died when she was a child."

"Then she must seem like part of the family?"

"Certainly."

"Why couldn't she take care of the little girl?"

It was the first sign that he was reluctant to see her go, and Brenda hesitated before she answered, but he said no more. He walked beside her, waiting.

She said, 'Ummm . . . my dad is probably hard for most people to understand. Although Mrs. Archer seems like an aunt or some close relative to me, I'm sure to my dad she's only a servant. He's kind of a throwback. You know, the old southern gentleman, where kids, dogs, and servants stay in their place. And, of course, *women*. He's probably written Diane off for good just because she wants a job. My work is acceptable because I can do it at home." She paused. "It makes me feel oppressed just talking about it. That's one of the reasons I've stayed so far away, I guess. I hadn't thought of it until now, though. But, I guess I'll go. For the summer, anyway. If you feel a need for a change of scene, drive on out. You could find a lot of interesting animals in the swamp. It comes up within a block of the house."

"I've been thinking of moving on soon," Rick said, with no emotional change in his gentle voice that she could determine. "It's that time of year when the north becomes beautiful and green."

A voice shouted from across the street, "Hey! Brenda and Rick! Come on over and join us. Stewart and Dale brought a couple of bottles of wine."

Brenda waved at Rachel. She lived in the flat beneath her own, and was now standing at the end of the walk that led back into the private garden around which the apartment building bent in a U shape. She was wearing a muu-muu and standing in her bare feet under the street light.

"I came out just now to go up and look for you. Hi, Rick."

For the first time Brenda felt slightly annoyed at the group that would be surrounding her and Rick for the next several hours. They had just started to talk, for the first time, alone. It might have led to something. She looked at Rick, to see if he might be holding back, as she was. But his face was turned toward Rachel, and he was beginning to cross the street. Then he glanced back, and reached out his hand. Brenda shrugged inwardly and accompanied him over to Rachel.

They went into an apartment much like her own, with more unframed paintings than furniture. Large cushions on the floor served as chairs and sofas, placed around the only really good piece of furniture in the room, a round, low cocktail table made of rich, dark pine. There was a woven straw mat on the table to protect the wood, and upon the mat the bottles of wine and a collection of glasses that looked as though they'd been purchased at a variety of garage sales, just like Brenda's own.

The conversation was lively and art oriented, as always. Trade talk. All of them were artists, most of them barely managing to hang on from one sale to the next. Among them the most financially successful was Stewart, who had set up a tiny studio in the aisle of a shopping mall and sat all day long doing rapid-fire portraits in acrylic or oil, charging from ten to fifty dollars. But he was growing to hate it. He called it prostituting his talent for that old necessity, money, and he was looking for a rich woman to marry, and he didn't care how old she was. The older the better, in fact; especially if she would write him into her will. It was a continuing source of amusement in the crowd, the topic used as a kind of joke. Stewart elaborated on it at each meeting, sticking in various proposals he'd had that day. Laughing until her stomach was sore, Brenda doubted most of what he said, feeling he did it for effect.

Another in the group, Jennie Blockman, taught art in a valley high school. Since she had taken the position, she came back into the neighborhood only on weekends. Slumming, they all claimed, hilariously, laughing, getting more out of the comfort that none of them were off poverty row yet than any one of them would admit. The third most financially successful was Rick, whose marvelous paintings were beginning to sell for big bucks. Brenda's own, built from her dreams and her ideas, were the kind that a buyer raved over, or a viewer stood back and frowned at, trying to figure out why the trees were blue and the fish were flying just slightly above the water. Brenda couldn't have told him why either, except that by making it that way she satisfied something deep within herself. It was *right*, somehow, this dream-world she put on canvas. It felt right. It was a good feeling, the kind she got in her perfect dreams, where the most beautiful landscapes imaginable were hers for those brief hours at night.

Before she knew it the cuckoo clock on the wall was squawking twelve. She got up, feeling slightly dizzy when she stood, and told everyone goodnight. Rick watched her go out the door, somehow apart from the others, not yet joining in again when she looked back at him. She gave him a smile and a wave, and comforted herself with the fact that he at least knew she would be leaving, but that it would be another two weeks, she hoped, which would give him a chance to grab her and beg her to stay. She might have done it to him, if she hadn't felt so deeply about it. That very depth of emotion, that stranger to her, made her seem cold, perhaps, but she couldn't help it. There was something old-fashioned in her too, she decided as she went up the stairs and let herself into her own dark flat, that was after all like her dad. Something in the genes, maybe. Something her southern belle great-grandmother had bequeathed her.

It was ten o'clock at home, she thought as the phone rang. Her dad would still be up. But the phone was ringing, and ringing. She was ready to hang up and have the operator test the number to see if something was wrong somewhere along the line, when a sleepy voice answered.

"The Norris residence," it said.

"Mrs. Archer?" Brenda began searching for reasons why Mrs. Archer was answering the phone. She never stayed overnight. "Isn't Dad there? This is Brenda," she added.

"Oh. Brenda. How are you?"

"I'm okay. Dad called today and asked me if I could come and spend the summer with Jessica. He said Diane had left. I told him I'd call him back. At least I thought I had."

"Well, he had to leave on business. I guess it was urgent. Is there a message I can give him?"

"Yes. Tell him I'll be there as soon as I can get there. But I have paintings scattered around on display, and I have others that I have to pack away and that kind of thing. It will take me at least a week to get ready."

"Don't worry about it, Brenda. I'll stay here nights until you get here. I can go home and feed my cat and dog, and come back when Mister has to be away. They've got the fenced yard, and they'll be all right."

"Isn't Dad going to be available at all? I mean, he was always able to turn things over to other people whenever he wanted to, it seemed. I hate to impose on you like that. Whenever he's there, I should think you could go home."

"I will. But otherwise, don't you worry. Go ahead and do whatever you have to do. I'll tell him you'll be here when you show up."

"Thanks, Mrs. Archer. Give Robert and Jessica my love."

Jessica would be fine, Brenda told herself when she broke the telephone connection, so why was she feeling guilty? Yesterday she didn't have a care in the world, to speak of. Now she was feeling as if she were letting everyone who loved her down. Thanks, Dad.

She thought of Belle Lake, the large brick house her father had named, designed, and built for his family. She could easily visualize the five-acre grounds, with the rose gardens, the border beds, the carefully arranged and planted shrubs as well as the large trees. The rear corners had been left to nature, a wildness her mother had loved, with the huge old oak trees and the long streamers of moss, with the vines and undergrowth making passage as difficult as any jungle. At the inner edge then, there was the duck pond, and the bench beneath the trees where she used to sit and dream. The entire rear area was enclosed by fences, both heavy, sturdy chain link, and tall brick walls. Only the front yard, carefully mown grass, was exposed to the public. And what public? It was all very rural. Major highways bypassed the area. It had started as part of an old plantation, and had stayed that way. The small town hadn't grown much except for one convenience store. The public passed in a hurry five miles away. No more than a thousand people lived in and around Pinewood, and all of those were deeply rooted there, well known. There were no murderers or kidnappers among them.

Besides, Mrs. Archer was there, and o was Robert. Jessica was in no danger.

But anyway, thanks a lot, Dad.

CHAPTER FOUR

Jessica stood in the meadow looking at the tower of the castle. The sun was in the east, rising high above the trees, eating away the shadows that slanted out from beneath the trees into the meadow. On Jessica's cheek was a tiny spot of jelly. She had skipped out without washing her face after breakfast, but Mrs. Archer was busy, and this morning she had forgotten. Mrs. Archer had told her to run along and play and not bother her. She couldn't do her work with a chatterbox at her side.

Jessica listened for the voice, but there was nothing except the frogs in the swamp, not so many as there were in the evening, and the birds in the trees. Down the meadow toward the swamp a cow raised its head and mooed softly, drawing Jessica's attention for a couple of moments. The cow stood looking at her for a long while, questioning her presence in the cow meadow, then lowered its head and began eating again.

Jessica began to run, her progress impeded by the

tall grass. Like an awkward swimmer, she floundered through it and reached the fence that surrounded the jungle of the castle grounds. She had wanted desperately to tell Mrs. Archer about the castle, but Mrs. Archer didn't have time to listen. "Yes, yes, you've been reading stories about castles? Run along, run along, child." Of course Mrs. Archer knew that she couldn't read, didn't she? Mrs. Archer herself had read to her from the big book called *The World's Best Fairy Tales*. It was a book out of the library, a book that had belonged to somebody else. Maybe Brenda.

She thought of Brenda for a while as she peered through the fence into the jungle of vines and bushes. She almost couldn't remember her face, it had been so long since Brenda had come to visit.

Jessica went along the fence to the gate. It was standing open, the way she had left it yesterday when she heard her mother calling for her, but no cows had gone in. The cows wouldn't like it in there where it was dark and damp. She had run, yesterday, and she had ruined her new dress, but her mother hadn't waited anyway. Jessica felt as though she would start crying again, with a huge knot of sadness and loneliness swelling in her chest and throat. But it stayed there, dry and hard and hurting, and finally it began to dissolve and spread out into her body, rising to her brain and making it feel dull and unhappy. She had been excited about the castle until now. Now she stood there, seeing it was no castle at all, but a terribly old house, that was all, that was all.

There was no magic. There was no beauty. There was no fine singing voice welcoming her. No, welcoming Annabelle.

Nobody lived here at all.

Jessica stood on the narrow path looking through the limbs and moss streamers at the sagging roof of the front gallery. Everything beyond the green of the trees and vines was gray. The moss was gray, and so was the house. Even the pillars at the front of the house, at the sides, all around the galleries, were now gray. If there were curtains at the windows, she couldn't see them. Someone had closed all the shutters, but they were rotting away, so that the glass of the windows stared through the cracks like secret eyes.

Jessica turned to leave, all the excitement, all the anticipation turned to gray dust in her heart.

Annabelle.

She stopped, her small face concentrated in a frown. Had she heard the name spoken, or had she thought it in her mind?

She turned back, facing the house. A dozen heartbeats later she began to go toward it, along the path, over the log that was squishy with green moss, under the spiderweb she had torn, but which now the spider had mended. She reached the stone steps that went up to the long gallery floor. The door of the house stood halfway open, just as it had yesterday. No one had closed it. She thought now that no one lived there at all, there was no lady in the tower. No one. And yet . . . there might be.

She crossed the porch and stood on the threshold of the door. The leering face of the door knocker looked down at her, but after one hasty glance she refused to acknowledge its presence. It was saying to her, *if you enter this house you will die,* but it was

61

only an old iron door knocker, an ugly face, and she was not going to listen to it. She put out her hand against the wood face of the door and pushed it wider. It had opened silently yesterday, but now the hinges screeched, their strident sound echoing back from somewhere in the depths of the dark rooms. Chills ran up Jessica's arms, leaving goose bumps in their wake. As the sounds and the chills subsided she rubbed her bare arms. She was cold. A cold, dank air came from the interior of the house, as if it had never been warmed.

"Lady," she called in a small and timid voice that was too faint to be picked up by the house and returned to her in an echo.

There was no answer. There was no sound at all. Jessica crossed over the threshold and into the room. It was a large hall with no source of light except through the door behind her. To her left a door was closed, and to her right there were two more doors, both closed. In the darkness at the far end of the hall a stairway rose against one side wall, then crossed over part way up and continued to rise against the rear wall. Beneath that rise was another door, closed too, and in an alcove farther on a door that was halfway open. There was not much furniture in the hall, just a couple of chairs, like dining room chairs, and a small table between them, and a sofa, and a tall bookcase with glass doors.

Jessica tried again, in a stronger voice. "Lady?"

She waited for an answer and when none came she hesitantly ventured farther into the house. No one lived here, so it was all right if she went upstairs.

She held tightly to the banister, for the stairway was

different from the easy wide ones at home. It was steeper, and narrow, and the banister seemed wobbly. Halfway to the top, some of the steps were gone, and she looked down into a black hole and a terrible sense of danger came over her. Something moved there in the dark, a soft, sliding like something being dragged or pulled across a floor. A brushing of material, of fabric against wood. Or of fur brushing as it moved, making a sound so soft Jessica's ears, thudding with fear, almost missed it. She hung onto the banister in terror, frozen, staring into the black hole. She was standing on the edge of it, but there was room to step around, for only one end of the boards was hanging down, broken. The hole began to gray as she stared at it, and she could see boards crisscrossed down below, and beneath that a dungeon of darkness. She squeezed away from it, facing out over the drop into the hall below, her hands gripping the banister. She had to move away from the hole, get away from whatever was in the hole. It was the dungeon beneath the castle where scary creatures lived. But if she didn't go in there, didn't fall, they couldn't hurt her. With her feet sliding along the board at the edge of the stairway, she climbed until she was on solid steps again. She looked back only once before she reached the turn in the stairway. It rose again, up, up, seeming to climb forever, before she finally found herself in another hall, this one narrow and long through the second story of the house.

A door stood open, and she went into a bedroom that was gray with light coming through broken shutters. In the corner of the large room was a round area and a stairway that went up into the tower.

Jessica climbed the short, creaking stairway and came out on the round floor of the small room. The uncovered windows let light in, and even streaks of sunshine turned the spiderwebs brilliant above the shadowy gloom that hung in the air off the floor. The windows were too high for Jessica to look out, but a lady could have stood here yesterday looking out at her, thinking she was Annabelle.

It was a very dirty room, with dust and webs and big framed pictures leaning against the wall in coatings of dust. There was one chair, a rocker, but one arm was broken and hanging askew. No one had been sitting in the chair. Dust covered the sagging wicker seat.

Jessica knelt in front of a painting. With her hand, she tried to brush the dust away, but it seemed only to spread it around, so she took the tail of her shirt and used it to clean the painting.

She sat back on her heels and looked at it. A mother holding her baby. Such a pretty mother, with hair as pale gold as her own, hanging in long curls down over her shoulder and her breast. And the baby, sitting on her lap, had soft yellow-white curls too, just like Jessica's own.

"That's me," she said aloud in surprise, "and that's my *mother*." With her fingers she traced the straight nose, the curving lips, and cleaned the dust from the corners of the blue eyes. "Her eyes are the color of my eyes. That's me, with my mother."

She sat back on her heels, pleasure pulling the corners of her mouth and making dimples. The eyes of the mother looked out at her, and her arms held the baby she once was. Jessica patted herself on the chest.

"Now I'm big. I live here in this house with you, my mother."

The mother smiled at her, lips pink and soft looking. The hands holding the baby had long, lovely fingers with tapered nails. The fingers lay lightly across one plump leg of the baby, and the other hand was on the baby's arm. The baby sat with its back against the mother's breast and was looking at a blue bird that was perched on the gallery railing. Vines curled around the railing, and pink flowers dangling from the vines opened here and there. Beyond the edge of the gallery roof was the blue sky. "Out there," Jessica said, pointing downstairs to a door that was closed against the light on the broken-down gallery. Out there was where she had sat on her mother's lap a long time ago while someone painted their picture.

Were there others? A daddy? A grandmother? Some kids had grandmothers. She'd had one once when she was that other little girl . . . but she didn't want to think about that. That grandmother had gone away to heaven, and had never come to see her anymore. Now she was this girl; this was where she lived. This was her real mother now, and that was her own real picture when she was a baby. She didn't need anyone else. No brother or sister or daddy. No grandmother.

She turned the other paintings so that she could see their faces, but they were all pictures of flowers, or fruit, or trees. One had two large birds. She left them leaning against the wall, and turned swiftly at the sound of a footstep behind her.

She looked through the dim, slanted rays of the sun

65

and saw the open hole of the stairwell, and the rocking chair back in the corner. She saw a long group of spiderwebs swaying in the corner behind the chair, as if they had been moved by the person whose footstep she had heard. She stood up, squinting into the strange light of the tower, but there was no one else, no one hiding behind the chair or the tall chest against the opposite wall. The doors of the chest stood open, and there were things on the shelves dark with dust, things that looked like folded clothes. She put her hands behind her. These were someone else's things. Her mother's? Was this her mother's special room?

She squatted again in front of the painting, her back to the room, the furniture, the stairwell. There still was dust sunk deep into crevices of the paint, and with her shirt tail she began cleaning again, going up into the corners of the painting near the heavy frame, and finally onto the carved gold frame itself, digging into the grooves, cleaning, cleaning. She murmured aloud as she worked, growing happy as this new world grew.

"And we will go down the stairs together—the back stairs away from the hole in the dungeon—did you know there is a terrible, terrible dungeon beneath the castle, Mother? And something lives down there. Perhaps it was put there a long, long time ago. But we will go down and out onto the gallery and to the garden and you will talk to me and tell me about the flowers. I already know what bluebells are. Mrs. Archer told me." She stopped and frowned, feeling as though she were separated into two people, two worlds. She pushed the old world away. "But I want

66

you to tell me. You—"

Creeeak. Creak . . .

Jessica whirled. The rocking chair was moving slowly, forward, back. Forward. With each movement a loud creak rose from it, swelling in the room, going into Jessica's head and thundering there, making her clasp her hands against her ears and cry out softly. She ran toward the stairwell, trying to escape the sounds of the chair as it rocked. The empty chair that was rocking, rocking, faster, faster, *faster. . . .*

Jessica felt like screaming, but they were moans instead of terror that made her skin feel like ice. She started down the stairway, and then saw the painting with the smiling lady and the baby that was—*remember*—herself. Herself and her mother. She must not leave them behind in this room that she no longer liked. She dashed back, chilled by the coldness in the room, driven half mad by the sound from the rocking chair that buzzed in her head like thousands of insects, sounds swelling to torture. She grabbed up the heavy, unwieldy painting and dragged it with her. It bumped against the floor, one corner making a long scratch in the wood, as the rocking chair rocked madly, faster, faster, and the sounds from it vibrated from wall to wall. Jessica got the painting to the stairwell, and there she lost it and it fell, bouncing from step to step and finally crashing to the floor below to lie face down. Jessica, frozen on the step, watching it fall, gasped in silence, her head ringing with the screeching of the rocking chair. She glanced back at it once before she too half fell down the steps, and she saw something in the chair, a gauzy outline, someone sitting there, hands gripping the broken arms, and a terrible insane laughter rose to mingle with the other sounds that filled the room. Jessica let go of the floor of the tower room and hurtled down the steps, missing the bottom three entirely.

She fell beside the painting.

Fear brought her eyes to the hole above, where the stairs ended, where the floor of the tower room began. The thing in the chair was not following her. The noise had stopped. Only the echoes of it were left in her head, and gradually that too ceased. Slowly she got up, first to her knees, then to her feet, not once taking her eyes from the hole in the tower floor. The light there seemed to glow, filled with dancing dust motes and narrow little rays of sunshine.

Jessica began to back away; then she remembered the painting again and she rushed to lift it off the floor. The mother smiled at her, and the baby looked eagerly toward the blue bird. It wasn't broken.

Jessica looked around. There was a large bed against the wall, a bed so high there was a little step at the side of it. Across the room were heavy chests and one dresser, the oval mirror so dirty it reflected only its own dirt. There were other things in the room, a desk that had a tall back, and some chairs. But Jessica didn't like the room. It was dark, and it was cold, too, and it also had the round corner that was part of the tower and the stairway to the tower. She didn't like any of it.

Groaning with the burden, she lifted the painting clear of the floor and carried it across the room, letting it down as she needed to in order to get her breath, then, once again lifting it and struggling with it toward the door into the hall. By the time she had put it down in the hall, her arms were too weak to move it again. She leaned it against the wall and then pulled shut the door to the bedroom that she didn't like. She would never open it again, not that door, no. That room didn't exist in her castle.

She went down the hall, opening other doors, seeing bedsteads, some of them with mattresses, some bare. All of the rooms had windows barred with the closed shutters, and some of the shutters were still intact, making the rooms dark. She left the doors open.

The last room she entered was different. She knew immediately it was a little girl's room. The bed was still made with pillow and quilt. It was a narrow bed, back in the corner. But she only gave it a glance, for there was something in the opposite corner, the dark corner. Something big, that took up all of the corner and much of the room. A big, big doll house.

With a cry of delight she ran to it. It was like a real house, with real furniture, two bedrooms above and a living room and kitchen below. And, best of all, there were dolls in it. In the living room a large doll sat, a man doll. On the floor beside him was a funny black hat, as if he had just put it there when he sat down. On the hearth in front of him were two more dolls, a girl doll and a boy doll. And in the kitchen, a mother doll, so tall her bonnet touched the ceiling. She was standing by the table, looking toward the front of the house, toward the bedroom.

Annabelle.

Annabelle. Annabelle.

They were cries of delight. Cries that sounded in Jessica's head, spoken there, or carried there. The voices were fine and small, like the voices of elves.

But it was so dark.

She drew back, afraid and yet not afraid.

Annabelle, they had called her. Someone had called her Annabelle, and it was from the doll house. The dolls were talking to her.

But it was so dark she could hardly see them.

She went to the window and tried to open it, but it didn't budge to her efforts. She found a chair and pulled it close and stood on it and saw that the window was latched at the top of the bottom section, but her fingers prying at the latch only dislodged the dust. She got down from the chair and looked at the window, and saw there was a long crack in the glass. Without planning, she picked up the chair and pushed it against the glass, and the crack gave. She stepped quickly back just as a triangular portion of the glass fell to the floor beneath the window. It cracked into three pieces and Jessica pushed it aside with her foot. She stood for a while looking at the broken pieces.

"That's really all right," she said aloud. "It's my room. It's all right. My mother won't care."

She stood on the chair again and carefully picked the rest of the broken glass out of the window and put it on the floor with the rest, then she reached through and unlatched the shutters that closed in darkness in the room, and pushed them open. Sunshine flooded in, sweeping a wide path across the room to the bed against the wall, showing here as it had in the tower the clusters of webs in the corners of the rooms and swagging across the ceiling.

But there was light now, and she could see, and

70

when she climbed off the chair and turned, she was startled to see that the papa doll was no longer sitting in the living room in his chair. He was standing now, in the middle of the room, facing her.

Annabelle. We've waited so long.

CHAPTER FIVE

"My name is Jessica."

Annabelle.

She felt a little scared, icy little rivers running up and down her back, and she remained standing by the chair, looking at the tall papa doll. He was dressed all in black, and he stood with his arms down at his sides, and his face frozen in white, his eyes painted on, and a fine, black mustache painted above the pink, round lips. The eyes did not move from side to side. They weren't made of glass like her dolls at home. Like Jessica's dolls. Jessica's dolls had eyes that rolled from side to side and closed, too, with long lashes sweeping down. Of course there were her Cabbage Patch dolls, with their wide-open eyes, and her Raggedy Ann and Andy dolls, who just had cloth eyes. Mrs. Archer had told her about the glass eyes, when she — when Jessica — had wanted to know if the doll's eyes were like her own, and if the doll slept, like she did. Mrs. Archer had said, "Dolls don't do anything, Jessica. They're not real. Their eyes are made of glass, and their eyelashes of nylon, or some such stuff. They can't do anything that you don't make them do. Their eyes close when you lay them down. Talk? Well, when you pull their string. Or punch the button. It's that computer thing that makes them talk."

She remembered well what Mrs. Archer had said, but this doll, standing in front of her, was different. He was real. A real doll. Somehow, she didn't know how, something made him walk and talk.

But she really wasn't afraid.

Not really.

He thought she was someone named Annabelle.

A really terrible, really scary thought was edging into her mind, unwanted, but not going away. What would he do if . . . ?

What would he do if he knew she was not Annabelle?

For a long time then she was unable to breathe, and her mouth got dry and crusty feeling. The doll was standing between her and the door, and the sunlight was moving, and now it touched upon his head, and she saw beneath the gray dust that covered him and his black clothes even his hair was painted black, and parted in the middle, waving down toward his ears, toward the stiff collar of his coat. He stood staring past her with his painted eyes.

There was movement in the doll house, a sliding of feet, a thump as the mama doll almost fell from the floor of the doll house to the bedroom floor. Her long skirt brushed the rug as she moved out and turned, reminding Jessica of the robot that now stood unnoticed in her brother's bedroom. It had moved like the mama doll, gliding smoothly, and then stopping, and raising its arm with short jerks. And turning, too, with little jolts of movement.

Until it faced her.

Now there were two of them, facing her, standing between her and the door.

Annabelle.

They still thought she was Annabelle. The mama doll had painted eyes, too, but her hair looked real. It was parted in the middle and drawn back and pinned to the back of her head in double coils. She wore a bonnet, too, that covered the top part. The dress she wore went all the way to the floor, but not like a robe, or a gown. It flared from the tight waist, and stood out around the doll's feet. Only the pointed toes of the doll's shoes stuck out beneath the dress. There, too, was the lace edge of the doll's underslip. Jessica's slips had lace at the bottom edge, too.

They had ears, Jessica saw, just like her own dolls. They were formed of the same white as the rest of the head. And they had real hands, with fingers and thumbs. They stood still in front of her, the mama doll slightly behind the papa doll. Jessica took a step forward, tentatively, but the dolls didn't move. Her fear began to lessen. They thought she was someone named Annabelle and — suddenly a new thought struck her. Was Annabelle a doll, too? A doll that someone had taken away? Or a doll that was broken?

She hurried to the doll house and looked in. The kitchen and living room ceilings were high enough that she could stand with only her hair touching them, and she moved into the room that wasn't so dark now, to the two dolls on the floor. One of them, a girl doll, was sitting in a small chair that was like the papa doll's large chair, and Jessica pulled her up. The doll's arms and body crinkled under her fingers, made of cloth and some kind of filling that was solid and firm and made faint paperlike noises, but the head and hands were like the larger dolls', white and solid. A glass of some kind. A pottery. China. Yes, china. Jessica remembered now the old, old dolls she had seen at the museum where Mrs. Archer had taken her once. They were called china dolls, and they were the kind of dolls Mrs. Archer's grandmother had played with. They, too, were dressed in these funny old dresses with the lace on the stiff skirts that stuck out like an upside-down umbrella. These were very, very old dolls, like the ones in the museum.

Vesta.

Jessica drew back, surprised. No one had spoken. There had been no sound beyond the birds and frogs outside, and other, quieter movements in the house, in the floors, the walls; yet the name came to her mind, as clearly as if it had been spoken aloud. Vesta. That was the name of the doll. Jessica *knew*.

Jessica held the doll in front of her. This doll was not Annabelle. She stood the doll aside, carefully, balancing it on its dainty black slippers. It stood without falling or swaying, but it hadn't moved yet by itself. Maybe it couldn't. It stared at her from its painted blue eyes. They weren't as pretty as glass eyes. The painted eyes were flat and hard and Jessica wasn't comfortable looking at them. She turned back to the doll house.

The fourth doll looked as if it had been thrown, or

kicked, back into one of the corners, and she drew it out, going in on her knees to get it. Its head lolled awkwardly to one side, and she realized when she sat down and pulled the doll onto her lap that its neck was broken. The china had pulled away on one side from the material of the body, and bits and ends of straw, stiff and old, were sticking out. This was a boy doll, dressed in boy clothes, even though it had real hair that was as long as the whole head and neck on one side, and gone from the scalp on the other, as if it had been pulled out.

"Oh. Oh," Jessica murmured in sympathy as she tried to straighten the poor head and the broken neck.

Vi-Vi-Vic . . .

Not Annabelle. Not this doll. He was a boy. Annabelle was a girl who looked like her. Or was in some way like her, because the dolls thought she was Annabelle. But of course they couldn't see her, not actually. If their eyes had been made of glass they might have been able to see through them and see her, but since they were painted eyes, and especially since some of the paint was gone, like in this boy doll's eyes, then of course they couldn't really see her.

"Who are you?" Jessica asked, then bit her tongue. Wouldn't Annabelle know who he was? She felt a struggling movement in her hands, something deep within the straw working in terrible effort. Jessica pulled her hands away, swiftly, and pushed back against the wall of the doll house. She stared open-mouthed at the doll as it struggled to rise.

Annabelle.

76

It was a cry, as soft as the whisper of a mouse in the wall, a fine-voiced chatter. Not in her head this time, but there, coming to her ears. The voice of the dolls, and this one pleading, somehow, she knew, for her help.

She put her hands out again and straightened the doll, stood him on his feet, but his head hung brokenly to one side, and even as he gained his balance he spun sideways on one leg, as if permanent balance were impossible for him.

"Oh poor Vic," Jessica whispered. "I'm so sorry."

Victor. Victor.

"Victor. I know. That's your name. And that's Vesta, and that's Mama and Papa doll. But . . ."

Where's Annabelle?

She came out of the living room of the doll house and looked at the ladder at the corner that went up to the top floor. She climbed it, and found beds and a cradle, and within the cradle, still covered by its dusty blanket, a baby doll. This one, too, had a china head, but there was something different about it. The eyes were small glass beads that opened when she climbed down the ladder and held the doll upright.

For a long time she sat playing with the baby doll. It was not like the others, it was just a plain little doll with a cloth body, even cloth feet and hands. There was something about the hands of the big dolls that she didn't like. The fingers were too long and too pointed. Too sharp. She was aware of them standing together, side by side, facing toward her as she sat with the baby doll, even Victor, with his head hanging all wrong; but they didn't move, and their strange

77

little voices were still. She was aware of them all the time, a bit uneasily, and she gave all her attention to the baby doll in its long, long dress, and to the things in the kitchen. With her hands and her shirt she wiped dust from little iron cooking utensils and from the top of the black iron stove, and the table and the cupboards. She straightened the chairs and set them close to the table. She set the table with dishes and cups and saucers, and even put out the silverware. It was tarnished and old, and she tried to polish it on her pants leg, but the tarnish had been there much too long.

The sunlight moved, shrank to nothing in the room. Warm air came in through the unshuttered window. Jessica was growing tired of sitting there, and she remembered the painting she had left in the hallway.

She stood up. The dolls had closed in on her. They were poised in a half-moon from one corner of the doll house to the other. Victor stood so close to the corner of the house that his head leaned against it. She stood, feeling uneasy again. Would they let her through?

She took a step forward, and the papa doll moved aside, making a path for her. Jessica drew a long breath, and went to the bedroom door where she stopped and looked back.

They were following her, all in a line like the ducklings at home, first the papa, then the mama, then Vesta, and at last, several paces behind, Victor, with a sideways, lumbering movement, as if the wound in his neck went all the way to his feet.

78

Jessica went down the hall without looking back again, but she could hear them behind, small dragging steps, the swish of long skirts, the faint, very faint rustle of straw. And most outstanding, the crooked stride of Victor, with a step that was heavier than the others, and a *sli-ide*, as he brought his wounded side along.

She stopped at the painting and squatted in front of it, one hand going to touch it gently. She smiled. "Mother. My mother. This is—"

There was suddenly noise from the dolls, a chattering, as from small animals alarmed, and they swooped in to surround her, to squeeze between her and the painting of the beautiful mother with her baby. Their bodies, arms, hands were pushing her, and she fell backwards, her head striking the floor. She sat up, the pain radiating from the back of her head to the front and almost blinding her, but even so she saw him, Victor, poised in front of the painting, bending forward, raising his arms and reaching out to the face of the mother. She saw his sharp, china fingers stretch out like claws and rake down over the mother's face, and when he drew away, chattering, chattering, the painting hung in shreds.

Jessica came forward on her knees, and with her arms swept the dolls aside. "No! No!" she cried out, tears blurring what was left of the painting. With trembling hands she tried to stick the strips of ripped canvas back, but they kept falling down again.

She whirled upon the dolls, who stood now in a close line behind her. She began striking out at them, feeling the thud of her hands against yielding bodies.

"Go away! Go away! Go away!"

Annabelle.

"I'm not Annabelle, I'm Jessica! Leave me alone! You've ruined my mother's picture. You've ruined my picture. That's me, when I was a baby. That's my mother! Go away!"

Annabelle.

She heard the sadness in the cry, but she had sadness of her own, and so she turned away from it. She ran to the top of the stairs and began to go down, sobbing, her throat convulsing. Why had Victor torn her painting? Why had he done that?

At the hole in the stairway she paused and looked down, and through the blur of tears she thought she saw a white, white face looking up at her, but she turned her head away and, clinging hard to the banister, crept past the hole. At the foot of the stairs she turned and looked back.

They were still at the top, looking straight ahead, lined up together, shoulder to shoulder. Only Victor, with his broken neck, was not looking toward her. His eyes were trained somewhere on the wall, his fine china face with its small nose and tiny pink mouth still the face of a doll, beautiful and set in its beauty.

Annabelle, come back. Don't leave us again.

Jessica turned away, running to the light beyond the open front door of the house.

On the stone porch she paused and drew a long breath of fresh air. She felt as though she had just awakened from a dream. Sometimes, then, she couldn't tell what was real and what was not real for a while. Mrs. Archer had told her that dreams, the lives she lived when she was not really awake, were not real. But still sometimes it was hard to tell. And now she felt that way again. She had stood here, on this porch, a long time ago. Her name was Jessica. Then she crossed the threshold into the house and she became someone named Annabelle. And in that house were dolls that were connected in some way to Annabelle, and they were real. Partly real, anyway. They talked. But in a strange way. In a way that she heard in her head more than in her ears. And they moved. And they thought she was Annabelle. Even when she told them her name was really Jessica, still they called her Annabelle. Did that mean they hadn't heard her? That their ears, made of china, couldn't really hear? Had it all been a dream?

"Jessica! Jessica!"

The call was real. It was Mrs. Archer's voice, though it sounded different. Strained, that's what it was. And mad? But Mrs. Archer never got mad at her, just impatient; she had said, "I'm not mad, Jessica, I just get a bit impatient with you sometimes. Now go out and play." So that was the trouble now, Mrs. Archer was impatient. Jessica was running even as the thoughts came to her mind.

The weeds and grass in the meadow scratched her legs she tore through them so recklessly. Even before she was halfway across the meadow she could see Mrs. Archer's face pressed against the chain link fence at the back of the yard, watching her. Yards before Jessica came to the edge of the meadow, Mrs. Archer was screaming at her.

"Where on earth have you been, child? Look at

you. My Lord, but look at you!"

Jessica reached the fence in front of Mrs. Archer's appalled face and began to climb. Mrs. Archer's hands tapped at her fingers from the other side.

"Get down, get down from there! What on earth are you trying to do, climb over that big high fence? You'll rip your clothes to shreds, to say nothing of your skin. You'll fall and break your neck! Get down from there!"

Jessica dropped back to stand in a patch of sweet-smelling clover, its leaves and flowers soft against her scratched legs. She stared through the wire at Mrs. Archer.

"But there's no gate," she said.

"Then you'll just have to walk around the wall to the front, won't you? Oh Lordy, how did you get over there, Jessica?"

"I climbed over."

"Over this wire? Well, then climb back, this one time. Carefully now. I'll help you down when you get to the top. Be careful of those twisted wires at the top. Do you know what those wires are up there for, young lady? They're there to keep people from climbing over, that's what. How on earth did you get over without cutting yourself to pieces? Do you know what time it is? Where have you been all day? I've been looking for you for at least an hour, me and your brother both. Robert's been looking around the front and down the roads, and I've been combing the back grounds, and all the time we were just about ready to call the police! If I hadn't seen you in the middle of the field, I'd have gone right back to the house and called the police. Now get yourself over here and tell me where you've been."

Mrs. Archer's hands reached up to hold on to Jessica as she climbed down the fence inside the yard.

"I was at the castle."

"The *what*? The castle?"

"Yes. It's my castle."

"Don't tell me you were over at that old place! Good Lord, Jessica! Don't you ever go close to that old house. Why, there ain't been a soul lived in that house for almost a hundred years that I ever heard of. You come on down here and," with Jessica on the ground, Mrs. Archer clutched one of her arms and shook her, "and don't you ever stay away from the house like that! What if those cows in the pasture had took after you? There wouldn't be enough of you left over to make sausage with. Come along, we have to tell your brother that he can stop looking."

Jessica went along beside Mrs. Archer awkwardly, her left arm still in the grasp of Mrs. Archer's large hand, and pulled up so high that Jessica at times had to tiptoe. As they crossed the back yard, Jessica saw Robert standing at the corner of the kitchen porch.

"Where's she been?" he asked.

"Oh Lord, who knows. Anyway, you can go now. We don't have to call the police after all. You might bring me a box of crackers back from the store. I saw there weren't but a few, and I need some for the casserole I aim to put in the oven for your suppers. The mister will be back on time this evening, he said when he called, so I'll be going home at five. When the bell rings on the oven you can take out the dinner

83

if Mister isn't here by then. I'll put this young'n in the tub and clean her up, and Lordy, you can tell the mister about this shenanegans if you want to—"

Robert had left, and through the holes in the brick wall of the breezeway, Jessica saw him get on his bike and pedal off down the driveway. Mrs. Archer gave her a jerk.

"Come along, little lady. You've got some explaining to do."

Jessica was upstairs, undressed and sitting in a tub of almost-hot water when Mrs. Archer asked the question again.

"All right, tell me about it now. Where were you all those hours, Jessica?"

"In the house," Jessica said. "The castle."

"Castle! *Castle*?" There was a long silence as Mrs. Archer slopped water and soap onto Jessica's stinging skin. Then she said, "Well, I hadn't thought of it before, but I can see where it would look like one of them old medieval castles, all right. With its round room sticking up at the corner, and all that gray stone it's built of. But that old place has been abandoned since Lord knows when, Jessica, and I expect it's a very dangerous place to be. No telling, the roof could fall in on you. Surely you didn't go in it, did you?"

"Yes, ma'am," Jessica said so softly that Mrs. Archer said, "What?" loudly, and Jessica had to repeat.

"Well, don't you ever do it again. You might find something in that house that you don't want to find."

Jessica raised her head. "What?" Did Mrs. Archer know about the dolls? Were they real after all, and not a dream?

"Hants. Spooks. Ghosts."

"What's that?"

"It's dead people and animals that come back in spirit form and hant the places where they lived. They walk around night and day, but mostly where it's dark and gloomy like that old plantation mansion there. It was called White Oaks in its day, and nobody has lived there in all my lifetime, and probably not in my mother's. I expect that old place is filled with ghosts, and you'd better stay out of there."

"What do ghosts look like?"

"Oh, mercy. Ghosts take many forms, so I've been told. They can turn into bats at night, and rats in the daytime, even birds. Crows, and blackbirds, not the pretty ones like bluebirds and wild canaries. But mostly they're gauzy, white, something you can see through. But don't you think for a minute they can't hurt you, because they can."

Mrs. Archer scrubbed Jessica's back vigorously. Jessica was pushed forward by the force. She leaned her elbows on her knees for support, rested her face in her hands and thought of ghosts.

"I didn't see any ghosts, except—" She thought of the rocking chair, and the way it rocked by itself, and then the slow appearance of something she couldn't remember very well.

"Do they rock in rocking chairs?"

"In old hanted places, they do everything."

"Well, I didn't see any," Jessica decided cautiously.

"Of course not. They don't just pop out the first time. But don't go there again. My grandmother told

85

me about White Oaks. There was a family there once, a man, wife, and three children. And the wife and children disappeared, and the man died from a broken heart, or some such malady. No one ever knew what happened to the woman and her children."

"Was there a girl named Annabelle?"

Mrs. Archer rinsed Jessica, holding the spray that was attached to the wall by means of a long, flexible tube over her head and letting the fresh, warm water fall over her.

"Why on earth do you ask that?"

Jessica shrugged. "I don't know. I just thought someone named Annabelle lived there."

Mrs. Archer grunted, turned off the spray, released the bath plug to let the water drain, and pulled Jessica out onto the rug. She reached behind her and brought down a towel that was twice as long as Jessica was tall, and wrapped her in it, toweling as vigorously as she had scrubbed. When the toweling was finished she reached for the hair dryer and blew Jessica's hair into a cloud of flying curls.

"Now," she said. "Get into your pajamas. It's past time for me to go home. I have to run down and get the supper on to cook."

"I don't want to go to bed," Jessica wailed.

"You don't have to go to bed. You can go into the TV room and watch cartoons from now on until your daddy comes and sends you to bed hisself, or else if he don't get here by that time, Robert can send you to bed. By any rate, you get to bed by eight o'clock, you hear?"

"Yes, ma'am." And then, "Maybe my mama will

come home and put me to bed."

Mrs. Archer snorted. "Don't hold your breath." She patted Jessica's head, and gave her a quick, rare hug. "It'll be all right, don't you worry, it'll be all right. You're young. A five-year-old's memory ain't much longer than a snail's ear. By the time you're grown up, you won't remember."

Jessica lifted her head. "Do snails have ears?" She'd seen many snails out on the walk in the grass, some of them tiny and cute, no larger than the nail on her little finger, and some of them almost as big as her hand. And she had seen their heads sticking out of their shell, but ears? Dogs and cats had ears, and cows, too, and so did she, but—

"Of course they have ears. How else would they hear you coming? You look close the next time you see one, and you'll see two little horns sticking up. Well, those are ears."

Jessica laughed, not really sure but that Mrs. Archer was telling one of her jokes, which she did sometimes. But Mrs. Archer's wrinkled face wasn't smiling, and her dark brown eyes weren't twinkling the way they did when it was a joke.

"I'll look," she said, promising herself and Mrs. Archer.

"Good. That should keep you busy tomorrow morning. Whatever you do, you must not go back to the old White Oaks place. Come along now. It's getting dark outside. I need to get the lights on, and get started home. My cat and dog will think I've deserted them."

Jessica ate a snack in the kitchen while Mrs.

Archer was putting food into the oven to cook, and then later she went to sleep in front of the television before her father got home. She was curled into the soft leather chair, with a stuffed animal in her arms. She woke briefly as she was being carried up the stairs, just enough to know that it was her daddy's arms that held her. She didn't know when he put her down into her bed and pulled the light blanket up to cover her.

The room she was in wavered, as if it were under water. The walls were indistinct and the furniture moved. She was finding it hard to breathe, and there was a terrible pain in her head. She put her hands up, to feel her head, and her hands groped in empty air. She began to scream with the panic that seized her, that flooded into her and controlled her so that she was nothing but fear, terror, panic.

"Annabelle, stop that this instant."

The room began to clear with the woman's voice. She looked up, but she could see only the full skirt. She knew it was her mother's skirt, and she was wearing a green dress today with a cream lace edging, and her petticoats stood out beneath, as was the fashion, with more lace showing, and only the tips of her green slippers peeking through. Annabelle shoved back, walking backwards to get away, and came to a wall where she could go no further. She heard her own voice crying out.

"Why did you hit me, I haven't done anything." She hated the sound of her voice, the whining sound of it, the half-crying, half-wailing, but the fear and the

pain were so intense she couldn't help it. "I was just going to get my embroidery basket, Mama. I wasn't doing anything."

"I didn't hit you, what are you talking about?"

Annabelle began to cry, frustration building. Was it her mama who was insane at times, or was it she? She reached up, groping for her head again, and her hands touched her head and felt the broken skin where her mother's ring had struck her.

"Oh, have you hurt yourself?" *the mother's voice said with deceptive softness.* "Come and let me see."

"No, no—"

"Don't say no to me."

The skirt was swishing closer, closer, angrily, the footsteps quick. The hand with the rings was reaching out, long and white. The other hand slipped for a moment from behind the skirt and it was holding shears, the points open and sharp.

She whirled, running, and struck the corner of the doorway. She fell, and struggled to regain her feet, to run, run toward somebody, somewhere safe, but the hand reached down and caught her by the hair. She screamed, and screamed. . . .

Jessica woke screaming, seeing the hand with the open scissors, feeling terror such as she had never felt in her life. She fought the blanket that covered her, and threw away from her the cuddly stuffed animal that was keeping her from escape. After a long time of fighting to rise from the strange, terrible dream, she heard footsteps pounding in the hall and felt the slight vibration from them.

The bedroom light came on, and Jessica stared through tears at the man in the doorway whose face was almost as white and twisted as her own.

By the time he had reached her side, she recognized her father, and she threw her arms around his neck.

CHAPTER SIX

"What is it? What is it?" He held her against him, felt the trembling of her small body. She was still sobbing, and he absorbed her panic. It washed into him, and he felt stunned by it. Under his breath he muttered, "Damn you, Diane. Why aren't you here taking care of your baby?" She'd never screamed in her sleep before, and he knew it was happening now because Diane had left.

"Did you have a bad, bad dream, baby?"

Jessica began to relax, the dream fading so that she had only pale visions of movements. Was it the ghosts? The hants? "Daddy," she said. "What are ghosts and hants and spirits?"

Paul was still for a thought, then he demanded, "Ghosts? *Hants?* There's no such thing, Jessica. There is no spirit world. I think you've been watching too many cartoons lately on television."

"No, Mrs. Archer told me about them. There really are ghosts and hants, Daddy, I know."

"And how do you know?"

"Because Mrs. Archer said so, and Mrs. Archer knows. She's — she's real old, Daddy, even older than you, and she knows about ghosts and hants."

"I think the word is haunts, and Mrs. Archer was only joking with you, Jessica, that was all. Now do you think you can lie down and sleep? Look, I'll leave a light burning for you, if that will make you feel better. We can leave on this light over here."

Jessica lay back on her pillow and gazed over the edge of the blanket at her daddy. "Are you mad, Daddy?"

"No, I'm not mad."

But he was. He was more than mad, he was furious.

"Goodnight, dear. Daddy's here, and so is Robert. You close your eyes and go to sleep."

He stood in the doorway watching until her eyes had fluttered shut for the third time and stayed, then he slipped away, leaving the bedroom door open so that he could hear if she cried out again.

Damn that woman. After all these years she pulled something like that, and right at this most crucial time — when the child's mother had left. Damn the bitch.

He called Mrs. Archer from his downstairs office, the corner room in the northeast of the house. Its window looked out over the front lawn and across the side lawn to the brick wall. The shrubs were glazed with light from the entrance, and he looked out on them, not seeing, not bothering to pull the draperies. It was past midnight, but it didn't matter. He was going to talk to her tonight.

The phone rang eleven times before she answered, and then she sounded more alarmed than asleep.

"Yes? What is it? *Elaine?*"

No, not Elaine, whoever that was.

"This is Paul Norris," he said, and she interrupted.

"Is something wrong?"

"Yes, some things are wrong, and one of them is I dislike very much being interrupted when I am trying to say something. I want you to know, Mrs. Archer, that your employment here has been terminated tonight. If there is anything in this house that belongs to you, you may come and get it tomorrow. I'll put a check in the mail that will, I'm sure, settle payment for your last days here, as well as two weeks' termination pay. But I also want you to know that your ridiculous stories about ghosts and haunts and other impossible phenomena had Jessica screaming with nightmares tonight. I hope that you haven't done permanent damage, madam. But what you have done is unforgivable."

"Jessica had a nightmare? Children have nightmares sometimes, Mr. Norris."

"Jessica has never had a nightmare before. Your stories about ghosts came at a very bad time, and I don't want you telling her those ridiculous stories anymore, do you understand? If you must return to this house at all, simply take your possessions and leave. Goodnight, Mrs. Archer."

He hung up the phone with an emphatic thud. On a note pad he made a note to call the agency and have them send out a temporary housekeeper tomorrow, then he made another note to call Brenda again and insist that she come home for a while. Didn't she actually owe him that much?

Mrs. Archer was still trembling. She sat on the edge of the living room sofa in her flannel nightgown. Even though it was June now, the nights were cool enough that she froze if she tried to wear a summer gown.

How long had the phone rung? She had first heard it in her dreams, had woven it around Elaine, and had created a situation where anxiety grew in leaps toward she didn't know what. Elaine on a dark street, running from something, and the ringing phone somewhere in a dark house behind her. Waking to hear that the phone was in her own living room was the only thing that had kept her from having a nightmare herself. Maybe this was the night for nightmares.

Elaine had wanted her to put in another phone, right beside her bed. Maybe she should. When the phone rang in the middle of the night, it was a terribly scary thing, especially when you've got one daughter and she's just got a divorce from a man who was as mean when he got drunk as an old billy goat on soured mash. He had threatened Elaine more than once that he would come back and "get her and the kids, too," so the ringing phone at twelve-thirty at night brought only one thing to Mary Archer's mind. She had half a notion to call Elaine and see if she and the kids were all right, but that would only scare them half to death if they were all asleep. Besides, Troy's threats so far had only been threats. A couple of times, Elaine said, he had come around when he was drunk, but she had called the cops and told them he was out in his car in that condition, and they had hauled him off to jail. That last time he had lost his driver's license, and she hadn't seen him since. He hadn't even tried to see the kids. The rumor was, he was living with an old gal down on the river, fishing and making his own liquor. He didn't need to go to town anymore.

Mrs. Archer got up and went into her kitchen, clicking the light on, and looking around with satisfaction. It was a small kitchen, but clean and white, with just a touch of color here and there in things hanging on the walls and a strip of bright border paper around the top of the cabinets. Janey, her oldest granddaugher, had pasted that up, and done a very good job of it, too.

She made a cup of coffee, even though she knew she shouldn't. But she also knew she wouldn't sleep another minute this night.

A scratching came at the back screen door, and Mary opened the wood door and then the screen. Amber, her big yellow cat, meowed up at her and undulated in when the screen door was open wide enough to allow room for his well-fed body. He went straight to his dish in the corner to check out the food supply, and when he found it empty he came back and curled around her ankles coaxingly. She stooped and rubbed his fur until it crackled.

"It's not time to eat, you old fat thing. It's the middle of the night."

But she poured him a few drops of cream, nevertheless, when she took out the pitcher to put some in her coffee cup. He lapped in his bowl, his small pink tongue making soft plop, plop noises as she sat down to sip her coffee. Through the screen door, she saw the dark muzzle of her dog, Rover. She had gotten him from the animal shelter three years ago after her fourteen-year-old shepherd died, and she had never seen anything so grateful for the freedom of a fenced back yard. He had run around it barking joyously, and she had let him bark. After a few days he had settled down, and everytime she looked at him he wagged his tail and smiled. Don't let anyone try to tell her dogs didn't smile. It was true cats didn't. But dogs did.

"You want something too, Rover?"

She got up and took a dog biscuit from the box in the cupboard, opened the screen door, and handed it to him. He took it daintily, careful not to close his teeth on her fingers. She watched him as he lay down on the stoop and began chewing on the biscuit.

When she sat down again she faced the thing that had kept her shaking as if she had a chill.

Fired.

And where else in this little burg would she find work? She'd been a widow for ten years, but she had worked for the Norrises since long before that. She wasn't old enough to draw her Social Security, and though she had a few thousand in savings, it wouldn't last a year if she had to start spending it for living expenses.

Jessica having nightmares? It was probably because her mother had pulled out, bag and baggage, as it was said. Ghost stories? Hants? When had she told Jessica any ghost stories? Never. *Never.* She had

96

only warned her about the old house, that was all. And who was Mister to say she was wrong about it? How did he know what roamed the halls and byways of that old ruined mansion? *Her* hurt little Jessica? Scare her, even? Mister should know her better than that. Why, she loved little Jessica almost as much as she loved her own grandchildren.

Her daddy woke her when he kissed her good-bye, and she sat up and blinked at him. The sun was shining on the trees across the driveway, and so many birds were singing that her ears rang.

"Robert's going to be with you this morning, Jessica, until the new maid comes. I'll be home this evening as early as I can. You be a good girl."

He was gone before she could understand, before she could wake up and ask him why there was going to be a new maid. Was Mrs. Archer taking a vacation? Once she had, Jessica remembered. Then, her mama had been here, but she hadn't liked being here so much. Jessica had clung to her too much, and her mama had grown impatient and angry and had pushed her away, and then told her if she didn't stop crying she would go away and not come back. Jessica had stopped crying, though she felt as if she would burst, but her mother had gone away, after all.

Jessica got out of bed and went to her window that looked out over the back yard and the duck pond, and across the meadow to the castle. It was still there, the tower almost invisible among the trees.

It was her castle. That was where she belonged. Her real mother was there, in the painting, holding

97

her when she was a baby. That was her house, not this. *That* mother, that real mother, lived and wanted her.

Jessica dressed in jeans and pullover cotton shirt, and went downstairs to the kitchen. Robert was there pouring himself a bowl of cereal. He grunted when he saw her. In one hand he was carrying his radio and Jessica knew he couldn't have heard her if she said anything because he was also wearing the headband with the ends in his ears. He mumbled at her from around something he was chewing.

"Here. Eat some of this. Mrs. Archer's not working here anymore, Dad said, and there's someone else coming. Want milk? Here."

She sat at the table long enough to eat the cereal he had poured in her dish, but she ate alone. Robert had gone back through the door toward the front of the house with a tray holding a bowl of cereal, a glass of milk, toast, and fruit. Jessica gazed at the fruit bowl on the table as she ate. There were oranges, apples, bananas, grapes, but she saw none of it. The painting of her beautiful, blond mother stood between her and the fruit, ripped and ruined. She mashed her eyes shut and opened them again, and saw the fruit bowl with the grapes hanging over the edge, but she knew what she was going to do.

She ran to the television room and the small desk in the corner where her color books and all her crayons and pencils and things were, and took from a drawer a small bottle of paste. She poked it down into her pocket and ran out of the house.

At the fences she was careful, first, to climb the

chain link at a place where no one could see her, where the tall, fully leafed magnolia tree sheltered her from view of the house and most of the grounds. Then, at the barbed wire fence that surrounded her castle, she was careful to shut the gate. When she went up the walk to the front door, she knew she was completely alone, and no one knew where she was.

The big, thick front door was still open, but when she crossed the threshold, she turned to it and pushed it shut. The door knocker made a small sound, a *plink*, but the other sounds were all shut out, even the songs of the birds and the frogs.

The big entry hall seemed darker than it ever had, so dark that she began to feel uncomfortable. Where was the stairway? Finally it appeared out of the darkness, the black banister showing up like a picture beneath the shadings of a lead pencil. She remembered the hole in the stairway. If there was too much darkness up there she might fall in the hole. She relented, and pulled the door open again, part way, so that light came in and she could see the steps upward.

She climbed the stairs as cautiously as she had climbed the fence. When she came to the hole she faced away from it, looking out over the banister to the hall, and clung to the dark, cool wood and inched past the hole, the place where the steps were hanging down.

There was more light in the upper hall, a gray, gloomy light, but light enough for her to see that the painting was ripped after all, that it wasn't a dream. She kneeled in front of it and then turned her head to look down the hall. The dolls weren't there today.

There was no sound from them, no call.

She pulled the paste from her pocket and began to dampen and press the strips of canvas to the wooden back of the frame.

When all the strips were in place again, and the face of her mother was together as well as she could manage, she looked around for a safe place to put it. A few steps away a table stood against the wall. Although the table looked narrower than the painting, it would do.

Jessica began to struggle with her heavy burden, lifting it, grunting with it toward the table, using the wall as support for the top of the carved frame. As she lifted the burden grew lighter and lighter, the top scraped against the wall, the bottom of the frame wavered and wobbled in her hands, rising, slowly. Jessica's hands followed it, and then poised suspended in the air as she watched the painting rise along the wall until the top of the frame bumped the ceiling. It hung there. Slowly, the bottom of the frame settled against the wall.

Jessica stared up at it, puzzled. Then she patta-caked her hands in delight and giggled. The pretty picture was going to hang there. Her mother had helped her, and her mother could do anything.

She stood in the hall for a while longer, but then she began to notice the silence, the gray light, the webs along the ceiling and down the walls into every doorway, and the length of the hall itself. She was beginning to feel a little lonely.

Were the dolls still here or had they left? She decided to go play in the doll house. It was, after all, her very own doll house. Her mother had given it to her.

She went to the last door along the hall and opened it. The room was filled with the light from the window that was still open, and the dolls were in the doll house, like real dolls, the papa sitting in his chair, the mama standing at his side, her bonnet touching the ceiling. Vesta was standing there too, and Victor. Their China faces with the little round dots of pink on their cheeks were still and cold and staring straight ahead. Jessica began to feel a deep sadness.

She sat in the edge of the living room and looked at their faces. Victor, with his broken neck, was staring at the floor.

"I'm sorry," she said, tears forming in her eyes. "Come back, please come back. I won't leave you anymore, except just for little whiles."

Mrs. Mary Archer woke up with a snap. Her neck felt as if it were broken. She had walked the floor last night until her legs were tired, then she had gotten dressed at four in the morning and sat down to wait for the sun to rise. She was going over to Belle Lake, get the few things she had left there, see about the child, and say something, she didn't know what, to Paul Norris if he hadn't left for work. She had planned to go early enough to be sure to catch him before he left, and now here it was after ten.

Grunting, rubbing the back of her neck, she got up. Well, Mister would be gone for certain, but he'd given permission for her to get her things. And besides that, she wanted to see Jessica. A child having nightmares wasn't unusual. It happened once in a while. Night terrors. The child woke up screaming, and then could remember nothing. Her own daughter had had a few of those. Not many, thank goodness. It was an unnerving experience for both parent and child.

She grabbed her overloaded purse off the small table by the front door, the table that held the telephone, telephone book, gloves for winter wear, and scarves. Her purse was old and black and so heavy it made her shoulder hurt after lugging it around the grocery store or shopping center on those days when she had to go shopping, and one of these days she was going to sit down and go through the contents and see what she could throw away. She'd be having time now, she guessed, what with no job to go to every day. She'd be able to do her washing again on Mondays instead of Sundays, and her ironing, what little there was to it, on Tuesday. If her husband were still alive she might even enjoy this forced vacation. Maybe, if she talked to Mister, he would relent and give her the job back. Especially if he couldn't find someone else suitable.

Her small car was parked in the driveway right beside the house. She went out onto the porch, locked the door behind her and thought about the locking process. That was something new. She'd never locked her doors, nor had anyone else in town that she knew of, until the burglary at the feed store. Then her locks, old and rusty, were oiled and put in use. Now, it was habit. Her back door, though, was wide open. Only the screen was hooked. But she wasn't afraid of anybody's going to that door. They'd have to go through the fenced yard, and who knew just how fierce Rover could get? He'd probably smile and wag his tail, but a stranger bent on thievery wouldn't know that.

Her car started on the first try, like always, and she felt pleased, like a parent with a child who had done something right. Thank goodness the car was paid for. She'd made the last payment just three months ago. She had the little Omni serviced regularly with proper oil change and lube job, and she hoped it would help the car to last her from now on. Of course if it didn't she could walk, she supposed. She was only one block from the post office and two blocks from the supermarket now that the new one had been built. The old grocery store on Main Street was boarded up now and had a For Rent sign tacked to the front.

Scared Jessica into having nightmares? Told her stories of ghosts and hants? More than likely he had magnified it all. Jessica wouldn't have told him that, she knew, when it wasn't true. Very little had been said about ghosts or hants. Lordy, she was only trying to keep the child from ever going over to the old Blahough plantation mansion anymore. Didn't Mister know that? And besides, what did he know! How could he be so sure such things did not exist. Was he willing for the child to play around the old Blahough ruins? A stone could fall on her, if nothing worse happened. But there were mysteries there, and everyone who'd lived around here long enough to know anything knew that. The trouble was, Paul Norris was

103

a newcomer. He'd only moved here around twenty-five or thirty years ago, when he had married June Havel. Now June, if she were still alive, could tell him there were strange things about the old Blahough place, because she'd been born here, as had her people before her.

Mrs. Archer turned the corner onto Main Street and followed it to the end where it became a country road, a two-lane blacktop that curled around the edge of the swamp of the old Blahough plantation land. There were a couple of very sharp turns and then the road straightened out and headed due north, and the grounds of Belle Lake opened up on the left. There was no lake on the Norris place, just the big duck pond in the huge back yard, but if Paul Norris wanted to call it a lake, Mrs. Archer guessed that was his right. But today, as she pulled into his driveway and eased her car quietly up toward the garages, she felt peevishly critical of Paul. He ruled his small kingdom like an old monarch, one of those old French or English kings who hadn't hesitated to chop off someone's head if they displeased his lordship. By the time she got out of her car she was thumping mad, and instead of going to the kitchen door where she always had before, she went instead to the private brick terrace that was in the corner of the family's favorite room: a combination family room and library, a large room with books, desks, a bar, a fireplace, large, soft, comfortable furniture. Connected to it was the smaller room where the large television screen set into the wall, made a room called the TV room. That was where Jessica spent a lot of her time, at a little desk in the corner.

The double French doors weren't locked, and Mrs. Archer stepped through onto the deep pile of carpet, and silence. The room was empty. She looked into the TV room, but it was empty too. She went into the hall. It stretched toward the front of the house, dim, cool, silent. She gave up and turned toward the kitchen, and stopped just inside the door. A strange, dark face stared at her.

"Oh," Mrs. Archer said, feeling invaded. "You must be the new maid."

"Yes ma'am."

Mrs. Archer looked at her rocking chair and saw that her embroidery basket was still there beside it, and on the small table was the rest of her stuff, an extra pair of reading glasses, a couple of novels she had brought with her. She never went anywhere for long without one of her romance novels, the sweet kind without all this disgusting sex.

"I'm Mrs. Archer, and I've come to get my things." She gathered them up swiftly, poking the books and the glasses down into the basket, and last of all taking the cushion out of the rocking chair, for it was her cushion, bought with her own money, and she had no intention of leaving it, though she doubted that Mister would have done anything with it but throw it in the trash.

"Where's the child?" she asked.

"The child?" The dark face, no more than twenty years old, was blank.

"Yes, Jessica. Haven't you seen her?"

"I've not been here but a short while. I saw the boy,

105

Robert."

"Well there's a little girl, too, just barely five years old. You're supposed to be looking after her, aren't you?" The young maid merely stared at her, and Mrs. Archer added, "Never mind. I'll go look for her. I want to see her before I go."

She went through into the hall and to the service stairs just off the washroom, and up. The music from Robert's room thudded dully in the hall. She looked into Jessica's room, but it was empty. And undone. The bed was just as the child had left it, and her pajamas were there, hanging half off the bed, dragging the floor. That new maid had better start looking around and doing her job, or she wouldn't last twenty-four hours.

Mrs. Archer knocked, then pounded, on Robert's door. She gave up and went on in without invitation. Robert, flat on his back on his bed, looked at her, then reached over and fiddled with a button among dozens of other buttons. The resounding music softened.

"Hi, Mrs. Archer." He sat up, looking pleased to see her, then the smile left his face as he looked at the basket. "Just come to get your things?"

"Yes, and to see if Jessica is all right. Where is she?"

Robert shrugged, his thin shoulders arching up and down like wings. "I don't know. Playing somewhere, I guess."

"Ummm." Mrs. Archer pictured the back yard in her mind. All the play pretties back there, and in the house, and what had the child done but climb over that tall fence and get herself in jeopardy. As well as Mrs. Archer herself, right along with Jessica. And that, Mrs. Archer was afraid, was exactly what she had done.

"Good-bye, Robert," she said. "Keep that noise tuned down a little, will you," she added out of habit.

She went out the front door and stood for a long breath on the front stoop. The lawn was as smooth as artificial turf, having been mowed just yesterday by the half-worthless handyman. But at least he did keep the grass mowed, even though he tended to let the weeds grow in the flower beds. He showed up only two to three times a week. Had other jobs to do, he said, but Mrs. Archer snorted her doubts.

She cut across the grass to the driveway and went down it to the gate in the breezeway. She crossed the breezeway between the garage and house and then stood in the middle of the back lawn and looked and listened. Birds, frogs, toads, even a cow lowing, and then the cry of a peacock down by the pond, but there was no sight or sound of Jessica, and Mrs. Archer didn't feel like shouting for her.

She spent several minutes trying to find her in the yard. She even looked into the shrubbery by the pond. The little railroad track and train were about to rust from never being used anymore. The swings hung silent. Last winter's leaves had gathered in the sandbox. Mrs. Archer's worst fears were being confirmed. Jessica had disobeyed her. She had climbed that fence again.

But *she* wasn't going to climb it, not she. And she wasn't going to wander around the yard like a lost duck screaming, either. Not today. There was an easier way.

She returned to her car, got in, and drove it out onto the road and turned left. Just beyond the brick wall of Belle Lake the trees began again, and a narrow road went back through them to the edge of the fence that surrounded the meadow in which the old Blahough mansion was fenced off. She had walked through this dry woodland many times looking for wild greens. And she had seen the farmers' fence and gate, and even knew the man who rented the meadow from the surviving Blahough sister, the only one left now of the old Blahough family. John Reilly came a couple of times a week in his pickup truck to drive along the little road into the woods and through the gate in the meadow to check on his cows. He wouldn't mind if she parked her car by the gate and used it to let herself into the meadow. And when she got hold of that child, she was going to upend her and give her a paddling, and she didn't care what Mister thought about it. Maybe it would help to keep Jessica away from those old hanted ruins. Yes, *hanted*. Nobody could prove to her they weren't.

She crossed the meadow in long strides, not pausing to sniff the fragrance of the flowers. She glanced back only once, and saw that her car was almost out of sight in the trees beyond the wide wire gate of the meadow fence. She opened her mouth to call out for Jessica, but found herself too breathless. When she reached the fence that surrounded the grounds of the old mansion she was swept by a strange chill of warning. Even the red-lettered sign warned her,

KEEP OUT. And the tangle of the growth that hid the crumbling old mansion was like a cloak of evil thrown up to keep in the secrets of its past.

She wanted to stay safely on the outer side of the fence, to call out to Jessica and have her answer and come, but her voice was stuck in her throat. She dreaded to break the silence of the interior of the matted growth.

The gate was a few inches open, hanging lopsided on its hinges, and the path, as narrow as the path of a deer, disappeared within a few feet into the briars and vines beneath the trees. That small child had gone through here, she thought with a rippling chill going over her skin, she had gone through that growth as if she knew where she was going. Mary Archer had no doubt that she had gone there again today, even though she had been told not to yesterday.

If a small child could go in unafraid, so could a fifty-nine-year-old woman.

The only difference was the woman knew the dangers of things not often seen in the world, and the child didn't, and that, Mary Archer told herself, was why she was having trouble breathing. She was nervous. When she reached the house, she promised herself, she could call out for Jessica. By then, maybe she'd have her breath back again.

She picked her way along the path. The trees were enormous. The thick horizontal limbs of a live oak, with all its silver-gray moss trailing down, hung above the path, and Mrs. Archer had to bend low to get under it. There was a log, covered in moist green moss, that she had to climb over, and the remains of several large, sticky spiderwebs tangling in her hair. The shadows were deep and the air cool, almost chilly. She was glad of the sweater she had wished she'd left in the car when she crossed the meadow. When it was beginning to seem that she had become lost in some unknown forest, she came suddenly upon the gray stones of the gallery. Pillars that once had been white stretched tall, upward to the upper gallery and on to the roof of the house. The windows were shuttered. The far end of the gallery ceiling had fallen, and it was held up from the stone floor only by the pillar at the corner. The front of the house seemed to stretch endlessly away to her left, and the side, with its double galleries, disappeared into the darkness of the encroaching growth of vegetation and trees toward the rear, in front of her.

She wanted to turn and tear her way out of there, but she went instead to the steps, halfway along the front, and went up onto the stone floor and across it to the deeply recessed front door. An ugly iron door knocker leered down at her, but after a startled stare into its glaring eyes, she avoided looking at it. It was but another warning to stay out, to keep away, lest the dangers and the evil never let her go.

She pushed the door wide open. Jessica would never hear her call if she didn't.

The squeak of the door hinges was magnified by the hollowness of the large, dim hall beyond. Mrs. Archer squinted into the darkness, curiosity overcoming fear. There was not a lot of furniture, she saw, just a table, a few chairs, an old settee, and near the door a piece of furniture that would have been a treasure if it had been taken out before it became so mildewed and rotten, and a coat rack combined with an umbrella stand, with a mirror that still reflected the rest of the room in ghostly outline.

If ever in her life she had seen a place that was hanted, this was it.

She longed to call out, to bring Jessica to her from wherever she'd gone in this monstrosity, but something warned her to keep silent, to dare not break the cold silence, to leave the spirits as undisturbed as possible.

She crossed the threshold and felt a definite chill in the air, several degrees lower than that out on the gallery. It was more than cold air, she knew. It was the spirits of the mansion manifesting, growing in power, spreading their cold from the grave as they came back, had long ago come back, into the only home they knew.

She walked softly, thankful the floors did not yield and give away her presence. Her ears were sharp and sensitive to the sound, and she listened to every movement of the house, and listened hard for Jessica. She opened the door to her left, and saw a large, dim, corner room that probably had been the parlor. The furniture remained, it seemed, covered by old sheets that were dusty and gray. The shuttered windows let in only thin cracks of light. Jessica was not here.

She crossed the hall and opened another door. That room was smaller, though it too was in the corner. An old organ, its sheet half fallen to the floor, was the only furniture left in this room, except a couple of straight chairs. The music room, Mrs. Archer said silently to herself. She went back out into the middle of the entry hall and faced the stairway. Weren't children always attracted to a set of steps, no matter where they were? She had a choice of either going up or going deeper into the house where she suspected she'd find nothing more than dining room and kitchen, and maybe a sewing room or office or something of that sort, and she figured that Jessica would have chosen the stairs. They looked dangerous. They went up one wall, crossed over, and swept even higher, and disappeared into a tunnel of gloomy light and shadowy darkness, and she had no heart for climbing them.

With curiosity drawing her again, she went to a doorway at the rear of the hall and found another, shorter, narrower hall. At the end of that she found the kitchen, a large, cavernous room that looked as if it would never warm up on a cold winter's day. The iron cookstove was still there, against the outer wall. The cupboards were painted a dark, dull, old green, and stretched from floor to ceiling. The table was long, as if it had been intended for many people, a trestle table with long benches on each side. There were cook tables, too, made of thick, solid oak, their tops stained with old flour still caked and small black flour bugs that searched even yet for food. Mrs. Archer shuddered. She looked out the back door, which stood open, and saw there was a back gallery too, but the posts were mere posts, not pillars as they were down the front and sides. The back yard was overgrown with vines, bushes, and tall trees, but over in one corner of the fenced area she caught a glimpse of tombstones. The family graveyard, that was what it was, and she shuddered again at the thought of having the burial ground so close to the kitchen door.

She retraced her steps out of the kitchen and down the hall, not bothering to open the door she figured was the dining room door, nor the others that probably included a washroom as well as who knew what. Closets, maybe, if they had closets in those days, or a pantry. She didn't want to see the remains in a pantry that was a hundred years old, or the bugs and rodents that probably lived there.

She didn't want to climb those stairs. Something inside her warned against it. She wanted to get out of the house and go home, to feel the warm air and the sunshine on her body and in her soul.

To her immense relief she saw that she wouldn't have to go upstairs for Jessica was standing at the bottom of the stairway, against the newel post, so still and quiet that it took Mrs. Archer a moment even to see her, in the dimness of the room. She started toward the child, her heart easing in thankfulness.

"Jessica, my child," she said, and started to reach out, but now she had come closer and she could see better, and she saw the child's head was hanging unnaturally to one side, and in the instant she saw that she also was stunned with shock into stopping and staring. This was not Jessica, but a small boy with half a head of hair and a pale, painted face, whose neck was grossly deformed or . . . *broken*.

And immediately afterward she saw it was not a child at all, but a large doll that had been leaned against the newel post.

But who would do that? The doll had not been there, she was sure, when she first came into the house. But of course, Jessica had put the doll there. She had probably come downstairs, bringing it with her, and had leaned it there while she went up to get another. It was not unthinkable that a child's dolls had been left in this old house if so much else had.

Mrs. Archer put her hand on the newel post above the doll's head and started to call upstairs at Jessica, to order her down from there, even though she no longer had the right to try to see to the child's welfare. Even so, she loved the little girl, and would do what she thought she should. But even as she opened her mouth she became aware of someone else on the stairs, up several steps just at the bend, looking down at her. She gaped at it, her mouth open. She was not fooled this time into thinking she faced a small person, even though it could have been. This was a large doll dressed in old-fashioned men's clothing, a black coat and trousers. But instead of being leaned against the wall, it was standing free, on the step, and was facing down toward her as if it could see.

She took a step backwards and then stopped again, still.

She heard a movement, and looked down, and saw that the doll with the broken neck was no longer leaning against the newel post, but now stood at least three feet away from it, between her and the door. Ripples of fear and warning moved over her, too heavy and too cold to be mere chills. She had to get out of this house of ghosts and hants and dolls that moved from one place to another as if they were part

114

. . . something. Yet she couldn't leave Jessica here. If she were here. How did she know the child was here? *What if . . .* but she couldn't think that. And she'd been wrong about the movement of the dolls. If they really were dolls. *What if . . . they had found Jessica, instead of Jessica finding them?*

She threw a desperate glance back toward the stairway, and was transfixed by horror. The large, man dressed doll was coming down the stairs, his leg bending slowly and straightening as he felt for a lower step, his arms reaching out from his sides and the white china hands and fingers looking sharp as claws. His sweet, painted face had a terrible set look of no feeling, no conscience, no mind; yet he was coming down the steps toward her, and she knew in her terror that it was she that was drawing him, for some reason she didn't know. She couldn't even cry out, or move. He had come within two yards of her, his painted, chipped eyes gazing expressionlessly up at her, his sharp fingers reaching up as if to hook onto her face, when finally something within herself sprung her into movement.

She whirled toward the open front door and fell over the doll with the broken neck. She felt it move beneath her body, a writhing of softness, of crackling straw, and the hardness of old china; and the revulsion that reared up in her came into her throat in bitter vomit that she swallowed desperately. She pushed herself to her hands and knees, and felt the sharp dig of the thing's fingers pierce her thighs. She kicked out, and heard its body slide across the floor and thud against the wall. Then she was clawing her way to her feet and out the door. She didn't search for the path, but tore through the brush and vines into the thickest part of the growth.

She threw a glance backwards and saw both of them on the gallery porch coming toward her, their white faces in doll sweetness, with pink cheeks and pink rosebud lips, but their hands out, white claws of death, and she knew she must run, *run*, or there'd be no mercy.

Jessica had been searching. For things that had belonged to her mother. She had found in a dresser drawer a small box of jewelry that had been hidden back beneath mouse-chewed pieces of old, yellowed clothing; and this she brought out into the hall to the table near the painting. She removed the jewelry carefully from the box and arranged it on the table. A pretty necklace of green beads, a bracelet that matched. Another necklace of white beads.

Close by her Vesta and the mama doll followed, their movements so quiet that Jessica almost forgot they were there. The other dolls, Victor and the papa, had slipped away. Perhaps they had gone back to the doll house, where she had rocked the baby doll and put it to sleep in its crib.

She took from the small pile of jewelry that she had yet to arrange a matching pair of clip-on earrings. She was making a curved arrangement of the jewelry, so that all of it would show, so that her mother, above in the painting, could see it. The painting bumped against the wall, softly, as if a wind were blowing it.

A sound, something all wrong, reached Jessica and drew her attention away from the jewelry. Something was downstairs, outside in the trees and the brush. She could hear the snap of twigs, the tearing of limbs, and a grunting, animal sound.

The front door stood open. She could see the spread of light from it, now that her attention was drawn that way, and when she went down the stairs to the bend, she saw that it was standing wide. Yet she had left it open only part way when she came in.

She hurried down the stairs, passing the hole in the stairway with scarcely a thought, turning her back to it, putting her toes between the balusters, clinging hard to the balustrade; and in just a few small steps, half a dozen or so, she was past the hole and running down the steps. Behind her came the dolls. At the hole they paused, bent at the waist, and leaped without hesitation, balancing on their soft-soled shoes with the grace of ballet dancers. They kept closely behind Jessica, one on each side, sentinels. And reached the door seconds behind.

Jessica paused on the gallery and stared out into the cool, moist, green tangle of growth. She could hear something there, but couldn't see it. Something was trying to get through. Then she glimpsed movement, and flashes of black, and she knew it was the papa doll and Victor. She put her hands to her cheeks in sudden dread.

"Come back! Come back!"

It could be a bear out there, or something else as terrible, that would tear apart her dolls. As her imagination gathered possibilities, her anxiety increased.

"Come back!"

She saw their faces rise from the undergrowth and vines and turn toward her, unharmed, and then they disappeared once more and came in sight again closer to the porch. She waited, her anxiety decreasing. They came to her, unscathed. Victor's head lolled, and he walked like the Crooked Man, and there was a small tear in his coat sleeve, but that was all, and she was glad neither of them had been hurt. Jessica drew back nearer to the door, to the safety of the house, while in the jungle in front whatever it was the dolls had chased away grew still.

Mrs. Archer stared through the protection of the trees at the front gallery of the house. The child stood there surrounded by the dolls that were nearly as tall as she. Jessica had called, and the dolls had responded, drawing away from her, where she, fallen, was trapped by vegetation and an ankle she felt was either broken or severely twisted. She stood on one foot, supporting herself with a hand on the trunk of a huge tree and considered if she had gone mad and was imagining this. But no, as she had always known in her heart, strange and terrible things happened, could happen, in a house allowed to sit and turn sour with the ghosts and hants and evil spirits; like mother growing in vinegar, things grew. The house was bad, everything in it was bad. If Jessica weren't gotten out of there, it would draw her in and absorb her, for already she could see that Jessica wouldn't die from the things that grew in the house. Instead she would come to something more horrible than death.

If she hadn't already.

She had to go back. Instead of running to her car and fleeing this terrible thing, she had to go back and get the child.

Jessica was turning now, going back into the house, and the dolls spun delicately round on their feet and still surrounding her, moved along.

Mrs. Archer crashed through toward the porch, crying out, "No! Jessica! Don't go back in there! Oh, my Lordy, Lordy, child, don't go back!"

Her ankle twinged with pain when she let her weight fall on it, but it held, and she knew it was neither broken nor sprained. Just twisted. And even though it hurt, it would hold her.

"Jessica!"

But the doorway was empty when she could see it again, and the gallery stretched away into its drooping jungle, empty too. Mrs. Archer stumbled up the steps and to the door.

She was blinded briefly by the gloomy light of the large hall. Then she saw Jessica huddling on the stairway several feet up, looking through the balusters. Mrs. Archer blinked to clear her vision, and moved closer, looking up. Behind the child stood the two female dolls, but the others were not there. Fear rolled up Mrs. Archer's back with cold ribbons unwinding, as if her clothing had been silently torn away, but she didn't dare think of that, or turn and look behind her. She held out her hands instead, imploring, desperately trying to reach this child who she feared was already gone.

"Jessica," she said slowly and distinctly, trying to keep the quiver of fear out of her voice. "Come down from the stairs, and come home with me. There are terrible, terrible things in this house, and they're going to hurt you."

"No. This is my house. I live here with my mother. Go away, Mrs. Archer."

"I won't go until you come with me. You must listen to me, child. Don't you know it isn't right if dolls move like real people? Don't you know it's bad, bad spirits in this old house that cause them to be that way? What if they should turn on you? They could hurt you awful bad, Jessica, child."

"No. They're my friends. And I'm not Jessica, Mrs. Archer. I'm Annabelle."

"You're . . .?" *Oh Lordy, Lordy.*

Suddenly, as if a switch had been flicked, noises began. From somewhere above came the squeak of a chair rocking, and the thud of something against the wall. *Thud, thud, thud,* a rhythmic sound that stripped Mrs. Archer of all but fear that grew as the sounds grew. A door, out of sight upstairs, began slamming shut repeatedly, as if thrown by the raging winds of storm.

She saw Jessica turn her head and look up the stairway, but she saw also that the dolls didn't move, and yet there was a finely pitched chatter beginning, voices that almost uttered words, yet did not; and Mrs. Archer knew it was coming from the dolls. She could hear it all around her, the fine, chipmunklike sounds, so faint it was hard to separate them from the other noises in the house. There was something

120

making them do that, she realized as she stood frozen, and it had to do with the wild rocking of the chair somewhere above and the bumping of something else against the wall, and the door, slamming, slamming.

She had to have help, Mrs. Archer knew then. This dangerous and evil spirit that had Jessica thinking she was someone named Annabelle, would not allow her to take the child from the house.

She hurried toward the open door, and saw it was no longer wide open, and it was moving, moving, closer and closer to the frame. It slammed shut just as she reached it, and she began to struggle to open it again when she saw in the darkness the movements of the two dolls dressed in black. They were closing in on her.

Mrs. Archer whirled and ran toward the back of the house. She flung doors open and clambered through, seeing them there, keeping up, like spots of blindness in the outer corners of her eyes. In the kitchen she bumped into a cook table, and bruised her side. She stumbled on, across the kitchen and onto the rotten boards of the wooden floor of the back porch. They caught her when she fell down the stone steps.

They were on her back like huge insects, but the terror she felt was worse than the pain when the nails of their sharp fingers ripped into the flesh of her back and her scalp. She heard the materials of her slip, dress and sweater tear, and felt the rush of warm outdoor air upon her skin, and the dampness, the trickling wet of blood down her back. She struggled up onto her hands and knees, but they were clinging round her neck, and she screamed once, a tortured, desperate scream when pain ripped through her eyeballs, and she was blinded.

"I can't see, I can't see, Oh God I can't see."

She put one hand to her face and felt wet cavities where her eyes had been.

Maddened, stricken with hopelessness and terror, still she began to fight. She rolled on the ground, and dislodged one of them. On her hands and knees again she felt for and found a loosened stone from the step, and she began to pound at them with it. She heard it strike, and felt the impact. Suddenly she was free, and she stumbled to her feet and ran, bumping into trees, tearing through tangled vines, briar and brush. She came to a fence with three strands of barbed wire at the top and felt the barbs rip through her palms as she struggled over it, but she could hear and feel them behind her, so she did not draw back from the pain.

She fell into the meadow and ran, sensing their presence, always, at her heels, hearing her own desperate gasps of breath as she tried to find her way across the meadow to her car. How could she drive, blinded? She could crawl into it, lock the door, and be safe. That was all that mattered.

From breathlessness only she kept silent, for the pain seemed unbearable, as if she had ceased to exist in any form except pain, burning pain, and darkness. *Darkness*.

She came to another fence, another stand of trees, and burst through them, her hands out to guide her from striking the trunks head on. *The car . . . the car*

. . . where?

Her foot sank into something soft and watery, but she did not think of the swamp, that she might have gone in the wrong direction. She went on, finding the way harder, the water deeper and sometimes reaching her knees as she pulled her feet from soft mud. All around her the voices of frogs paused, and stopped entirely as she approached and passed.

It seemed hours had gone by. She was breathless, and there was an added pain in her chest, ripping through her, going into her shoulders, her arms, up into her jaws. She struggled on, pulling her feet out of mud, sloshing through water, and then suddenly she was trapped. Like an insect in honey, she couldn't pull her feet from the soft mud beneath her.

Slowly, she was sinking, and she realized she had stumbled into quicksand. The water had reached her waist now, and the coarse, sandy mud was swallowing her.

She had an additional moment of torture, of sudden mental clarity, and knew she had run the wrong way. She was now deep in the swamp, a place where few humans dared to wander.

She put back her head and screamed, reduced to a lost animal drained of all hope.

CHAPTER SEVEN

Jessica uncovered her ears. The house was quiet again. The bumping of the picture against the wall had stopped, and so had the rocking chair and the door. And Mrs. Archer had gone away.

Jessica stood up, and Vesta and the mama doll moved back from her to give her room. She climbed the stairs again, and went to the table where the jewelry was and began to sort it out. The pin here, and the other pin there. Another necklace, strung straight and long. It had both white and red beads. These were her mother's things, and she was going to take very, very good care of them.

When she had finished with all of those, she went into some of the other bedrooms looking. In one bedroom she found clothes that had belonged to a boy. There were old black trousers and white shirts with ruffles down the front. They were folded in a dresser drawer. The white looked dirty now. And the underclothes were funny long things that she laughed at. There were holes in all of it, and beds made of bits of cloth and lined with fur. Mice beds. She knew about mice beds because she'd seen one in the garden shed once. But the mice were gone. There were no babies.

Wherever she went, the dolls followed along, all four of them. The papa doll and Victor had been gone for a while, but that was the way of men people. They often went away and left the girl people and the mothers.

Sometimes the mothers went away, too.

But those were other people's mothers, not hers. Her mother lived here, in this house, in her very own house, and she didn't go away.

She had to go. To the house where Jessica lived. If she didn't, they would stop her from coming here, just as Mrs. Archer had tried to.

"I have to go now," she said to the dolls as she led them back to the doll house. She climbed the ladder to the upstairs and lifted the baby doll from its crib and hugged and kissed it, then she tucked it away in its dusty blanket and climbed down again. "I have to go now," she said again, "but I'll be back. You stay right here and wait for me. I'll always come back to you. And someday, I won't go away anymore."

She went out and along the hall, and it seemed darker than it had before. When she passed the painting it began to thump lightly against the wall and she paused and looked up at it. It wavered against the ceiling as if it would fall, but it didn't. It hung there on its invisible nail, touching the wall, making its sounds. But something was different in the hall, and her attention was drawn to the big bedroom where the tower room rose. The door she had shut so carefully was open, and as she watched, it began closing, opening, closing, but in soft silence, as if it were beckoning to her. But the dark in the house was increasing rapidly now, as if a cloud were gathering, and she had to hurry away, and go to the house where Jessica lived.

When she reached the meadow, she saw that the sun was low over the tall trees of the swamp, and the frogs there were picking up their songs by the millions, so that her ears buzzed with it. She had missed lunch again. Would they be mad at her? Would Mrs. Archer spank her? She never had yet, but several times she had said she would. This might be one of those times.

At the fence she was careful not to tear her clothes. She climbed up apprehensively, listening to the quiet in the yard. Someone had fed the ducks and they were eating the bits of grain out of the grass at the edge of the pond, and quacking softly among themselves. The peacocks and peahens were there too, eating, sometimes chasing the ducks, who squawked, ran, and then came right back to eat again.

Jessica wanted to stay and watch them, but she ran on to the house instead.

In the kitchen she stopped and stared at the stranger in a white apron and little white cap who was cooking supper. She was black, and young, and at last she noticed Jessica.

"Well, hi," she said. "Where've you been?"

Jessica didn't answer. She continued to stare.

"My name's Della, and I'm gonna be here until your daddy can find a full-time housekeeper and babysitter. I been so busy today I didn't have time to go looking for you, but your brother said you're not supposed to stay out and play so long without lunch, but he said you been doing that lately. How come?"

"Where's Mrs. Archer?"

"Mrs. Archer? I don't know no Mrs. Archer, honey. Who she?"

"She cooks for us. This is *her* kitchen."

Della went on working with fresh vegetables at the double sink. "Oh, yes," she said, "well, then I expect she's the one who quit yesterday. I guess she's the one I met this morning. Anyway, here I am. I expect you'd better talk to your daddy about not showing up for lunch."

"I wasn't hungry. I forgot."

"Well, you talk to your daddy about it."

Jessica hesitated. "Can I go out and watch the ducks eat?"

"I don't see why not."

There were benches placed at scenic spots around the pond. Two were white wrought iron with intricate carving. On each side of those benches were matching iron chairs, and in front of the bench a table, just like a furniture arrangement in a living room. Two other benches were built of pine, curved and comfortable. The fowl had been fed near one of the pine benches, and Jessica climbed onto it and tucked her feet under. On each side of the bench flowering shrubs perfumed the air, and the limbs of a large oak tree extended over her head and trailed moss toward the sparkling reflections of the pond. A soft breeze rippled the water, edging out from one narrow inlet a small ship with white sails. Jessica watched it for a while. Robert's. He had several boats on the pond, and sometimes they sailed on their own into the middle, which to Jessica seemed a long, long way off. And very deep. She was sure the pond was as deep as the ocean. Her daddy had warned her never to go into it, for she might drown. She had seen Robert go in though, last year, when he was still playing with his toy ships and boats. He had waded toward the middle, with the water coming up to his waist. But he hadn't gone all the way to the middle.

He used to swim in there, he told her. But he also told her that never, never should she go swimming there.

So Jessica sat on the bench with her legs up and watched the ducks and peacocks feed, and then she watched the water with its ripples, and its toy ships sailing out and then back in to the grassy banks. She grew sleepy watching, and the sun went down and long shadows fell across the grass. The ducks gathered together on the banks, sitting, picking at their feathers, quacking softly. Somewhere across the yard the peacocks cried out.

Then Jessica's daddy came and picked her up and carried her back to the house, and she put her head on his shoulder and her arms around his neck.

"Have you been a good girl today?"

"Yes, Daddy."

"Fine. In to your dinner now, then up to bed."

Jessica made no objections. She was tired, very tired.

At ten P.M. the phone rang, and Paul answered it to hear a woman's voice say, "Mr. Norris? I'm sorry to bother you this late, but I'd like to speak to my mother, Mrs. Archer."

Paul sat up. He'd been half asleep in front of the television waiting for the commercials to end and the news to come on.

"Mrs. Archer?" He frowned at the phone, a sudden feeling of something wrong invading the quiet he had been enjoying. But that, he decided immediately, was probably because he'd been half asleep when the phone rang. "I expect you'll find her at home, Mrs. uh — Miss — "

"Elaine. Elaine Brown. Mrs. But she's not at home, sir. I called there first. I thought perhaps she was spending the night at your place again."

"No, indeed. In fact, Mrs. Archer doesn't work here anymore. Her services were terminated yesterday." In the middle of the night, he amended in silence. No need to go into detail.

There was a long silence in which Paul longed to hang up the phone. He yawned and waited for Elaine Brown to get over her surprise. Obviously Mrs. Archer had not told her daughter that she'd been fired.

"I don't understand," the daughter finally said. "You fired her?"

"Yes, I did. She'd been telling my four—uh—five-year-old daughter ghost stories and causing her to have nightmares."

"Mama?"

"Mrs. Archer, yes. I have not seen her. We have a new, temporary housekeeper."

"But . . . where is she? My mother. Her car's gone."

"Then obviously she has decided to take a trip or something like that."

"Oh no. Her cat and dog are there. She'd never do that. Not without telling me. She'd never do that, anyway."

"Then perhaps she went someplace to a shopping center and just isn't home yet. I'm sorry I can't help you, Mrs. Brown."

He hung up and settled back to listen to the news.

She was crossing a back porch made of wood. Beside the door to the house was a bench, and on the bench potted plants. The one at the end drooped pink flowers all around it like tiny bonnets. She took one in her hand and looked at it, searching it for beauty and peace, trying to shut out the sounds of screams that echoed somewhere within the house.

She searched the deep pink within the flower and heard the awful, terrifying screams settle to anguished sobbing. It was her brother. Mama was being mean to Zachary again. Annabelle had been searching the back yard for a way to freedom, and found no escape. She could run through the fields in search of

130

her papa, but she would never find him and would be deserting her brother and baby sister.

She slipped through the doorway into the big, cavernous kitchen. The maid, Dandy, was working in silence at a cook table, her black hands trembling. Big, big eyes looked at Annabelle, but they were helpless eyes, terrified eyes. Annabelle slipped on by, as silent as a wraith, and went into the dining room. She saw the long tablecloth move, and knew where Zachary was. She knelt and lifted the tablecloth, and looked into the twilight world that he occupied beneath the table.

"Come on, Zachary," Annabelle whispered. "She's gone. Together we'll run until we find Papa, and we'll tell him what she has done to you."

"No. No." He shook his head, whispering in timorous hisses. "Don't ever tell Papa."

"Zachary, you're a fool. Why would you not tell Papa?"

"Because — because he would send her away again to that bad place."

"Oh, Zachary, Zachary, don't you know we would be free? That she couldn't hurt us anymore? Maybe the next time they would keep her, forever."

"Oh no, no."

Tears were falling down his face again, and Annabelle crept in to raise the hem of her dress to wipe his tears away. She grew still beside him, feeling the sudden tension in his posture as he turned his head away, listening.

The footsteps were coming, along the hardwood of the hallway. They paused at the dining room door *and a voice called softly, "Zachary, oh Zachary darling. See what Mama has for you . . . see . . . what . . . Mama . . . Annabelle . . . Annabelle . . . are you with Zachary? Are you filling his head with bad things again?"*

The footsteps came nearer. The tablecloth, hanging down all around to the floor, trembled, and one corner lifted, and a long, slender hand reached under, holding something clasped in the palm. "Here, Zachary, darling, Mama has something for you." The fingers opened, one by one, and blood dripped from the fingertips, and the small object rolled out upon the floor and trailed toward Annabelle and Zachary, its tiny dead eyes staring at them, and only bloody tissue left where the body had been.

Jessica screamed, fighting the tablecloth. It covered her face, smothered her, trapped her in terror and helplessness.

Paul stood at his bathroom mirror shaving. Sometimes he thought about letting a beard grow again to get rid of the nuisance of having to shave twice a day, and in the evening with lather and a sharper, keener blade than his morning electric shaver gave him. Sometimes he used the shaver at noon, trying to avoid the old four o'clock shadow. But those few times he'd had a beard he had itched, and it had annoyed him to put his hand to his chin and feel that crisp hair instead of the round hardness of flesh and skin.

Ah, well.

The razor scraped down the side of his face, clearing away the white foam on one side.

A feeling of apprehension settled between his shoulders and he paused, frowning at his image, seeing a face half covered in white and thinning gray-streaked hair waving back from a high forehead, but seeing it without awareness, his mind trying to grasp the reason for this sudden feeling that something was very, very wrong.

Was it Mrs. Archer? It did seem damned odd that the woman hadn't said something to her daughter before she left, if they were as close as it sounded like they were. Considering all the years Mrs. Archer had worked here at Belle Lake, he didn't know much about her. But he had a lot of employees that he didn't know much about. As long as they did their jobs, that was all he asked. Their private lives were their own business. He didn't even know if Mrs. Archer had one child or a dozen.

He shrugged it off and went back to shaving, and took a clean swipe across his chin. Crisp whiskers gave way beneath the blade and left the little strip of skin velvet smooth.

Diane . . . his thoughts kept going back to her, but in anger, nothing else. The love he'd felt for her was buried, he hoped forever. He didn't want it to surface. Even if she wanted to come back sometime, which he doubted, he'd not take her. He hated the feeling she had given him, of being out of control. But he had sense enough to know that if he brooded about it the detriment would be his, not hers. So he had lost this one. Well, he'd lost before. A man didn't stay in business these many years without losing a few.

And Brenda. She had said she'd call back, and maybe she had, but the message hadn't reached him. He wasn't going to worry about his loss of control over her, either.

Jessica . . .?

The sound reached him, at last, coming more into his continued awareness of something's being wrong than becoming actually audible. Several walls separated him from her, but he knew finally that she was screaming again. Gasping, breathless, desperate screams.

He burst out of his private bathroom, flinging the doors back as he went, through his dressing room and at last out of the large master bedroom. In the hall her cries reached him clearly, and she sounded chillingly, helplessly trapped by something she could not emerge from. He pounded around the balcony of the stairwell, and turned left down the hall to the rear of the second floor. In the dim hall night light he glimpsed a shadow entering her room at the end of the hall. He reached her doorway to see it bending over her bed. He paused long enough to flick the switch, and the room suddenly was softly lighted, every small lamp in the room turned on.

Robert was bending over her, as if he didn't know what to do next. He reached out to her. "Jessica? Jess?" He looked over his shoulder, his face pale, his eyebrows lifted questioningly. "What's wrong with her, Dad?"

Paul pushed past him and pulled Jessica into his arms, yanking away the tangle of sheets and blankets.

134

Jessica was fighting weakly, as if she had been fighting a long time. Her cold skin was damp with perspiration. Paul sat on the bed, holding her tightly against him.

"Jessica! Jessica, it's all right. Daddy's got you. It's all right, baby. Wake up!"

Her eyes changed, blinked rapidly and looked around, as if she had just regained consciousness. Her fighting stopped, but her body remained tense in his arms. Her hands closed over his, small fingers digging in. A soft moan took the place of the loud cries.

"Did she have a nightmare?" Robert asked.

"Every night since her mother left," Paul said, not trying to hide his bitterness. "What did you dream, baby?"

Jessica looked at him, her eyes as blank as if she had indeed been unconscious. She slumped, the tenseness going out of her, and leaned her head against his chest. Her eyes closed. Almost immediately, she was asleep again.

"I wonder what she was dreaming," Robert said nervously. "It must have been really bad. It woke me up. Her screams. I thought somebody was kidnapping her or something grosser."

"She's all right now. Maybe she'll sleep the rest of the night without incident."

Incident. What a weak word. Paul continued to hold her, though he was growing uncomfortable and restless. This was a woman's job. A relative's job. Damn these young, modern women who had to get out and *live*. Why didn't they rear their children first?

He settled Jessica in bed and pulled her blankets up. She sighed, turned onto her side, and tucked her hands under her cheek. She looked like an angel, Paul thought, with her pale hair spread out on the blue pillow, and her long, golden lashes on her soft cheek making tiny patterns of shadows. He touched her forehead, but her skin was still cool and damp, drying fast in the air now.

He turned to find Robert still standing there staring with parted lips and puzzled eyes at his little sister.

"She's all right," Paul said again, for his son's benefit. How long would it be before she really would be all right? How helpless the child must feel, unable to draw her mother back again. How deserted she must feel. If he ever got a chance he'd tell Diane about all this, but he doubted if she'd care.

Paul turned out the bedroom lights but left the door open. The one ceiling light down the hall a few yards made pale tracks into the child's bedroom, enough to make her feel safe if she woke, but not enough to disturb her sleep.

Robert backed out of the room ahead of Paul, and smiled, actually noticing his appearance for the first time. "Hey, you look funny. Half and half."

Paul put his hand to his chin, and felt the foam on the one side. He didn't feel like smiling. "I suppose," he said. "Goodnight, Robert."

"Goodnight, Pop."

Paul returned to his bedroom and to the desk in the corner. He pulled from the drawer the little blue book of addresses and searched out Brenda's number. He pulled the phone across the desk and began dialing.

136

At this time of night, out there, she would probably be gone, he thought morosely, as he let the phone
ring. But he'd keep calling if he had to stay up the rest
of the night.

To his surprise she answered after only a few rings,
and he was robbed of feeling angry at her for not
answering her phone.

"Brenda, this is Dad. How are you?"

"Fine, Dad, and you?"

"I thought you were going to call me again to let
me know if you could come home for the summer."

"I did call. I got Mrs. Archer, and she said she'd
tell you. Haven't you talked to her?"

Paul hesitated, trying to remember if he'd given
Mrs. Archer a chance to tell him about Brenda's call.
Well, even if he hadn't, why hadn't she left a note?
Because, something whispered beneath his irritation,
she had planned to tell him. But even so, he argued
silently, why hadn't she told him? She could have
called, at least.

"Was it important?" he asked.

"I just told her it would take me a couple of weeks
to get arranged for leaving here, with paintings to
gather up and stuff like that. She said not to worry,
that she'd stay there with Jessica until I could get
there."

"I see. That's impossible, however, Mrs. Archer
does not work here anymore."

"Why on earth not? Is she sick?"

"No, she's fired."

"But why?" Brenda wailed. "Mrs. Archer was
like — is like a grandmother to us all. Why would you

137

fire her?"

"You needn't be so adamant, Brenda. I did what I had to do. She was telling Jessica ghost stories. Telling her about haunts and spirits, for goodness sake. And the child has been having horrible screaming nightmares ever since. I had to get rid of the woman. We've got a temporary maid, Della, but she's not yet twenty years old, and just working for college money, so she won't be here long. Even though she lives in, she's in the maid's room in the service wing and I'm sure she didn't even hear the poor child screaming tonight. If Jessica has many more of these, she's going to be ill. We need you now, Brenda, not two weeks from now. Surely, you can make room for this emergency?"

"Yes, Dad, of course," Brenda said, her voice fading away in the distance. "I'll leave tomorrow."

Well, that's that, Paul thought as he finished giving his elder daughter a few good words of advice about driving cross country alone. He hung up the phone feeling somewhat placated. Brenda was a woman now, and it took a woman to give proper care to a small girl. Perhaps it all wouldn't be quite right without Diane, but the situation would be improved.

He went to bed, and began making plans for tomorrow. He'd get up early and drive over to his office in Alexandria, and from there fly to a board meeting that he was pretty sure was set for tomorrow afternoon. Or was it the day after?

He yawned and closed his eyes, blanking out his mind the best he could. There'd be only a few hours for sleep. Maybe he could grab a nap in his office mid-morning. He was tired. Sometimes he worried about his heart. And at times he thought about cancer, it was such a sneaky bastard. But mostly, his heart. There was a breathlessness . . . and he had stopped smoking years ago, so it wasn't emphysema, he hoped. The pillow wasn't just right. A bit too flat. He pounded it into renewed plumpness and settled down.

The knock at the door was timid, and the voice so faint he couldn't hear what it said.

He sat up in bed and shouted, "What?"

"Mr. Norris —"

"Oh for Jesus Christ," he mumbled as he threw back the covers and strode toward the door. He opened it to find Della standing there looking scared. She was wrapped in a snow-white robe that looked like silk, but was probably polyester.

"Sir," she said. "Excuse me for disturbing you, but there are police downstairs asking to see you. I tried to get them to wait until morning, but they won't. They say it's because of someone who is missing."

"Ah. Yes. I'll be right down."

He grabbed his own robe. There was no question who the missing party was. Mrs. Archer.

Della had the two uniformed men waiting in the foyer. Although there was a small settee and a couple of chairs, the men were standing. Just as Paul went down the stairs, the grandfather clock against the foyer wall struck one-thirty. It was even later than Paul had thought. He'd watched the Carson show, and then something else that hadn't kept his attention, and then he'd showered and shaved— Suddenly he remembered that he hadn't finished shaving. He paused at the foot of the stairs and put one hand to his face. The foam had disappeared a bit, but it was still there in spots on the whiskered side of his face. Part of the shaving cream no doubt was on his pillow. Ah well. He faced the police officers with as much dignity as he had left.

"Gentlemen?"

"Sorry to bother you at this time of night, Mr. Norris, but we understand that Mary Archer is under your employ, or was until yesterday, is that right?"

"Yes, it is. She no longer works here, however. Her daughter called and said she wasn't at home, and I assume the lady took a trip without telling anyone. After all, it's the first unemployed time she's had for many years." He mentally examined the two men as he talked, trying to remember if he'd ever seen them before. They were from the sheriff's department, which was located in another town. One of them was young, dark, and not very tall. The other one made the younger man look short, probably, for he was almost as tall as the old grandfather clock. Paul wished he could step back upon the stairway so that he'd not have to look up to him.

The younger of the two did most of the talking, and he said, "Her car was found in a wooded area just beyond your northern brick wall, sir. The farmer who has the meadow behind your place rented, went in earlier this evening to check on his cows, and found her car parked right at his gate. The daughter of Mrs. Archer said she often went there to pick wild greens. We thought you might have seen her."

"No." He found himself surprised now, and disturbed. "I didn't even know she picked greens there. I can assure you none of us have seen her. Maybe she — uh — had a heart attack and is somewhere in the woods there."

"Did you know her to have trouble with her heart?"

"Of course not. Mrs. Archer didn't discuss her state of health with me. But a woman her age might have that problem. Why else would she have abandoned her car? She must not have been able to get back to it."

"Those were our thoughts. Is it all right if we search the grounds of your property?"

"I don't know why on earth she would have come here. As you probably know, my place is surrounded by tall brick walls, or fences, except for the outer front, with walls and fences set back near the house. Of course if you want to look around, that's all right. Just be sure to close the gates behind you. I have fowl I don't want out on the road, and a small child as well."

"Of course." They nodded and went out, the young one looking back at him from the front stoop. "If you hear anything, of course you'll let the sheriff's department know?"

"Certainly."

Paul stepped out onto the narrow porch and watched them go to the car parked in the paved driveway at the side of the house. Thank God they didn't have the lights on top on. He closed the door, locked it thoroughly, and went back upstairs. But he was beginning to feel almost too weary, and knew a good night's sleep was lost.

Jessica woke with no memory of her dream, just a feeling that she'd been asleep for a very long time. She felt tired, although it was hard to identify how she felt. Her head was — not wanting to talk, or do anything. She didn't want to watch cartoons, and she didn't want to draw or color.

The new maid came into her room and helped her with a bath and with dressing, but the new maid didn't talk much either. Not like Mrs. Archer. Where was Mrs. Archer? Why wasn't she here? Why did she have to go away on vacation?

But Jessica didn't feel like asking. Her head was tired. There. That described exactly how she felt.

She had no appetite, but Della didn't nag her about eating breakfast the way Mrs. Archer would have, and she said nothing when after a few minutes Jessica slid off the breakfast bench and went outside.

She was going to her castle. Then maybe her head would stop being tired.

But at the tall, chain link fence she stopped and stared, for there were men in the meadow. Three of them, one in uniform, stood talking together. They were too far away for Jessica to hear what they were saying, to hear their voices at all. But she could tell by the way they faced one another and the movements of their mouths that they were talking, and looking around. When they looked toward the fence she drew back and hid behind the trunk of the magnolia tree.

After a while they walked away, back toward the

trees and out of sight on the other side of the brick wall. But Jessica remained hidden, watching. She was afraid to cross the meadow today. She didn't want anybody else to find her castle.

CHAPTER EIGHT

Brenda lost no more time in packing to leave. Rick had known for a few days now that she was leaving, or thinking of leaving, at least for the summer, and he'd made no move toward her. To throw herself at him just wasn't her way, and although she'd never been in love before, and might never be again, she knew that if Rick was not in love with her then it was better to chuck the whole thing right now. She'd survive. She'd never forget him, and she'd regret that not once had she felt his arms around her or his lips on hers. The desire she had for him was not to be fulfilled, or whatever, but to stay here and yearn for someone who didn't love her was the most foolish thing she could do.

So maybe her dad had done her a favor. If it hadn't been for his insisting that no one but a relative could take care of Jessica, she'd have stayed on, yearning, dying a little more each day that her love and need grew.

She'd made a big deal out of collecting her paintings, packing others away and all that. Excuses. Actually, all she had to do was call the places, the very few places, that were kind enough to hang her pictures on their walls, and give them the address where she would be in case of a sale. Big deal. The few others she could haul in the back of her Rabbit.

She was up at dawn carrying things down. By nine, she was ready to go. She had only to make one phone call before she turned the apartment key in to the manager.

Rick answered sleepily.

"Did I wake you?" Brenda asked with a savage sense of glee. Punish him a little for not caring. "I could have gone on, but I wanted to tell you good-bye."

There was silence on the phone. Brenda was beginning to think he had put it down and gone off to have breakfast, when he answered her.

"*Goodbye*? You're not leaving now, are you?"

"Yes, didn't I tell you my dad had called and wanted me to come home for the summer?"

"Yes, but I thought it was going to be a couple of weeks before you left. Didn't you tell me that?"

What were they going to do, have a fight over it? Brenda wanted to fight with him. If she couldn't love with him, then fighting was the next-best thing, especially considering her feelings at this moment. Her frustration. Her anger at him for not loving her as she loved him. Yes, it was better never to see him again. She tried to see him through the telephone. He'd be leaning on one elbow, blankets shoved down exposing his nude body. He was well-muscled, not too brawny, just right. His dark hair would be tousled and falling down over his forehead like a little

145

boy's . . . .

"Good-bye Rick," she murmured, feeling as though her heart was being pulled out of her. She put the phone down, and left the suddenly empty apartment. The furniture that had made it look homey when her things were on and around it now simply looked like old discarded furniture.

She closed the door quickly.

Five minutes later she was driving away, putting the ocean, her friends, and Rick behind her.

Rick watched the red VW Rabbit pull out of the courtyard drive and speed away, going in the direction opposite from him. Breathlessly he shouted, but she didn't hear. He sagged, his bare feet stinging. He had run like hell. First he had tried to call her back, precious time wasted, for she didn't answer her telephone. Then he'd pulled on his jeans and run down to his car. The old sweetheart wouldn't start. So then he'd started running, barefoot. At the last minute he'd decided he couldn't let her go. But his last shout was noticed only by other people, who stared at him, and the small, dark-haired girl in the red Rabbit zipped around the corner and was out of sight.

He sat down on the curb. His one chance had been if she'd driven toward him on her route to the freeway. But she hadn't. She was gone, and he had only a very vague idea of where she was going.

She hadn't even looked back. Didn't that mean that she was headed toward a new chapter in her life and was leaving nothing behind that mattered to her? How did he know but that she had an old boyfriend

146

back home who was waiting for her? A fiance, even. Maybe an old relationship would claim her forever.

What he should do, he told himself as he rose from the curb and started back to his flat, was get his own stuff packed and head north. Work called. At least work endured. The restless lonely heart found sanctuary in work.

Robert stood near the small group of men in the woodland next to his house, hands in pockets, listening to bits and pieces of what was being said. He had first been attracted by the unusual activity, and the towing away of Mrs. Archer's car. Then, when he had ventured into the woodland, the police had approached him with questions. But he didn't know anything. He had not seen her since she'd left early yesterday morning. He had gone to his window and watched her drive away, first turning her little car around in the area by the garages. But he hadn't seen which way she went when she reached the road. Home, he had assumed.

There were men around the area all day, and into the next. They didn't seem to mind if Robert hung around. Nobody seemed to be doing much. Robert himself had tried to help with the search, going over and over the ground between the car and the gate into the meadow. What footsteps and broken twigs there were probably belonged to the men who had been walking back and forth. A lot of them had wandered out into the woodland, a fairly open area where the pine and oak trees had room to grow, and the grass beneath got enough sunshine to flourish. Robert knew that Mrs. Archer had picked greens here because he could remember coming with her. But that was a long time ago. If she had come here for greens since Jessica was big enough to go along, he didn't know of it. Of course he had grown up, and no longer went with her, so she might have picked greens here every day for all he knew. Only the tops of the trees were visible over the wall, and his own room was on the other side of the house, facing toward the swamp and town.

"Maybe she went into the swamp and got caught there," he said to a small group of three men who were talking of pulling out and giving up the search. "There are a lot of bad places in there."

"She wouldn't have done that," a man scoffed. "Nobody in his right mind is going in there unless he knows where he's going. I know a few people that still hunt and trap in there on the other side, but they're experienced. I doubt a woman like Mrs. Archer would go in. What for? She knew better."

They walked away and paid no more attention to him. Robert stood by the gate and gazed across the meadow toward the dark tree trunks that marked the beginning of the swamp. Behind him cars and pickups started and turned around in the spot that fast was becoming another road, and drove away. Behind was silence, with even the birds seeming to wait, to see if all the unwanted commotion was finally at an end. A crow called, then another. They flew, and were joined by others, above the meadow. They lowered and perched on the tiptops of big trees in the middle of the meadow where one arm of the swamp came up almost to the cluster of trees that surrounded the old Blahough mansion. Robert glanced away from them, wondering about the swamp, when something moved there at the jungle of the Blahough place. A suggestion of something. Not high in the trees, but on the ground. Robert squinted through the sunlight, trying to spot it, separate it from the dark growth. Nothing now. Maybe it had been a trick of his eye.

He wondered if anyone had looked around the old mansion. Of course he knew that Mrs. Archer wouldn't have gone there. She had told him a few times about that place, and she truly believed it was haunted. There was no reason she would have gone there. Still . . . he didn't feel like giving up the search yet. He liked Mrs. Archer. To think of her being gone put a hollow place in the middle of him. She'd been around all his life, and had kind of taken the place of his mom. As much as anyone could, she had.

He let himself through the wire gate, fastening it behind him to keep the cattle in. The grasses of the meadow were from knee- to thigh-high, some of them blooming and very fragrant. The clover that had once filled it was now only in spots, and there were other things with white flowers, and some with tiny blue ones. Down underneath, soft, fine green grass was like a cushion. He saw the cows were after the grass beneath, mostly. He went out of his way to go past a cow that raised a gentle head and gazed at him, chewing her mouthful of grass. She had a clover sprig, too, and as he watched it disappeared into her mouth, the purple bloom gone. He patted her, rubbed her thick neck, and scratched between the

149

spots where her horns would have been if someone hadn't cut them off .

He went on across the meadow to the fence that surrounded the Blahough place. There were NO TRESPASSING signs all around, he saw, as he circled the ruined mansion, following the enclosing fence. He found one gate, closed, and passed it by. Through the thick growth of trees, underbrush and vines, he caught only occasional glimpses of the gray stone of the old building, and he had to admit Mrs. Archer was probably right in a way. It was damned spooky. She wouldn't have gone in there.

At the back he had a better view of the house. The trees were huge, but the undergrowth seemed thinner. He could see a wood gallery or porch built on, a rotten structure that didn't look as if it would hold a squirrel. Shingles had dropped from the roof, leaving holes. The remaining shingles were green with moss. There were two back doors, one closed, one partly open, and four windows, heavily shuttered. The upstairs windows were shuttered, too. Vines grew over most of the wall, going up the porch posts and trailing across the edge of the porch roof.

Naw. Mrs. Archer wouldn't have gone in there, and he wasn't going to either.

He went on along the fence, touching it occasionally. It was good and tight, with sharp barbs at the top, three strands. The farmer probably kept it up as part of the deal. The owners, Robert knew, lived on the other edge of town. They had a big old house that was almost as old as the Blahough mansion, and they were two old maids that must be close to a hundred years old now. They'd been there all his life, looking just like they did now. He used to see them in church. He'd seen one of them just last week in the supermarket. They were tall and skinny as poles and went around together like two old birds, ignoring everyone else. Somehow or other they were related to the Blahough that had owned all this land, and they had inherited it. He couldn't remember all the details. Mrs. Archer had told him about it. Mrs. Archer liked to tell local history. She knew everyone and everyone's business. And she had been positive that this old mansion was haunted. Only she had called it *hanted*.

Robert smiled. He liked her. He hoped she wasn't gone forever.

Where had she gone?

He started off across the meadow toward the swamp, when he was stopped abruptly by a noise. Something barely heard, but something creepy that made the hair on the back of his neck and arms rise. He stood very still, listening. *Bump, bump, bump.* A steady, rhythmic sound dull and deep within the house. If there had been one bump, he would have figured something fell, a board, part of a ceiling, or even the roof, but the continued bumping sound meant that something else was going on.

He retraced his steps to the fence and stared at the mossy, gray stone. The sound drifted away, softening until there was silence. But still the hair stood stiff on his body, and a sudden urge within him shouted *run*.

He began to back away.

Suddenly he was seeing something else. Just across the fence, in the corner of the back yard, more gray

151

stone. But these were part of a small cemetery.

It was like an omen.

And he knew damned well he wasn't going to hang around there any longer.

He followed his urge to run and sprinted like mad across the meadow to the edge of the swamp. Feeling relatively safe, he turned back to stare at the Blahough mansion with its weird sounds and the graveyard within yards of the back door. He shuddered. Some of the kids had been wanting to sneak in there because it had the reputation of being a haunted house, and he'd half gone along with it. They hadn't set up a date yet, but he knew now they'd not set up a date. Not with him.

He turned his back on the Blahough ruins and ventured into the swamp. The ground grew mushy almost immediately. A million frogs serenaded him. Once, when he was younger, he had gone into the edge of the swamp, the place just beyond the wall of his own yard, and caught frogs. But now, he just listened, and tried to spot a few. He saw several pairs of bulging eyes sticking up above black water.

He began walking along the edge of the swamp. It had come out in places beyond the fence that had been erected to keep the cattle from going in and dying there, and he knew there was no point in his climbing over. Mrs. Archer would never have gone over that barbed wire into the swamp.

He followed the fence on back to his own back yard fence, where the tall chain link joined the end of the brick wall. It looked good in there, and safe. The trees in the corners and around the edges, the grass in the center, the flower beds, the pond, all looked so familiar and so good. The little railroad track curling in and around the trees in the far corner, a toy that his dad liked more than anyone else did, had a special look, too. It was a good place to be, in contrast to the hell of old White Oaks.

He came suddenly upon Jessica. She was sitting on the ground at the base of the big magnolia tree, just a few feet from the fence. She looked startled, her eyes round and big, as if she hadn't seen him until he spoke.

"Hi," he said. "What are you doing here?"

"Nothing." Her eyes left his, going to gaze instead across the meadow toward the Blahough place. "I saw you in the meadow," she added. "Lots of people have been in the meadow. Why?"

"We've been looking for Mrs. Archer."

Jessica's big eyes rounded again and flew back to stare at him. "Where is she?"

"Nobody knows. She's gone."

"Is that why she doesn't work at our house anymore?"

"Yes, that's why, I guess. I got to go now. See you."

He glanced back after he had gone a few yards along the fence, and she was still sitting beneath the tree staring off across the meadow.

They were all gone now, and she could go home. She had been waiting and waiting for them to leave so they wouldn't see her going to her castle. That was her home now, not this. That was where her mother lived.

She climbed over the fence and when she was a few yards out into the meadow she turned and looked all around, to be very, very sure the men were gone. To be sure, too, that Robert was gone. She had watched him when he had gone to the fence of the castle, and had seen him go along by the wire and stop and look at the gate, and she was so glad she had remembered to close it. She must always close it, to keep the dolls from wandering out. Even though she always gave them orders to stay near the doll house when she was gone, she was afraid they might forget, and wander away. And get into the bad swamp and drown. Or get onto the highway and get hit by a truck or a car, like Mrs. Archer said the cows would if they got out. She was very careful to close the gate for that reason, all those reasons. Nor did she want them to follow her and be seen by any of the people who lived in this house where she must return at lunchtime and at night. It was important they stay in the castle. They were part of the castle, part of her life there.

And so she had watched Robert, and had seen him go out of sight around the fence, hidden by the trees. And she had waited, her arms tight around her knees. She didn't want him to go into her castle. That was hers, and nobody else's. It was *her* mother who lived there, not his.

After a long time, he had crossed the meadow on the other side of the trees of the castle and gone to the dark edge of the swamp, and after that he had come on along the fences. Now he was gone. She looked and looked, but saw no one. She was alone in the meadow.

Running now, joyously, her arms lifted and skimming the tops of the tallest flowers in the meadow, she went all the way to the castle fence before she stopped and looked back. It was all very still. She could see the ends of the brick walls that were on both sides of Robert's daddy's yard, and she could see the red brick of the house in spots through the trees. They were still, like the dark trees of the swamp, and the woodland on the other side of the meadow. That was the thing about trees that she most liked. They stood right where they were planted. They never moved around. Only when the wind blew did they move at all, and even then only the tops moved. Unless the wind was hard and strong, as in a hurricane, then sometimes the whole tree fell over, with its roots in the air. When that happened the tree died. For trees were living things just like people and animals, only different.

She hoped no hurricane ever came to uproot the trees around the castle, for then the castle would be exposed, and everyone would know it was there. The trees protected the castle.

The gate was still closed. Robert hadn't undone the wire that looped over the top of the post. When she passed through she carefully fastened the gate again, then she slipped quietly along the path, ducking under limbs and climbing over the one old dead tree that had fallen across the path and was rotting there, with insects crawling all over and through it, and moss growing upon it like another small world all its own. She tried to touch it as little as possible when she climbed over.

She had remembered to close the door behind her, too, so the dolls wouldn't try to follow her. Sometimes they seemed not to hear what she said. Actually, all of the time. They never turned their heads to look at her when she talked. And they really didn't talk to her, not really. But she was going to teach them. She'd be a teacher, and have a classroom.

She closed the heavy entrance door and stood still, widening her eyes for better vision in the darkness. There was a smell that she hadn't noticed much before, a stinking smell that made her wrinkle her nose. As she waited the dark lessened, and she could see the foot of the stairs, the newel post with the carved knob. She began too to see the curve of the banister, going up, up toward the lighter area above. And someone standing where the stairs turned.

Had her dolls come to meet her? No.

Something else was showing up on the stairway, and she strained to see, to make a definite form out of something she could barely see. It was a figure, a tall figure, and it was wearing white. The white wavered like a candle flame, a huge, pale candle flame. Yet it stayed there, at the place where the stairway curved, halfway up. Gradually in the darkness the face appeared, as if the dark were gradually lessening, and Jessica saw that it was a woman, with long, long hair. She was very pale in the dim light, so pale that Jessica could hardly see her at all. But she knew who it was.

She started forward.

"Mother?" she cried softly, questioningly, timid and all at once afraid.

The coldness engulfed her, a terrible chilling cold that went through her clothes and made her chin quiver and her teeth chatter. The figure on the stairs above her moved away as she climbed. She stared up, seeing more clearly the long golden hair, like her own, and indistinct outlines of the face. It wavered, coming clear and fading again, with the eyes and nose outlined at one moment and faded to a featureless blur the next. The long white robe flowed down, covering even the arms. Then Jessica saw a hand reaching out from the whiteness, the fingers extended toward her, as if motioning for her to follow. The figure moved backwards up the stairway, floating above the steps, or gliding so smoothly it appeared to float.

Jessica was so intent on following the figure, her mother, that she stepped into the hole in the stairway, and felt her body going down, down into the darkness, the dungeon below. She screamed and reached out desperately for support, and her hand gripped a post of the banister. She clung to it sobbing. With one knee she gained further support, and after a few seconds of struggle, pulled herself up. She sat with her arms around the baluster for several heartbeats before she looked up again.

The lady was gone. No one stood on the stairs now.

But then she saw her again, so pale she was almost invisible, at the distant top of the stairs. Jessica stood up and carefully made her way past the hole in the stairs without looking down. The form above took shape again as she drew nearer, and then faded to the softness and thinness of a sliver of fog.

Jessica reached the top of the stairs. Light from

open rooms filtered into the hall and made deep shadows by the pieces of furniture scattered along its length, and the painting on the wall began to bump lightly against the ceiling, the bottom of the frame dancing a slow dance in the air as if it were going to fall. Jessica stood still, and there was no sound in the whole of the castle that she heard except that of the picture frame moving, as if a wind blew it.

She was still cold, but her teeth no longer chattered.

"Mother," she said, tears beginning. Her knees burned and hurt, scraped raw from her fall. She put her hands down to cover them, but that only made them sting worse. "Mother, come back."

Suddenly she was there, a tall, tall form in white, the icy cold spreading out and surrounding Jessica, and from the wispy folds of the robe a hand reached out, palm toward Jessica, long fingers stretched wide. It came suddenly, abruptly toward her.

Jessica felt it. The sensation of touch was on her chest, and the force of the push toppled her backwards, and she was falling, falling, the hard risers of the stairway scraping her back as she went down. She put her arms out to catch herself, yet she kept tumbling.

Annabelle. Annabelle. Annabelle.

The fine voices were crying, angels' voices, elves' voices, the sounds of harps. They cried in sadness, and they were rushing toward her, surrounding her, stopping her rolling tumble down the stairs toward the dark hole into the dungeon. She looked into the blank, pretty doll faces, and felt their bodies supporting her. The mama doll, and the papa doll. And Vesta and Victor, too, with his broken neck. She sat on the stairs and leaned against the wall, weeping, tears blurring their faces, yet she saw the white of the hard china and the spots of pink that were their cheeks and their lips, and she saw the blue of their eyes, even the flecks of whiteness where chips of paint were gone from some of them. She saw too that the hands of the papa doll and of Victor were stained dark, as if they had been playing with mud.

She stood up and looked toward the top of the stairs, but the figure in white was gone.

All around her came the desperate chatter of the dolls, alarmed, crying *Annabelle, Annabelle, Annabelle.*

CHAPTER NINE

Brenda arrived at Belle Lake in the middle of the afternoon, almost exhausted. She had driven straight through, except for a few naps stolen in the rest areas along the interstates. She had stopped for one restaurant meal only for each of the two days and one night it had taken her, and she was famished. She didn't want any more snack food, not for months to come.

No one greeted her. She drove her car nose up against the wall of the breezeway, as close to the gate as she could get. She carried a load of suitcases and elbowed her way through the black wrought iron gate, kicking it shut. The new maid answered her knock on the door that led from the breezeway into the hall at the back of the house.

"Hi, I'm Brenda. I'm expected, I think. Is Dad around?"

"No'm, he's not. He left this morning early, just like always. I'm the temporary maid, Della. Let me help you."

Brenda relinquished part of her load gratefully. "Where's Robert? And Jessica? The closer I came to home the more eager I got. I'm dying to see them."

"I don't know where they are, miss. They've been here for lunch. Then they always go on to their own business. Sometimes they don't even show up for lunch. Nobody said it wasn't all right."

"Well, then, Della, I guess it's just you and me."

"I'd had a room ready for you, but I didn't know you were coming today."

"Oh, that's all right. It won't take long to put sheets and a blanket or two on my bed. You might have noticed that one of the unoccupied bedrooms has a lot more junk in it than any of the others. That's my room. I always show up around here sooner or later."

The sober distance that Della had displayed evaporated. Though still reserved, she began smiling.

"I noticed that. I vacuumed and dusted in there same as the rest."

"I hope you have something good to eat, too. I'm starving."

"Oh, of course, Miss Brenda. Come on and let me fix you something to eat, and while you eat, I'll go up and make your bed and take your things up."

"Why don't you fix my plate and make a pot of coffee while *I* take my things up? Then you can make my bed while I go out to see if I can find my little sister and brother. They're probably out playing, don't you think? Or is Robert too big to play now? I keep seeing him the way he was, and it has been a year. I guess a fourteen-year-old boy can do a lot of growing in one year."

"He might be upstairs in his room. He's got a big collection of tapes and records that he plays."

"Oh, really? Last year he was into frogs."

They laughed and separated, Brenda taking two of her suitcases toward the service stairs, and Della going on into the kitchen.

Her old bedroom looked a little strange. She stood in the middle of it, feeling as though she was transported back to an old photograph where the colors weren't as brilliant as they used to be. It took a few minutes of quiet examination of things almost forgotten, of the silver dresser set, the framed photos, clothes she'd left hanging in the closet, for her to begin feeling the old warm, safe homeyness.

She brought a pitcher of water from the bathroom and poured part of it into the ceramic bowl on the table in her bedroom and washed her face. From the closet she chose a favorite old blouse, one she'd gotten for Christmas when she was a young teenager, and tried it on. It still fit, so she buttoned it. There'd been times when she could have hated her small body with its minicup-sized breasts and boylike hips, but then she'd philosophized that looks weren't, or shouldn't be, that important. Lots of people would like to be some other size. And to compensate, her skin was smooth, always had been. She'd never gone through the acne stage. Also, her features were nicely arranged, and her hair was thick and rich in texture. Another advantage was, she could still wear favorite old blouses.

She went down the hall to Robert's room. The door was halfway open, and she looked in. But she sensed before she reached it that he was not there.

Jessica's room was also empty. It had not been redecorated, she saw. The original crib was still in the corner, even though Jessica obviously now slept in the larger bed. The crib was full of stuffed animals, and had a small quilt hanging over the side. The toy box that had been her own, and then Robert's, was now in another corner of the room, overflowing. Yet the room was neat. Della's work, she guessed. Della might be as efficient as Mrs. Archer, but it just wasn't the same. Coming home had made Brenda lonely to see Mrs. Archer, to be hugged by those big, warm arms.

She went downstairs and ate, then went into the back yard and looked around. The sandbox didn't look as if it had been used for a long time. Leaves left over from fall had collected in the corners of the box. And nearby, grass was growing under the swing set.

A peacock screamed, its voice muffled slightly by the trees that stood between her and the pond. She skirted the shrubs and trees, paused to admire flowers that seemed to persist in blooming, even though it had been many years since her mother had been here to tend them.

Jessica was not near the pond either, nor was Robert. Robert used to sail small ships and boats here, and she saw some of them stranded in the weeds at the edge of the pond while one other floated without direction part way across the small body of clear water. Lily pads grew thickly on the far side of the pond, and frogs jumped into the water as she approached. The ducks came quacking to meet her, but she had forgotten that a visitor here was expected to bring goodies. She apologized to them, and after following her to one of the benches and standing around quacking a while longer, they went back into the water or sat down and started grooming their feathers.

She was so tired. She leaned her head back and rested it on the top board of the bench, sliding down so that comfort was not so compromised, and closed her eyes and listened. Peaceful and familiar old sounds: ducks murmuring, birds singing, frogs beginning to peep again. The peacocks and peahens were doing their own thing on the other side of the pond with an occasional ear-splitting call that didn't disturb her. It had been a long, hard drive, and every minute of it spent thinking about Rick. But he was two thousand miles away now, maybe more if he had gone north, and she'd probably never see him again. If she spent any more time brooding about him and what was never to be, then she was a fool.

A fool, she told herself, trying to make it penetrate whatever it was inside that ran one's emotions. It was like water off the ducks' back. Penetration nil. She was a fool for thinking of him when he was probably in love with someone else. Still, she couldn't get him out of her mind.

She tried blanking out everything but sound, and when she felt sleep coming on she didn't fight it, even though her neck was already beginning to feel cramped, and her tailbone against the hard seat of the bench was making itself known as one-half of two very hard objects.

She woke abruptly, aching, but with the pain of cramped muscles the lesser of her discomforts. She felt exposed, observed. Someone was staring at her.

She jerked up. Jessica stood a few feet away from the end of the bench, with no sign of friendliness or recognition on her face. And for a few heartbeats and a barrage of impressions, Brenda returned the stare. The plump little girl she had known, the baby, was gone, and the child who stood a few feet away was a slender, golden-haired beauty grown tall. Taller than she had been, at least. Taller than Brenda expected. She had come home ready to pick Jessica up and carry her around the way she used to. Last year she'd still had baby plumpness, and had been fully three inches shorter, it seemed. Her face had been rounder, the cheeks fuller. Had she lost weight recently?

"Jessica! Don't you remember me?"

The little girl kept staring, making no effort to respond. Brenda leaned forward with her hands out, but Jessica still did not move.

"I'm Brenda. Your sister. Didn't you know I was coming home?"

She shook her head.

"Didn't Daddy tell you? Didn't Mrs. Archer tell you?"

She shook her head again, and now at last she looked away. She went to the edge of the pond and threw a handful of something that looked like flower petals into the water. The ducks rushed to get it. Jessica stood watching them.

It had grown quite late, Brenda saw. The air was cool and the shadows long.

"I've come to spend the summer with you," she said, trying to feel as if this small person were not a total stranger. She reached down to take Jessica's hand. At first she thought her little sister was going to ignore her offer, but after a slight hesitation the small hand slipped into hers. It was cold, and Brenda took another closer look at Jessica. She saw scraped knees, dirty clothes and arms, with smears of dust on her face. Something that looked like cobwebs was in her hair.

"Where've you been this afternoon, Jessica?"

"Just playing."

"Well, you sure found an interesting place, I'd say, by the looks of you. Let's go up for a bath and clean clothes before dinner, okay?"

"Okay."

That was better than it looked like it was going to be there at first, Brenda decided as she walked with the little girl to the house and the bathroom upstairs. Although Jessica definitely was not enthusiastic about her big sister's being home, at least she was not uncooperative.

The evening would have been a very pleasant one if it hadn't been for the news about Mrs. Archer. Her disappearance laid a pall over Brenda's brain, it seemed, taking away much of the pleasure of being home. She had gotten more enthusiastic greetings from both Robert and her dad, and the hours after dinner had been spent in listening to them both at the same time, or trying to. Her dad was almost boyish in

166

his happiness at having her there, and Robert was running over with information on this past year. She got away long enough to put Jessica to bed, and then went back for another two hours. But finally she could hold her eyes open no longer, and she too said goodnight.

Her old bed was great. She'd forgotten how comfortable a bed could be. Della had dressed it in satin, pale blue sheets that had never belonged to Brenda, but probably to Diane. It was a luxurious feel that she didn't object to. Within seconds she was asleep.

Annabelle was trying to quiet the tears of her brother, Zachary. He had picked up the severed head of his tiny pet mouse, the little furry animal he'd found one day in the feed bin down in one of the barns. It had been wandering blindly, so young its eyes were not open yet, and he had shown it to Annabelle and told her it was his pet, and he was going to keep it in his room. She had warned him. Don't let Mama see it, Zachary, don't ever let Mama see it. But he hadn't listened because the eyes he saw their mother with were different from her own. When she had smiled and conjoled him into letting her see what he had, he had shown her. "Fine, you can keep a pet, my son."

And now he sat with its little head in his hands, cupping it, crying over it, with little drips of blood oozing between his fingers and dropping to the floor.

"Come, Zachary," she urged, for their mother had left the room, her footsteps sharp on the boards

between the rugs. "Hurry. She's gone into the kitchen, but she'll be back. Hurry, Zachary. Come with me. We must find somewhere else to hide."

He came with her, letting her pull him by the shirtsleeve, while he, blinded by his tears and his heartache, could only stumble along. She urged him to the safest place she knew, the small room beneath the stairs, the dark room with no windows and no light, the room without furniture except for an old desk and chair that she suspected her papa sometimes used when he wanted to get away and be by himself. Mama would not come in there looking for them. She'd never think to look there, unless she heard Zachary crying.

"You must hush, Zachary, hush."

He huddled in the dark beside her, and she could feel the trembling of his body, and the jerk of his sobs.

Outside in the hall the footsteps came, rapid, angry, growing even angrier.

"Zachary! Annabelle! Answer me! Don't you dare hide from me, you cruel, terrible children. Answer me, I demand you answer me!"

Zachary shuddered, and Annabelle tightened her grip on him. His sobbing continued, as if it were his only connection to life.

The footsteps came back and stopped at the door, and a long minute later the door was jerked open and dim light from the hall entered the room. She came toward them, her face hidden by the shadows in the windowless room, but her steps loud and quick on the wood floor. She reached down, her hand claws *that grabbed onto Zachary's hair and jerked him up. He cried out in pain, and Annabelle leaped up, her own hands claws that dug at her mother's arm.*

"Put him down, put him down!"

The other hand came around, a fist made of the long fingers and strong palm, and struck Annabelle on the side of the head, knocking her back to the floor. As their mother began dragging Zachary toward the door, Annabelle rose and screamed, "I'm going to kill you someday, Mother. I'm going to kill you."

She was screaming, screaming, words muffled and indistinct, "I'mgoingtokillyou, kill you, kill you," and then clearly, "No! No! No!" The room was dark, a dungeon of fear and terror and coldness, and she had been closed in, and the door locked, and she was beating at the door, but the door was not of wood, but soft and smothering, covering her head like blankets or pillows. . . .

The footsteps woke Brenda, and half asleep she listened to them coming quickly down the hall, the heels snapping down sharply on the wood floor. The steps passed by her door and went on down the hall. Brenda turned over onto her side, her back to the closed door, and snuggled her blanket up around her head. Disturbances in the night weren't totally foreign to her. After all, there were other apartments, other tenants, and many of them walked the halls and balconies one way or the other at night. Sometimes there were parties, loud and festive, and she had learned to sleep around it all.

And then she woke abruptly, completely, and stared at the pale rectangle of the window. She was at Belle Lake now, and the hall outside her door was thickly carpeted. She sat up, listening, wondering if she had experienced an especially realistic dream, feeling oddly chilled and frightened; then she heard it again, faraway, still walking with those quick, angry steps. Then suddenly it stopped, and was replaced by another sound. The gasping, almost unreal screams of a child, cloaked by many walls and closed doors.

Jessica!

She threw her covers aside and ran without grabbing a robe. There was a vibration of someone else running, whatever sounds were made on the carpet dulled under the sounds of her own rushing breath and pounding heart. She burst out into the hall just in time to almost collide with her father. He grunted as he dodged her, and seemed to slow, letting her go ahead. Robert stood sleepily in his doorway, and stepped back as they went by. Jessica's door was closed. Brenda herself had closed it. She had forgotten the real reason her dad had called her home, and it was worse, much worse, than she had even thought.

She ran into the dark room. The bed was only faintly outlined by the dim light from the hall, but she could see Jessica's pale face rolling from side to side, though otherwise she seemed to be lying perfectly still. The screams jerked out of her, half sobs, half strangled.

The room suddenly was filled with light. The lamp by the bed, the lamp on the small desk, and the lamps on the dresser glowed with welcome light. Jessica's eyes were open, glazed with terror, unseeing. Brenda pulled her up and found her body damp, her pajamas clinging to her, yet she was cold to touch, as cold as if she had been out in winter air.

"Jessica! Jessica!"

Brenda felt like shaking her, but only pulled her against her breast, enfolding her in her arms. She felt helpless, and with a growing fear of her own. She'd had no experience with a terrified child. What did a person do?

Jessica went limp against her, and her hands reached up and clasped behind her neck. The screams died away on the last gasp, and she was breathing normally. To her astonishment, Brenda saw that Jessica was sleeping again. She glanced up at her dad. He nodded as if it were all right now, and moved off toward the door.

Brenda eased Jessica back into her bed and tucked the blanket around her. Already a warmth had come back to her skin. Jessica drew a long sigh and turned onto her side, her face toward the wall.

Paul whispered to Brenda, "She's never had two in one night. But be sure to leave the door open, just in case."

Brenda nodded. She was trembling and weak, as if she had been through something dreadful right with Jessica.

Paul turned out the bedroom lights.

"Dad, can we talk a while? I don't think I can sleep

now."

"Sure. Get your robe, or you'll be freezing."

She realized she was wearing a very brief nightie, and she stopped by her room for a warm robe. It was not the air that was so cold, but herself, chilled by the experience.

They went down to his office, and left the door open. Paul poured himself a drink from the small liquor cabinet, but didn't offer a drink to Brenda. She would have been shocked if he had. To him, she knew, fathers and daughters didn't drink together, except on very special occasions, and then the daughter drank wine, or at least a very weak mix.

It was all right with her. She didn't care for alcohol anyway. It gave her headaches.

But she was amused by the old tradition still standing, even at a time like this. Then he surprised her.

"Would you like a little wine?"

"No thanks."

"I can get you a glass of milk or a decaffeinated soda from the kitchen."

"No, no. I don't want anything. I just want to talk about this. Has she been having these terrible nightmares every night?"

He looked thoughtfully at the wall as he settled back in his wine-red leather chair. "I don't think she's missed more than one since her mother left."

"Does she say anything about what she dreams?"

"Only the first time. She woke up and wanted to know what ghosts and haunts were. She called them *hants*. Mrs. Archer had told her about them, told her

172

they were the spirits of dead people and that sort of thing. I don't know what all. But since then she doesn't wake up after she dreams, and I haven't tried to wake her. I don't want her to remember whatever it is she dreams about. And since she doesn't fully wake up, doesn't it make sense that she might not remember them the next day? It was those stories that got it started, I'm sure. That and the fact that she has been deserted by her mother."

"You mean the stories Mrs. Archer told her?"

"Yes. The fool woman should have known better."

Brenda sighed. "Dad, Mrs. Archer was around all the years I was growing up, and she never told me a ghost story."

"Your mother wouldn't have allowed it. Besides, the lady is aging. I don't know how old she is, but she's been working here since you were born, and she wasn't young then."

"What has that got to do with it?"

"Some people can't take aging. It can be a difficult process. It takes a strong character to age sensibly."

"I always thought of Mrs. Archer as being very strong, and I really don't believe she was that old, was she? I mean old enough to be getting . . . uh . . . obsessive about some things. I wonder if there could be some connection between Mrs. Archer's disappearance and the nightmares Jessica is having?"

There was a silence.

"I don't see how they could have any connection," Paul finally said. "Although Jessica had her first nightmare the night I called Mrs. Archer and told her not to come here anymore except to get her things. It was the nightmare, and the ghost stories and non-sense, that prompted me to terminate Mrs. Archer's employment. There's no possible connection, other than that."

"Nevertheless, I wish I could talk to Mrs. Archer. She never told me ghost stories."

"Like I said, she's aging. Getting a little daft, maybe."

Brenda shook her head, but didn't pursue it.

"She went off with someone," Paul said. "You wait and see. She has a boyfriend, probably."

"In that case, she would have left her car at home."

"Maybe so, but she wouldn't necessarily have informed her daughter, contrary to what the daughter believes. She'll be turning up one of these days."

But Brenda saw no conviction on his face, and she knew he was saying that for her benefit. The mystery of the car and Mrs. Archer's disappearance might never be solved. And Brenda had a strong, uneasy feeling that in some way that disappearance and Jessica's nightmares were connected.

"Don't you think we should take Jessica to a doctor?"

"What on earth for? She's a healthy child."

"Nightmares like I saw tonight are not exactly what I call healthy, Dad. Why don't we make an appointment with her pediatrician, and have him recommend a psychologist?"

Paul got out of his chair so quickly it was set rocking. He thumped his glass down on the desk.

"A psychologist!" he shouted, as if it were a dirty word, an equivalent of bankruptcy. "My daughter doesn't need one of those! There's nothing wrong with Jessica except the women in her life! If her own mother hadn't deserted her, and then if the woman who's supposed to care for her when her mother is gone hadn't told her a bunch of nonsense, and if you had come on when I first called, none of these things would be happening now."

"Take it easy, Dad," Brenda said calmly. She was in no mood to argue with him, or to even consider arguing or trying to make him see how unreasonable his attitude was. He was Paul Norris, with ideas of his own that nobody would be able to change. To tell him he was completely unreasonable would be to miss several points that deep down she had to agree with. She was all for a woman's having a career, but she also felt that if a woman had children, she should be responsible for their welfare. She agreed that Diane should have waited, and that Mrs. Archer shouldn't have scared Jessica, if that was what had happened. But she failed to see how her own arrival a couple of days earlier would have made any difference in Jessica's nightmares. Certainly it hadn't stopped the one tonight.

"Maybe," Paul said, without relenting too far, "you should go up and take Jessica's temperature. See if she's running a fever."

Brenda smiled faintly at her hands, clasped in her lap. That was his way of giving in, just a little. If Jessica had a fever, then he'd rush her off to the doctor.

"She was cold as ice. She didn't have any fever."

"Maybe now that you're here, she'll be all right," he

said, the hope in his voice almost pathetic.

Brenda got up and kissed his cheek.

"Maybe," she smiled. "We'll try."

She was on her way up the stairs before she remembered the strange sound of footsteps hurrying down the hallway that was not carpeted. She paused, feeling it come back like a cloak of freezing darkness that settled over her.

But that, she thought as she hurried on to her room, was not something she could have told her dad. It had too much of a ghostly ring.

CHAPTER TEN

Diane had been having the same dream for the past three nights, and on this third night as she woke from it and sat in her bed trembling, she could no longer ignore it. A dream repeated three times held a significance that a single dream could not hold, and it terrified her. Not only was it a nightmare in itself, vividly imprinted in her mind so that she lived it over and over during the day, but now having had it again put it in a category she couldn't deny.

It was about Jessica, and a long hallway or tunnel, dark and frightening, and Jessica was running down it, away from her toward something or someone else. Diane tried to call out to her to stop, *stop*, that she was in terrible danger, but as in every dream of that type, the voice was mute. And so Jessica kept running, her arms held up and out, her golden hair trailing behind, going toward . . . what? Her death?

Diane raised a blind, and saw that the city lights were still glowing in a dark that had seemed to last forever these past three nights. She then looked at her clock and saw that it was only past four. Another hour before daylight. And at least four more before she dared call Jessica. She didn't want to wake her up, and she didn't want to call before Paul left for work.

The apartment seemed small and confining as she went around looking for something to do. The kitchen was tiny, and had nothing in its sparkling sterility but tea, coffee, and a loaf of thin sliced Earth Grains bread for toast. She wasn't hungry, but she made a cup of coffee, and took it with her to the tiny bathroom.

She could have gotten a larger apartment, and maybe she should have, she thought as she went to bathe and dress. But she had found this small one so attractive, with the wrought iron decorations over the private back gallery. It looked down upon an enclosed courtyard that had a fountain and flower beds, an area paved in brick, a few trees, and places for lounging, or just sitting, protected from the noise of the streets by the surrounding apartments.

Or maybe it wasn't the apartment at all that seemed confining, but something else that had come to her mind with the dreams. She missed Jessica. And worse, she was going back in her thoughts and memories and trying to snatch back days that were gone forever: when Jessica was a small baby and cried so much. Why hadn't she taken the tiny thing in her arms and sat down in the rocking chair and worked it all out, just the two of them? Why hadn't she touched her then, instead of waiting until now when the desire to go back made her feel ill? And later, when Jessica was a cute, plump toddler and clutched her skirts with those dimpled little hands, and cried when she pulled away and left, why hadn't she stayed and picked her up and cuddled her more? Now perhaps her arms wouldn't suddenly feel so empty.

And her new life itself, empty. All around her people were living their private lives, and she was not part of it. Nor did she want to be. Her thoughts kept straying back to Belle Lake, and to Jessica, and her heart seemed to be coming alive with a vengeance and yearning toward that which she had driven away from.

She wasn't sure she wanted to go back to live there just yet, but she was very sure that she wanted to bring Jessica here, to be with her.

There was a problem, though. Paul. Had he started divorce proceedings, and if so, would he allow her to take Jessica away? He would try to stop her, of course, but if she handled it right, what could he do? She was, after all, the child's mother.

But what had her dreams meant? Did her feelings of dread, her anxiety at making sure that Jessica was safe, really mean that something was wrong at Belle Lake, something wrong with Jessica, or was it only her?

She was going to be late for work, but it didn't matter that much to her. She had to make the call before she left. Of course, she wouldn't dare miss an entire day, not this soon after she had started work, but thirty minutes shouldn't matter that much.

She waited it out nervously, too unsettled to be pacified by music or anything on television. She stood at the window and watched the sky lighten and the artificial lights go out. At eight-thirty she made the call.

She expected Mrs. Archer's voice, and was made even more uneasy when an unfamiliar voice answered, saying, "The Norris residence." Mrs. Archer had always answered with an ordinary Hello, which had annoyed her dreadfully at times. The only time she had ever called Mrs. Archer down on it, the lady had snorted and answered, "Pshaw. The people who call here know whose residence it is."

"Is Mr. Norris there?" Diane asked.

"No, ma'am."

Diane breathed a sigh of relief. "Then I would like to speak to my daughter, Jessica, please."

"Yes, ma'am, just a moment. I'll see if she's up."

Diane waited. Time passed slowly. Seeing if Jessica were up entailed going upstairs, obviously. No one had answered the phone upstairs, or the new voice, whoever it was, would have been back by now. When the next voice came, though, it was neither Jessica nor the one who had first answered the phone.

"Diane? This is Brenda."

"Oh! Well hi, Brenda. I didn't know you were there. Who's the new maid?"

"Her name is Della. She's temporary, here for the summer. As I am."

"Did Mrs. Archer get sick?"

"No, Dad fired her."

"Fired her! I don't believe it. The old girl was a fixture."

"I know. I miss her. And to make it worse, she seems to have disappeared."

Diane had no time to question that one, so she said, "How's Jessica?"

"I haven't seen her yet this morning. She had a dreadful nightmare last night, but I'm sure she's all right now."

"I'm coming home to get her this evening, Brenda. I'm terribly lonely without her, and I've been worried about her. She's well, isn't she?"

"Except for the nightmares, she seems to be. I think she'll be fine when she's with you again. I came because Dad called and said Jessica was having severe nightmares since you had left, and he wanted me here."

"I really have to go now. I'm going to be late at the store. Did you know that I'm an assistant buyer now? It's interesting work, and I don't want to mess up so soon."

"It sounds very interesting, Diane. I'm sure you'll do well. Did you say you're taking Jessica with you tonight?"

"Yes. I'm driving up this evening as soon as I get off work."

"Have you thought this out, Diane? Who's going to take care of her while you're working? And as a buyer, won't you be out of town a lot?"

"Not a lot. Occasionally. And we'll work it all out, you needn't worry. At this point no one can stop me from taking my daughter."

"I'm not trying to stop you. I was just wondering if you had a day care arrangement and all that. And also, you're going to run into opposition from Dad, probably."

"I don't think he'll be difficult. He knows a child needs her mother."

"Yes, but—"

"Will you please just tell her that I'm coming after her tonight? I'll talk to Paul when I get there, if he's home before we leave. I don't want to keep her away from him entirely, but I want her to come with me now, at least for a while. Please tell her."

"Yes, I will."

"I think I can be there by seven at the latest."

"We'll see you then."

Brenda went down the hall to Jessica's room. This unexpected turn of events didn't make her as wildly happy as she had thought it would. Of course, not once had it occurred to her that Diane would want to take Jessica to wherever she was staying, but she had allowed herself a daydream on the subject of Diane's coming happily home and taking over, and freeing Brenda for trotting back West to see if Rick were still around.

Now, though, she felt a mental frown dampening her spirits. Was it really the best thing that Diane take Jessica? She shrugged. Jessica would probably be delighted, and immediately cured of whatever ailed her, and that, of course, was the best thing.

Jessica was not in her bedroom. Brenda went back out into the hall, and then she heard running water beyond the half-open door of the hall bathroom. She knocked.

"Jessica?"

"What?"

"Can I come in?"

"Yes."

Jessica was standing on a stool in front of the wash basin. There was a fleck of toothpaste left on the side of her mouth, even though it was obvious she had just washed her face. Pale, silky curls clung damply to her forehead. She stepped down from the stool and took a towel from a rack and dried her face. Brenda saw she was already dressed in jeans and a blouse that was buttoned crookedly.

Brenda sat down on the edge of the tub and pulled Jessica to her and started redoing the blouse.

"How are you feeling this morning, Jessica?"

"Okay."

"Did you know you had a bad nightmare last night and Dad and I came to help you?"

"No."

"You don't remember it at all?"

Jessica gazed at the wall, hesitating, then said, "I didn't dream last night."

Good, Brenda thought, a bad dream forgotten should cause less harm.

"Do you know who called this morning?" Brenda asked cheerfully.

"Who?"

"Your mother."

Jessica stared at her, her incredibly blue eyes as expressionless as if they were made of glass.

"Diane called," Brenda said. "She said she misses you very much, and she's coming this evening to see you. She'll be here before your bedtime. And do you know what else?"

"What?"

"Something really fantastic. She wants you to pack a few of your things and go home with her."

"When?" Jessica asked quickly, but the flicker of change on her face was not one that Brenda read easily.

"Tonight. She'll probably take you to all kinds of places this weekend."

Jessica said nothing. Her head dropped, her chin almost touching her chest, and her eyes stared downward. Brenda had a strange feeling that Jessica was trying to hide. Brenda finished arranging the blouse, then brushed Jessica's hair. It lay in long, beautiful ringlets. Brenda talked of zoos and restaurants and parks, of the ocean and the Mississippi River, and told Jessica of times she had been taken to those places when she was a child. And she wondered at Jessica's silence.

"Can I go now?" Jessica said when there was a lull in Brenda's monologue.

"Go where?"

"To play."

Brenda said nothing for a moment, wondering if she should just turn her loose and let her go wherever she wanted, or keep her near. "Where do you play?" she asked. "When I came yesterday I couldn't find you."

Jessica shrugged. "Just anywhere." Then hastily, as an afterthought and as if she had been scolded about it, "I don't go out of the yard."

"Have you gone out of the yard before?"

"No."

They walked down the hall together, past Robert's closed door where music was blasting the walls and there was a decided awkward squawk of an added instrument as if Robert were pretending to be part of the band. Brenda cringed and hurried her steps. She took Jessica's hand in hers, and felt it as limp as a fallen bird.

Through breakfast Jessica said nothing. She ate with her eyes lowered. Brenda was beginning to feel concerned about this change in her little sister. Last year she had been so talkative. Last year she had wanted to be right with her, sit beside her at the table, climb onto her lap at every opportunity. Now she was totally different, very quiet and withdrawn, and seemed to edge away whenever Brenda moved.

But of course, she reminded herself, two mother figures had walked out of her life in the past two weeks. Her own mother, and Mrs. Archer.

Having one of them reappear should have made a difference in Jessica's behavior, but so far it hadn't.

After breakfast Jessica sidled toward the door. "Can I go now?"

"Why don't you stay with me? Help me set up my studio? What do you think about that room upstairs with all the windows that nobody uses? It used to be my mother's sewing room, and I think it would make a lovely studio. You can help me carry in my things from the car. Will you?"

Jessica only stared at her.

Brenda tried to ignore the veiled hostility and reached for her hand again. "Come on, I'll show you my paintings."

She kept Jessica with her until lunch, talking to her, urging her to help in small ways that wouldn't tax her, encouraging her to be more like her old self. The sewing room was changed to a studio with her easels and mediums and canvases, with the finished and half-finished paintings leaned against the wall. Robert showed up finally, a muffin in each hand, jovial and loud, and Brenda no longer had to fill silences alone.

Left more to herself, Jessica began to stare moodily

out the window and, it seemed to Brenda, very sadly. Her heart ached for the child, but she had done all she could do to cheer her up this morning and it hadn't worked. She had stopped asking to go out, even after lunch was finished. But she looked yearningly toward the door, her eyes large and unhappy.

Brenda at last said, "You may go, Jessica, and play."

Jessica crossed the room sedately, but once she was beyond the door, she ran across the back porch and out of sight.

"Where does she play?" she asked Robert.

He shrugged. "Just around. She likes to be by herself, I guess. One day when we were still looking for Mrs. Archer I came along the back fence on the side of the meadow and there she was just sitting under the magnolia tree. That big one back by the fence. And Mrs. Archer damn near had kittens one day trying to find her. She even had me out looking. But there's a lot of hiding places around here. I used to hide in some of them myself."

That reminded Brenda of her own childhood. "Yeah, and I had a few. I had one in the corner behind a lot of bushes that Mother called my pouting place."

"Maybe that's what Jessica has. A pouting place."

"Does it seem to you that she's unnaturally quiet? Or is it just because she's older that she has changed?"

Robert poked an entire blueberry muffin into his mouth and mumbled around it, "I don't know. I hadn't noticed."

"Well, I guess she'll be all right. Diane's coming

this evening to take her home with her."

"What?" He swallowed the muffin successfully. "Hey, she can't do that. Dad'll shit."

"I don't know why. After all, that's been his main concern, that Jessica be with her mother."

"But here, not there. She can't take her away from here."

"Not even for the weekend? Christ O mighty, Robby, you sound just like Dad. Of course, Diane can take Jessica with her for the weekend. There's no divorce yet, and no legal custody given to Dad. And going away with her mother might be the very thing that Jessica needs."

"She doesn't need anything she doesn't already have," Robert said adamantly, a scowl on his handsome face. "She's got everything a kid needs right here." He waved an arm. "This is where she belongs. If Diane wants to be with her, she's got to live here."

"Hey! She doesn't. She has moved to New Orleans, and has a job there that she likes, and she wants Jessica to spend at least part of her time there."

"That's not right."

"That's the way it is."

"It wasn't that way with *my* mother. She stayed here."

Brenda sighed, tired of arguing, knowing the arguing would be much fiercer tonight when their dad got home. "I know. She was my mother, too. But Robert, if being with Diane would stop Jessica's nightmares, wouldn't you say she should go? If every weekend she could go down there, have that to look forward to—"

"I don't know. I guess. If it's only for weekends. "Hey," he got up. "Do you need any more help? I got

187

some places to go. I'm meeting my friends in town. We're going to mess around this afternoon."

"No, I don't need any more help. Thanks. Everything's in. Is it anyone I know?"

"I don't know. Kenny Blevins, Melody Rogers."

Brenda said, "Melody Rogers? Is that Anna Rogers's sister?"

"Yeah. And Cindy'll be there. She's always hanging around. I call her dopey."

Brenda could see his embarrassment, and laughed. "Not to her face!"

"No." Robert looked shy suddenly and grinned at his toes. "Actually, she's not as dopey as she was."

Suddenly he was gone, through the door toward the breezeway, whistling self-consciously, and Brenda sat smiling, feeling uplifted by the simple fact that her brother was self-conscious about his feelings for a girl.

Feeling better about everything, she went in search of a phone and phone book, to see if any of her old friends were still around town.

Jessica stood in the gloom of the upper hall looking through tears at the painting of herself in her real mother's arms. "Mother, Mother," she whispered. "I won't leave you, Mother."

The heavy frame of the painting angled out from the wall as if a wind blew behind it, and then thumped back heavily. And through the open doorway in the bedroom where the tower room rose in the corner, the squeaking of the rocking chair began.

The fear that these noises could sometimes bring to Jessica drew down around her, like a cold, dark cloud. She took a step backwards, and another, until she stood against the wall opposite the painting. She huddled in against a tall, old piece of furniture that had shelves behind a glass front, the fear washing over her, and coming up from inside her. Why didn't her mother make the bad noises stop? It was because somebody bad lived in the house, too, but Jessica didn't know who it was. Somebody bad.

The noises subsided, and the painting bumped softly, as if the wind that had blown it had subsided, too, leaving it to touch the wall easily just now and then.

Annabelle.

"I'm coming," she said, and ran down the hall toward the bedroom with the doll house. She opened the door to find the dolls in a semicircle around it. She always expected to see a change in their faces when they saw her, but the change never came. The painted eyes stared straight ahead, and the tiny pink mouths never smiled. The dolls turned as she entered, and went with her to the doll house.

She climbed the ladder to the upper floor, and took the baby doll out of the crib. She gazed into its glass-bead eyes. When she lifted it up the stubby lashes lifted and the eyes opened. When she lay it down the lashes went down, closing the eyes. She sat with it, rocking it, and then she put it back into the crib and climbed down.

"My other mother is coming tonight to take me away," she said. "I don't want to go away. I want to stay here with you, and my real mother. That other one is not my mother. She never was. She took me from here. She took me away from my real mother. I

189

don't want to go with her."

She sat in the midst of them, her fists in her eyes, weeping.

They stood silent around her, their arms raised as if to cradle her.

The footsteps started in the hall a long way off, a faint sound of high heels against wood, growing louder and closer. Jessica lifted her head listening, her mouth open in dread. Had Brenda followed her? Was Brenda angry, and was she coming to punish her for leaving the yard? The dolls began to move about in small steps, back and forth, coming in even closer, their movements jerky and nervous, their faces unchanging, cherubic.

The footsteps came to the open door and passed by, and Jessica stared at the hall beyond the door, seeing nothing. The footsteps faded, going on, even though the hallway ended just beyond the door.

The silence that was left contained a terrible chill that made Jessica huddle into her own arms. The dolls were still now, standing so closely around Jessica that she could feel them touching her. And she knew a truth suddenly. They were protecting her, protecting Annabelle. They would always protect her.

She began to play, turning her mind deliberately toward the joys of her dolls and her doll house. And the first thing she noticed, the room was darkening.

She ran out, remembering at last that she must go back, that she had another house, and people there who would come after her if she stayed too late. And she ran too from the darkness in the castle, for the darkness scared her.

When she left the house she paused, and then she

pushed the door far back, wide open. And she left the gate open, too, the wire and boards that it was made of leaned back against the inner fence.

She drew a long, deep breath.

Then she crossed the meadow.

CHAPTER ELEVEN

It had been an evening filled with tension, and the minutes seemed to delay in their passing. Robert, uneasy with the atmosphere, had gone upstairs shortly after dinner, leaving Brenda to deal with their father alone. To his credit, he hadn't said much. Jessica curled quietly in front of the television, a thumb in her mouth, and the Walt Disney channel was chosen for her.

At first Brenda had considered not even telling Paul that Diane was coming. Robert hadn't said anything, nor had Jessica. But it worried her, like gnats buzzing around her ears. So she had told him, at the dinner table, in the middle of his favorite dessert. He hadn't said a word, but Brenda could tell by the changing expressions on his face, the white, the bluish-gray, and then the red, that it was going to burst sometime during the course of the evening. As if the weather were gearing up to be a background accompaniment, heavy clouds had rolled in, lightning was flashing, and the thunder was getting louder and steadier.

She wished she could do as Robert had done and

simply skip out, but she went instead to the TV room and tried to get absorbed in the show. Their dad settled down in his chair and put the newspaper in front of his face.

At seven-thirty he said gruffly, "Better put her to bed."

"Now?" Brenda said, surprised that he would send Jessica off to bed before Diane arrived, before the child showed any signs of sleepiness. She appeared to be fully concentrating on Dumbo, the elephant.

"Yes, now."

"But —"

"It's pretty obvious she's not coming, or she'd been here by now. Diane's like that. She'll say she's going to do something, and then forgets all about it, or puts it aside, depending on what comes up to distract her." He was just short of gritting his teeth as he spoke in controlled inflections. He didn't take the newspaper down until he said, "Come, give Daddy a kiss, baby."

"The storm has probably delayed her," Brenda said, but Paul ignored her.

Jessica obediently got up from the fluffy throw rug in front of the television, kissed him, and went out of the room ahead of Brenda. She said nothing at all as she kept ahead of Brenda, up the stairs and to the bathroom. Brenda brought her pajamas from the bedroom and helped her change.

When she tucked Jessica into bed, Brenda hugged her and with her cheek pressed to Jessica's forehead, said, "She'll be here, darling, don't you worry. When you wake up in the morning she'll be here."

Jessica turned away without answering, toward the wall. Brenda pulled the light blanket up around her, and left the bedroom door open. The hall light that burned night and day, because most of the time everyone forgot to turn it out, just faintly illuminated a path from the door to the bed.

Brenda stood in the hall looking back toward the bed for a short while, frowning. Something just wasn't right, but it was only a growing feeling, nothing that she could really pinpoint.

Diane followed the curving blacktop road with increasing anxiety, fighting the darkness that seemed to swallow the car lights. When she approached a sharp curve, the light beams shot off into the trees, leaving the road dark and unfamiliar. The clock on the dash told her it was past ten now, and she was still thirty minutes from Belle Lake.

It wasn't her fault, she reminded herself. She'd had to stay at the store late, for one thing. There were delayed samples she'd had to look at before she could leave. Then she'd had to find a place where she could have the car checked and gassed up. And then, to top it all, there had been an accident on her route out of town that had blocked traffic for half an hour. Delays that she couldn't help. So it wasn't her fault. Jessica would be asleep, and she'd have to face Paul without Jessica to forestall his anger. He'd never say much in front of her.

Also, there was the rain, just enough to make the road black and glassy and render her lights almost useless. But it was a fairly light shower, though noisy, and stopped by the time she reached the village.

Pinewood was closed as tightly as an abandoned

motel. Street lights spaced widely apart made it seem all the more deserted, showing small puddles of water where the storm had passed by. Not even a dog wandered Main Street, and the houses on the adjacent streets were shuttered and without obvious lights. In the eastern sky through the tops of the trees she could see a continuous flash of lightning, as the storm gathered and grew more intense. Lightning flashed high in the clouds overhead, the thunder it produced partially drowned under the murmur of her car engine and the sounds of the tires on the wet pavement.

She drove through town without observing its speed limit, though she was still much below her normal speed. She swept around the two curves in the road that separated Belle Lake from Pinewood, going through the impenetrable darkness of the swamp. With her window cracked a couple of inches, she could hear the frogs in the swamp, was almost overwhelmed by the sound. She pushed a button to roll the window up, but reversed it instead. The frogs thundered in the dark, lightning-pierced night, a sound she associated with boredom and darkness and loneliness, a sound she hated. Every one of the hicks in the area talked about the marvelous sounds of the frogs, how they enjoyed it, which only made her hate it more. How could anyone find such a raucous noise marvelous? Her window was down, and the frogs were deafening her, but the driveway into Belle Lake was upon her, and she needed both hands to make the swing sharply to the left.

She drove along by the row of pine trees that edged the southern side of the drive. On her right was the lawn, lighted by fake-antique electric lanterns every thirty or forty feet. The house looked huge, a dark bulk against the rolling clouds with its spots of lightning. Was the storm coming back? Storms made her nervous, and always had. This was a bad night to have come, she suddenly decided. It was the worst night of the year for her to attempt to come back here.

Her tires squealed lightly, a sound feeble under the racket made by the frogs. She was driving faster than she had realized, she now saw, and braked slightly, heading back toward the garages.

Suddenly, unexpectedly the little man was there in the driveway, in front of her, boldly displayed in her headlights. She stared at him, disbelieving, slamming her feet frantically to the floor board, one on the brake and the other instinctively beside it. He was wearing a coat with tails, it seemed, and ridiculously, in the flash of the lights her car turned upon him, he had a round, white face like a child's, and was wearing on his head a tall, black hat.

Her car stopped with a screech just inches from him. The headlights shone full upon the ridiculous figure he made, and possibilities flashed through her mind: he was not a man, but a child, dressed for a costume party. *What was he doing here?* He was not real at all, but a trick that was being played on her. Ridiculous. He was moving. He was real. In her mixed fear and anger she stuck her head out the door window and shouted, "What the hell are you trying to do, get yourself killed—"

She almost strangled on the words, for into the car lights others were coming, a girl dressed in a gown of a century ago, the skirt hiding her feet, and a woman . . . a small woman no larger than the man. Midgets? People from a circus? *What—?*

They had such strange faces. All of them looked alike. Strange, white faces with full pink cheeks and tiny red mouths. They reminded her of something, someone, she had seen before, but . . .

Something struck the side of her car, and she jerked back, feeling it against the shoulder she had pushed against the door, seeing it and yet not seeing it clearly as it came in through the car window. She smelled it. A sickening, sweetish smell, very old, as of something that had been put away in a trunk for uncounted years. And she glimpsed from the corner of her eyes another of the white faces, just like the ones in front of her.

She began to fight it, trying to throw it back out the window. Her hands clutched old clothing, and something else as hard and cold as glass. *Its face.* Good God, its face! Her hand cupped its face and shoved it away from her, and suddenly she knew what they reminded her of: *antique dolls*.

Someone was playing a terrible, horrible trick on her.

She slammed her car in reverse and backed blindly toward the road, but she was aware that the little man with the top hat had leaped onto the hood, so that when she faced the front of the car again he was right there, against the windshield, blocking her view. The other one was still clinging to her door, though he was outside the car now. She fought the steering wheel, thinking only to drive as fast as she could to dislodge them, get away from them, throw them off.

197

Her car spun backwards onto the road, and then on almost into the ditch. She fought the wheel to straighten it, and pulled the shift into drive.

The tires screamed again on the damp pavement as they fought for traction. The car seemed to stand still for a very long time before it shot forward, going back toward town, along the edge of the swamp. The noise of the frogs almost drowned out the roar of the engine as she pulled the wheel, jerking it back and forth, trying desperately to dislodge the little man whose face was pressed against the windshield in front of her, and the boy who clung to the door at her side. There was something wrong with his neck, she noted with a part of her mind, and his glass head thumped against the car, a small sound under all the others, but a sound that drove her frantic with fear.

Her efforts to dislodge them were failing. The one at her door was climbing in again.

She gave the car a final, sudden jerk, turning its nose directly into the forest of the swamp. The trees loomed up, too soon and too close for her brakes to help, and she crashed, a slow-motion awareness in which she saw the hood crumple and rise and the car do a leap into the air and then turn slowly onto its side, the door at her elbow coming open.

She couldn't stop her fall. She was flung helplessly from the car, her hands out and grasping for something, anything to stop her fall.

Robert stood at his window looking down into the driveway, trying to see again what he'd seen just seconds ago. He couldn't believe it. He had to see it again to make sure he had seen it right. Yet he knew what he had seen.

Diane had come driving in, like she always did, as if her car didn't have brakes. And right there, in the headlights of her car were the . . . *robots*? They had suddenly appeared there in her lights, a little man, a boy with his head leaned to one side, and then, surprise. Two little women, dressed in old-fashioned clothes. They were like dolls, but they moved. He had seen them.

Robots.

Something new for Jessica? Something Pop had gotten for Jessica that he didn't know about?

And then crazy things had happened. The two men robots had leaped on the car, and Diane had slammed it in reverse and backed out, going seventy miles an hour it looked, so fast she almost hadn't made the road. And now she was gone, back toward town, and the robots had gone with her.

What in the hell was going on?

He opened his window, unlatched and pushed out the screen, and leaned as far out as he could without falling, searching below for some signs of what he had seen. The two women robots were still down there somewhere, but it was dark there now, except for a teasing flash of lightning now and then, and he couldn't see a damn thing. He'd think he saw something move, but he couldn't be sure.

He finally drew back and hurried out of his room and down the stairs. He went out the seldom-used front door, feeling a bit edgy about going out the door into the breezeway right where they might be.

Yet when he stepped onto the lighted front walk, he changed his mind and went back into the house and locked the front door. He ran down the hall to the door that led to the service quarters and the utility areas, and then into the short hall and to the door at the end of the breezeway. It, too, was tightly locked. Only the night lights were on in the hallways, and the kitchen and utility rooms were dark.

He opened the door into the breezeway cautiously and peered out. After a moment his eyes adjusted to the dark, and he could see the breezeway was empty. He went through. The gates on both sides were open. That was unusual. He walked out onto the blacktop of the wide driveway and stood with his hands in his pockets, listening and watching. Nothing unusual here, not now. Not that he could see.

Where had Diane gone?

Back to New Orleans like greased lightning.

He tried to laugh, tried to see the humor in it, but his smile turned to a frown.

What the shit was going on?

He walked the length of the driveway, seeing and hearing nothing out of the ordinary. He heard the sound of the car then, and he waited, standing beneath the shadows of the pine tree at the end of the grove. But the car was coming from the opposite direction. It couldn't be Diane coming back. And it was coming much slower, and furthermore, it was a pickup truck. A service truck of some kind, with lettering on the door that he couldn't read in the dark.

The truck passed by, leaving behind the sounds of the frogs and the faraway thunder.

Robert waited a few minutes longer, then he went back to the house, wishing he'd thought to bring a flashlight along. With a light he could have looked around and finally found the robots, maybe. Yet he wasn't sure he really wanted to. There was something weird and scary about it all, and he felt a sense of safety when he locked the breezeway door behind him.

When he reached his room and was latching the window-screen, he heard the siren. Police or ambulance, or both. Coming nearer, nearer. Stopping then, not far away. Somewhere between here and town. He remained standing at the window watching, listening, wondering.

He was still there when a police car pulled quietly into the driveway an hour later, but he stayed in his room, puzzled, chilled, and finally went to bed quietly and with a surreptitiousness that was new to him. With his ears wide open he listened, blanket up to his chin, but the house was deadly quiet.

It had something to do with Diane and the robots, he knew.

Brenda was still in the library downstairs when she heard the arrival of someone. There were muted voices, and a strange male voice among them. Her first thought, that Diane had arrived, was mixed with an anxiety that she had brought a man along. Of all the worst things she could do, that would be it. Yet she had a feeling, too, that something was wrong. She had heard the sirens thirty minutes or more ago, an unusual sound here at Belle Lake, with only the secondary road out front. Not many police sirens had ever been heard here. Her dad had gone upstairs early, but she could hear the deep tones of his voice, too, in the foyer. She put aside her book and went out into the foyer, and saw two policemen talking with her father.

Paul's face, turned toward her, had been drained of all color. For the first time in her life she knew the expression "white as a sheet" could be true.

"Diane has had an accident," he said. "She's seriously injured. She's been taken to the hospital." He turned back to the policemen. "We'll be there as soon as we can."

The two men in uniform left, and Paul closed the door. He was wearing a robe over pajamas, and he went immediately toward the stairway.

"Brenda and I will be gone for a good part of the night, probably, Della. Keep an eye on Jessica and Robert. If Robert wakes, you can tell him where we've gone."

Only then did Brenda see Della, standing back out of the light.

"What happened?" Brenda asked her. "Do you know?"

"All I know is the doorbell rang and they were on the doorstep. They said a woman named Diane Norris had had a wreck just around the corner, and is in the hospital."

"Just a one-car accident?"

"I don't know."

Brenda and Della were still standing in the foyer when Paul came running back down the stairs. Brenda followed him out to his car, remembering her purse too late, but deciding in silence that she didn't need it anyway.

Paul seemed not to want to talk. He drove faster than Brenda had ever seen him drive and she was forced to fasten herself in tightly and pray they didn't follow in Diane's wake and have their own accident. Less than a quarter-mile from the driveway they swerved around a police car, a wrecker, and the crumpled red metal that had been Diane's Porshe. Something about it struck Brenda as wrong, but the sight was gone, put behind them, before she could identify it.

They arrived at the hospital in a neighboring town, larger than Pinewood, which didn't have so much as a clinic, and went upstairs to the large white room where Diane, in a high bed separated from others by surrounding curtains, was drifting in and out of consciousness.

Shocked by the sight, Brenda stood by the bed. A nurse on the other side monitored devices that clicked and undulated at the head of the bed and to the side. Diane's face and head were bandaged on one side. Only one eye looked out, bloodied, closing again in weakness.

She seemed not to see Paul, and reached her hand toward Brenda.

Brenda heard Paul make some kind of choking noise, and she glanced at him to see that he was stooping forward, hand to his chest. A nurse near the door, who had brought them in, was alerted and returned, taking him by the arm and gently leading him from the room.

Brenda noticed the heart monitor was uneven.

Diane was not doing well at all. Probably, she needed no company, no one to agitate her. She started to draw quietly away, but Diane's fingers, fluttering weakly, closed on hers, tugging her near.

The nurse on the other side of the bed said, "I think she wants to tell you something. She's been asking for you. You are Brenda, aren't you?"

"Yes."

The nurse nodded. "She's been asking for you in her moments of consciousness."

The unbandaged eye looked imploringly at Brenda, and Brenda bent down nearer to the bed.

"It . . . it was like little . . . people," Diane whispered. "They . . . jumped my car in the driveway. Dolls. They were dolls that move. Big dolls. Child-size." Her eye closed. *"Don't let Jessica . . . outside."* She gasped and the heart monitor began a steady sound, and the red line straightened, with no bleeps, no further sign of a heartbeat.

Brenda stared, stunned, shocked by it all, absorbing it all in a deeper part of her consciousness, knowing that Diane had died, yet not knowing. Two nurses came rushing in through the curtains, and another came and led Brenda away.

Paul was in the waiting room just outside the large intensive care unit, with a nurse still at his side. He was bowed forward, an elbow on his knee, his hand supporting his head.

"Is he all right?" Brenda asked.

"Yes, he'll be all right."

The nurse moved away, and Brenda sat down. She put her hand on his arm. "Dad? Diane has died."

He nodded.

For a few minutes longer they were surrounded by doctors and nurses, trying to lend support, and at last Brenda urged Paul away. The air outside the hospital was clean and fresh, the pavement still damp. The clouds had thinned and stars peeked through in places, as brilliant as if they, too, had been cleansed by a summer shower.

"Do you want me to drive, Dad?"

"No. I will."

If he had let her, she thought, searching for the normal feeling amidst the sorrow, the shock, he would have been near death's door himself. But knowing that he was still himself, she sat back in the seat feeling somewhat reassured. For a while back in intensive care, when he had seen Diane, she was afraid that his heart wouldn't be able to take it.

He drove slowly, his thoughts obviously not on what he was doing.

They came, once again, to the place of the accident. There were deep tracks off the side of the road and into the trees and the swamp. Brenda saw them now, although when they had passed earlier, she hadn't seen anything but the other automobiles. For a moment the car lights fell upon the tree that had been struck, its bark peeled off, the wound white in the darkness of the forest. The wrecked car had been taken out.

The Mercedes slowed.

Paul spoke for the first time. "She was headed away, you know. She wasn't headed toward home, she was headed away. That's what the trooper said."

The light clicked on in Brenda's brain. That was the thing that had disturbed her when they passed the wrecked car earlier. Its trunk was toward them, toward Belle Lake, with the hood of the car headed away. Diane had not been arriving at Belle Lake, she had been leaving!

And that corresponded with what she had said just before she died, about being jumped in the driveway by . . . dolls. Dolls? Little people, she had first said. But none of that was acceptable. It was, it had to be, a product of a mind that was no longer right. The accident had injured Diane's head severely, and all she said was to be discounted. But it seemed very odd that she had been in the driveway, at least long enough to turn around. And she must have been driving very fast when she struck the tree.

"She wasn't belted in," Paul said in a low drone that indicated to Brenda that he wanted to talk, without interruption. He was speaking aloud his thoughts. He stopped the car, the lights shining on the wound in the tree and picking up in the damp, crushed grass bits and pieces of red metal, and glass. "She hit the tree at a high rate of speed, and the door came open. They don't know how she hurt her head so much. Not on the windshield, but on the frame of the door, they think. They didn't know that she hadn't been home. There must be a mistake of some kind."

"Hadn't we better drive on, Dad?" Brenda said, not wanting to be near this scene of destruction any longer. The forest, with its eyes of glistening, black water gleaming in the dark, in the car lights that pierced the dark, unnerved her. She was beginning to tremble all over, the shock of Diane's death invading her nervous system.

Paul started the car moving forward and drove without speaking on into the driveway and to the garage. Although they walked together into the house, Paul stopped at the library.

"I'd better go up and check on Jessica, Dad. If you need me, just call."

He nodded. He was already pouring a drink. Brenda felt like she could use one herself to stop her shaking, but she went on to the front stairs and up.

She stopped in the bathroom she used, and took an aspirin. When she went back out into the hall, Robert was standing in his doorway.

"What happened?" he asked. "Della told me Diane had a wreck. Is she all right?"

"She's dead, Robert. I'm sorry." She waited, to see if he might need her, but though his face grew pale also, just as Paul's had, it stayed that way only a moment before the color came back.

"Oh Jesus," he murmured. "That's too bad. Poor little kid."

She knew he was referring to Jessica, and Brenda nodded. "Yes. It's going to be hard to tell her. I'm going now to check on her. You'd better get some sleep, Robert."

"Where's Dad?"

"Downstairs treating his shock and pain with booze."

Robert shrugged.

Brenda went on to the room at the end of the hall, pausing outside the door to look back at Robert. He had disappeared, and his door was closed.

When Brenda looked into Jessica's room that sense of stunned reality returned, and she stood staring through the path of pale light that led to Jessica's bed. A woman, wearing a long white gown, was bending forward over Jessica. Her long, pale blond hair swung forward, obscuring the side of her face. The arms, white, almost as white as the full sleeves of the robe that fell away from them, were poised out toward Jessica, the hands not quite touching the child. The stance of the woman, the slowness of her movements, if any at all, enhanced the sense of unreality. Yet she was there, and as she reached for the little girl, Brenda saw her fingers, abnormally long, and curled like claws.

Brenda heard her own gasp, and the sudden whimper from Jessica.

The woman's head turned suddenly, a face of beauty and savage cruelty looking for one instant at Brenda. Jessica had begun to scream, but Brenda was paralyzed. As she stared at the woman there was a sudden shift in posture, and then she was gone.

The room was empty. The path of light was undisturbed. The white throw rug on the carpet beside the bed held nothing but the little pile of clothes that Jessica had climbed out of and that Brenda had forgotten to take to the hamper.

The screams of Jessica filled the space around Brenda, filled her head, yet not her awareness, not completely, not enough to move her forward. A woman had been in Jessica's room, bending over her bed, a woman in white, a woman of such beauty, and cruelty, as Brenda had never seen before.

Robert came running down the hall. His hand came up and struck Brenda lightly on the shoulder. "Hey!"

Brenda jolted forward, going to the bed and pulling Jessica up into her arms. The little girl clutched her with trembling hands, and pressed her face to her as her screams settled to sobs and then to silence. Brenda looked over her shoulder at Robert.

"Turn the lights on."

Robert pushed the switch, and the room was exposed. No one was hiding.

"Look in the closet," Brenda said. "I saw someone here, by Jessica's bed, just before she started to scream. Look everywhere."

But even as she gave him instructions, she knew he'd find no one. The woman had vanished.

And there was only one explanation, one that Brenda rejected even as she thought of it.

The hideous, unnaturally long fingers, curved, clawed, stayed before her mind, an image imprinted upon her vision like the residue of a white light.

CHAPTER TWELVE

It was up to Brenda to tell Jessica that her mother was dead. Arrangements were being made for the funeral, and Paul was subdued and distant, as if his sorrows had surrounded him and isolated him from the rest of the world. He seemed capable only of sitting at his desk and dealing with the problems by telephone, and lifting the leather carafe to pour himself another drink. Yet he never showed the effects of the alcohol in his movements or his speech. Brenda held back her warnings, though she wanted to say, Dad, it doesn't look good, the way you're holding your liquor. It's got the elements of alcoholism, this way that the effect is lessened, like water in your system instead of whiskey. But she said nothing. The house, large and of many rooms, most of them unused, had never been a noisy house, but now it became funereally quiet, with not even Robert's music to disturb the silence.

Brenda waited, dreading to tell Jessica, but the child couldn't be left thinking her mother might yet come to get her. Although, Brenda wondered, puzzled, Jessica had said nothing the morning after Diane's death, nothing at all about her mother's not coming when she'd said she would. It entered Brenda's mind, and left it again, as she delayed facing Jessica.

Finally, after what passed for lunch, a half-eaten meal that not even Robert had appetite for, Brenda took Jessica to the unoccupied TV room, and sat in front of her, the small hands limp in her own. She unconsciously massaged the tapered little fingers until Jessica drew them away, trying to find the right words. Finally, deciding there were no right words, she plunged in.

"Jessica, I'm sorry you didn't get to see your mother last night. She didn't come to get you because she couldn't. You see, something really—uh—bad happened. Her car hit a tree. She—Diane—died last night. She's gone now. I'm very sorry."

There was the slightest flicker on Jessica's face, but her features blurred beyond the tears that filled Brenda's eyes. She hadn't planned to weep in front of the little girl, and she hastily wiped away the tears and blinked back the ones that threatened. When again she had a clear view of Jessica's face, she saw no change of expression at all. The round pretty face looked as it always did, blue eyes wide, blond curls framing, lips closed. How she had changed since last year, when those lips were seldom closed.

"She's not coming to get me?" Jessica asked.

"No, I'm sorry."

Brenda expected more, but there was no change. No tears. No questions.

Didn't she understand? Had she never been told about death? Well, no matter, at least Brenda had done the worst part, she felt, and she could answer whatever questions Jessica asked later on. She had a sharp, lonely feeling for Mrs. Archer, and wished she would come back and handle this. Brenda had faith in her, even if Paul didn't.

"Can I go now?" Jessica asked.

"Yes. Why not," Brenda said relieved. Let her go and play, and find comfort however she could.

There was another problem concerning Jessica a couple of days later, on the day of the funeral. Paul had said nothing to any of the family that Brenda knew of, and she delayed in going to him. But the funeral was at two in the afternoon, and she could put it off no longer.

She found him at his desk. The somber colors of the room made a suitable background for him. The heavy draperies were almost closed, leaving only a narrow space to let the contrasting brightness of the sun penetrate the gloom.

"Dad," she said, hesitant even to add her voice to this silence. At first he didn't answer, didn't even glance her way, as if he hadn't heard her. Again she said, "Dad?"

Without moving he answered, "Yes."

"What about Jessica? Do you want her to go to the funeral?"

He drew a long breath and leaned back against his chair. "No. She's just a baby. It's bad enough that she's lost her mother."

Brenda wasn't sure she agreed with him. Robert had been just short of seven when their mother had died, and he had gone to the funeral. She opened her mouth in preparation for reminding him of that, and then decided against it. These had been difficult days for all of them. Only Jessica had gone on with her play. If she could continue with some kind of activity that kept her happy, then so be it.

But Brenda thought as she left the room, Jessica was just reticent, probably, because there was no way these things concerning her mother could not have left their mark. Why else would she have those nightmares? Thankfully, she didn't seem to have them every night. There had been none since the night the lady—the ghost—had bent over her.

Or had that been Brenda's own hallucination? Well, of course it had. But what had it meant? Surely there was a meaning, like an especially realistic dream or persistent dream; things like that just didn't happen out of the blue with no reason.

And there was the other thing: the footsteps. But that, from the distance of several nights now, could be put in the category of a dream. Although it had seemed at the time that she was awake, she must not have been.

Something occurred to her for the first time, and she felt the coldness of the unknown move over her arms and up the back of her neck. Both occurrences, the footsteps and the hallucination of the blond woman, had come just as Jessica was entering one of her night terrors. But whatever meaning there was behind that only made Brenda feel confused. Was it her own psychic touch with Jessica? Did she know, somehow, subconsciously, when Jessica was going into one of her nightmares?

213

She couldn't think of it, because when she did, a terrible feeling she couldn't identify came over her, chilling her with her own unknown terrors. There was a dark curtain here that she didn't want to open.

Robert was following Jessica.

He had slept very little since the night of Diane's death. He had kept his eyes open, and his ears tuned to every sound. His music was shut off, and so was his television. He hadn't given his attention to his comic books, either, or to anything else. He was watching. At night he watched out his window, and a couple of times he had seen something move in the shadows of the pines across the driveway, and he had crept downstairs, as quietly as he could, and out the door. And this time he had taken a flashlight. But he found nothing.

He wanted to talk to Pop about it, but hated to bother him at this time. Wait, instinct told him, until the funeral was over.

He watched Jessica, belatedly, even though he couldn't figure out who the robots belonged to if they weren't hers. If there were robots on the place, hadn't their dad bought them? For Jessica, not for him. Why would he want robots like that, that looked like real people?

And, or, he thought also, maybe they *were* real people. Midgets from a carnival. But he had scanned the newspapers, and there was no mention of any carnivals.

The whole thing was a crazy mystery, but he knew what he had seen.

So, after lunch on the day of the funeral he followed Jessica. Only that morning had it occurred to him that she might know more about it than he had given her credit for. He always thought of her as being just a baby. But she wasn't, really. And so he decided to see where she went so often and for so long. He knew Brenda had told her about Diane, but then Jessica had left the house. To play, he guessed, but he wanted to know where, and with what.

She went through the shrubbery behind the garden shed, and along a winding path to the magnolia tree. He stayed back, keeping her barely in sight part of the time, losing sight of her entirely at others. She was beyond the thick trunk of the magnolia tree and then she was gone.

The high chain link fence ended the back yard, and he slipped quietly along through the shrubbery and the trees to the duck pond, but she was nowhere. He stood listening, but heard only the ordinary sounds, the murmuring of the ducks, the blip of water as they dipped head down after food, the frogs calling in the swamp, a sound he wished now he could put a lid on so he could listen for his sister. Had she just plain disappeared? Had she climbed the magnolia tree? He used to climb it. There were a lot of good places to sit in it, all hidden by the large, glossy green leaves. He used to pretend he was Tarzan of the Apes.

He went back to the tree and looked up into its dark, greenish interior, but then a movement to his left caught his eye.

Jessica. Halfway across the meadow toward the old Blahough mansion. Was that where she was going? Unbelievable. *Weird*. Surely not to that old creepy place. He must be wrong. Maybe she was just out in the meadow to gather wild flowers.

He stood against the fence watching her, feeling like a spy. She was running, her arms out above the tops of the weeds and grass. She wasn't pausing to pick flowers.

She went directly to the fence that surrounded the abandoned old place, and down along it to the corner where, he remembered, he had seen a gate. She went through and was gone, swallowed by the wilderness of old trees, vines, wild growth.

A cold dread made him feel strange. He was scared for her.

He stood at the fence waiting for her to show up again. In all his life he had never gone any nearer that place than he had when he was looking for Mrs. Archer. Why in the hell would Jessica go there? And alone, too.

He didn't like it. Knowing she was there made him feel . . . really weird. He wasn't sure exactly how he did feel, but he didn't like it. Was that where she had been that day when Mrs. Archer couldn't find her? Was that why Mrs. Archer had told her about ghosts, and then got herself fired for trying to warn her away from there? He wasn't afraid of any ghosts, or anything like that. It had been fun to think there might be ghosts, but that was when he was still young. Younger, at least, than now. But still, he didn't like knowing that the little kid was over there all alone.

He started to climb the fence, a job not easy, for finding a toehold was almost impossible. The links were too small.

He backed down, thinking he'd just go around to the meadow gate, and then he remembered something. The funeral. It was this afternon, and he had to get dressed. He reluctantly left the fence, the outdoors, and went into the house. He looked through the house until he found Brenda.

He didn't tell Brenda where Jessica had gone. That was something he wanted to explore first himself. He only asked, "Isn't Jessica going to the funeral?"

"No. Dad didn't feel she should."

Robert shrugged and went upstairs to get dressed.

During the next two hours he couldn't get his mind off Jessica at the old crumbling mansion, or in the jungle that surrounded it. He tried to imagine what she did there. Maybe she just played in the yard? Maybe she was looking for ripe blueberries? Blueberries wouldn't grow in a jungle like that, but she was just a dumb little kid, she wouldn't know that. He sat through the funeral with his thoughts following Jessica, and making plans. They'd be home by three again, and he could have his clothes changed in ten minutes. He absented himself from the sadness of the funeral psychically, yet his thoughts of Jessica increased the uneasiness he was feeling, and made his hands cold and dry.

His timing was off quite a lot. It was four instead of three when they got home, but it took him only five minutes to throw off his black suit and white shirt and get into the jeans of the morning. He left the suit crumpled on the bed. He put on sneakers so that his footsteps would be silent, and he avoided the areas where someone would be, the kitchen, the library, the office. He slipped out the front door and ran across the front lawn to the verge of the highway where the wall ended, and slipped around it into the wooded area where the farmer's road went back through the trees to the fence at the edge of the meadow.

There, he got down on his knees and ducked under the wire gate. Then, he followed Jessica.

He felt exposed as he crossed the meadow, as if he were being watched. Especially after he noticed the old gray stone tower sticking up above the trees did he feel he was being watched. He ducked down, and ran hunched, with the tower now hidden in the treetops.

The gate in the hog wire with the three barbed top wires that surrounded the Blahough mansion was hanging askew. The top wire that had looped over the fence post was missing, he saw, remembering clearly how it had looked when he passed around this fence the day he was looking for Mrs. Archer. He edged through the opening in the gate without touching the wire. Shadows fell upon him immediately, dark, damp shadows. The path was a narrow little thing that disappeared beneath the first cluster of vines.

But as he progressed slowly along the path, he noticed it was still there, curling inward among the trees, but recently trampled, leading him deeper into shadows toward the house.

If the feeling hadn't been there, the sense of dread, like the threat of a bottomless hole hiding beneath the vines in the next few steps, he would have enjoyed the adventure of exploring. He wondered why he had never gone in there before. Or why none of his friends had ever insisted on looking around the old house. When they were still young and believed in ghosts, they would have been sure this was a haunted house, and would have explored it. But they hadn't. They hadn't even thought of it then. The old place had just sat here, growing more vines and more jungle with every season.

He fought through the growth at times, pushing hanging moss and vines out of his way. He came upon a log that had been scuffed on top, rotten bits of it knocked down, the moss that grew green upon the top side uprooted. The path led on beyond it, a little wider and clearer now. He stepped over the log, putting his hand on it for support. Something tiny and soft squirmed beneath his hand and he jerked it away with a shudder. Wriggly things here took on an aspect different from wriggly things in other places. He found suddenly that he wanted to leave, to tear out the way he had come and forget this. Jessica was probably back in the yard somewhere, playing. At the swing set, maybe, where she used to spend so much time. He hadn't looked anywhere for her. He'd been crazy to think she was still here after all these hours.

He stood still, staring ahead, his eyes straining. As if it were becoming visible gradually, he saw the gray stone, tiny bits among the camouflage of green. To his left a chorus of frogs began, and it comforted him. He hadn't realized until now how his heart had begun to pound, and how cold his skin was. The frogs made him remember that this was nothing but a place that had been left to grow into a jungle, that was all.

He went forward, and even began a low whistle,

just enough to show he wasn't scared, not enough to attract the attention of . . . whatever lurked.

The floor of the gallery was there suddenly, so suddenly he almost cracked his shin against it. He looked up at a huge gray stone front that seemed to go on forever toward the sky. The upper gallery floor was falling at the far end, had fallen, so that it rested within a few feet of the ground floor. The pillars were still standing, some of them supporting vines now. Green moss grew in cracks in the stone walls, and the trailing vines sent feelers in and leaves upward. The windows were shuttered. But the big, deep front door was standing part way open.

Robert stepped onto the porch and crossed it gingerly, eyeing the gallery floor that was hanging above. At the threshold he stopped, looking in cautiously, listening for sounds of Jessica. He opened his mouth to call out to her, yet breathed out in silence.

The foyer beyond the door looked like a dungeon, huge and dark. There were pieces of old furniture scattered about, and the foot of a stairway far back in the gloom. The stairs, though, seemed lighter as they rose, and he followed his gaze and crossed the foyer to the stairs and stood looking up. There was a landing above, and a turn in the stairs toward a lighter hallway. He listened, his eyes exploring every door within sight, and seeing nothing beyond but more darkness.

Crazy, he thought, that he would think Jessica was here. She wasn't. A little kid like her would be scared to death to come into a place like this. He didn't like it here, either. There was nothing but silence in the house, a huge, deep-holed silence. A dungeon silence. Not even a mouse had run when he entered. Nothing lived here. It was . . . a dangerous place for anything to live. An impossible place to live. Life would not survive here overnight.

He turned to go out, the doorway a beckoning pathway to life. Out there the frogs sang and the mice made nests wherever they could find a safe place. Things wriggled.

Abruptly behind him, upstairs or down, he couldn't tell which, there came a sound that caused the hair on his back to rise. Footsteps along a wood floor, fast, almost running. Too heavy and too sharp to be Jessica's. The sound of the steps seemed to pass over him and go on, fading. As suddenly as they had begun they were gone again, leaving a silence that pulsed with his racing blood.

It had to be Jessica, he decided. No one else would be in this house, and the steps had sounded like a woman's high-heeled shoes because they were magnified, somehow, by the hugeness of the house, the thickness of the stone walls, and the height of the ceilings. Jessica was somewhere upstairs. But even if he did yell at her, she probably wouldn't hear him. There must be forty rooms here.

Knowing he wasn't alone helped. If a little kid like Jessica could come in here, then so could he. No way was he going to chicken out of this. Besides, he was looking for something. And that was another possibility. Maybe it hadn't been Jessica running, but one of the robots. Maybe this was where she brought them.

He began to feel like his head was screwed on wrong. Something was haywire with the whole thing.

Where would Jessica have gotten the robots if their dad hadn't given them to her? And if their dad had given them to her, how come *he* didn't know about it? Yet, what could they have been if they weren't robots? Little people? *Real* little people, like from a carnival? Living here? Something was crazy, and he was going to find out what.

He was halfway up the stairs, and almost stepped into the hole where the steps were broken. He paused long. enough to glance down. There were fallen boards there, hanging, barely visible in the darkness. He pushed closer to the banister and stepped over, watching the steps more carefully. Some of them made noises when he stepped on them, and some gave threateningly. He kept close to the banister and went on, and finally came out into a section of hallways that branched. Narrow halls went off to the sides. The wide hall went back to the end of the upper story where a window, with shutters broken and falling, let in just enough light to keep the hall from the darkness of the others.

There was nothing in the halls but some furniture and a picture high on the wall. Silence had taken over again, and then, so softly he almost missed it, he heard the murmur of Jessica's voice. She was talking to someone, in one of the rooms back toward the end of the hall.

Light shone through an open door far down the hallway, and he hurried toward it. The picture on the wall began to waver and thump faintly as he passed it, as if his footsteps had vibrated it into movement. He only glanced up at it, and saw it was an old painting of a blond woman with a blond baby on her lap, but the woman's face was separated into three pieces, like a reflection in a broken mirror. Odd. It was a big, heavy frame. If it fell, it could kill a guy, he thought as he gave it plenty of room.

Jessica's voice guided him. She was in the room where the light came from, and when he reached the doorway he could see that the window had been broken out and the shutters pushed away. That was the first thing he saw. The second thing was the large doll house in the corner of the room beyond the window, with Jessica sitting in the top floor holding a small doll on her lap. Beneath her, in various parts of the lower rooms, the kitchen and the living room, were the robots he had seen in the driveway. At least four of them. He stared. Dolls, all of them. The boy doll had a broken neck, with something sticking out. Tiny wires? He hadn't noticed that the other night. He'd seen them for only a few seconds. But he hadn't been dreaming. Here they were.

But they were only big dolls. They weren't moving. Of course, they weren't being activated. Not at the moment. He frowned hard, looking from one to the other. Anger began building in him. What kind of deal was this, anyway? Did Jessica realize these crazy robots of hers might have caused the death of her own mother? It was because of them Diane had driven out of the driveway so fast. It was because of them . . . and Jessica? *Where did she keep the controls?*

He almost called out to her, to order her down from that old doll house and away from here. To demand to know where she had gotten the dolls and where she kept the controls that activated them.

He almost called out.

But some deep premonition warned him, and the hair on his back came up again, to stand in warning like the hair on an animal's back. *Get out of here. Go to Dad. Tell him.*

Get out.

Quietly.

CHAPTER THIRTEEN

Paul had gone somewhere, Robert found when he reached home. He felt like crying when Brenda told him.

"But where? Where did he go?" His face was screwed up and his voice was whiny. He knew these things, and hated it, but the fear in him made it impossible for him to act like he was anywhere close to fourteen. "Today was her funeral. Why should he leave today?"

"I think he left because of it. He said he'd be back tonight. Maybe he went to his office. He used to do that when something bothered him a lot. It's better than sitting here getting sloshed."

Robert shrugged, trying to bring back a bit of nonchalance. He was still nervous from hurrying so fast. He still felt like he was trying to get out of that terrible old house without making any noise. He still felt like he was going down the path in that green jungle with something—with *them*—right behind him. Of course, they hadn't been. When he reached the gate and looked back, nothing was there but the trees, the vines, the bushes.

He thought about telling Brenda about Jessica, where she was, what she was doing. He wanted to ask her if she knew anything about Jessica's getting robots to play with. But she wouldn't know. She hadn't even been around here much at all in the past several years. Just a little visit now and then every year or so. What would she know?

Well, he'd wait. However long it took, he'd wait.

But he didn't want to see Jessica.

He went up to his room and locked the door. At the window he sat on the floor and gazed out. He could barely see over the sill, but the window was open, and he could hear Dad's car when it arrived.

He sat there and watched the light of the sun fade and disappear. Brenda came up and knocked on his door.

"Robert, it's dinnertime."

"I'm not coming down."

"Why on earth not? Are you sick?"

"No, I'm just not hungry."

That wasn't quite true, but he was going to wait until Jessica was put to bed before he left the room. He had a funny feeling about her now, a feeling he couldn't identify.

He tried to figure it out as he sat in the growing darkness. It was like she had become one of *them*.

At eight, with streaks of red light stretching up like fingers of a dying fire into the black of the overhead sky, Robert heard Brenda and Jessica go past his room and down the hall. Their footsteps were muffled in the carpet, and Brenda's voice was a murmuring softness. A floorboard creaked, reminding Robert of the other house. After a few minutes Brenda came back. She paused outside his door. Then, as if deciding to leave him alone after all, she went on.

"Annabelle, Annabelle, where are you, dear? Mother has something for you."

She looked up from among the tombstones, where her mother had sent her to clean the graves. Every weed had to be clipped. Every twig removed. Zachary worked with his back to her. Fog swirled around them, so that if she hadn't known who he was, she would have been even more frightened than she was.

"Annabelle, come here, dear. Mother has something to show you."

Zachary's pale face turned toward her. His eyes were dark and huge and filled with silent terror.

"Annabelle."

She rose, brushing the twigs and leaves and dirt from the front of her dress and her stockings.

She went out through the spiked iron gate and across the back yard to the porch. Her mother's voice came out from the house, somewhere. She was being nice now. Maybe a good time was coming. She entered the kitchen, the fog coming with her to swirl in mists, obscuring the ends of the room.

"Come, dear Annabelle. Come, dear."

Mother was in the laundry. Her voice came from behind the closed door.

She put her hand to the knob, and pulled the door open.

It swung from a rope in front of her, its neck

227

broken. Her new doll, Victor, the doll her papa had brought her most recently.

Robert was awakened by Jessica's screams. He had gone to sleep by the window, and his neck felt as if it were made of wood. Something popped when he straightened, an alarming pop, but he felt better afterward, more awake, less as if he'd been crammed into a tiny cage for several hours.

Footsteps thudded past his door, and Jessica's screams ended. He went out into the hall and stood indecisively. When Brenda came back from Jessica's room several minutes later, she looked at him in surprise.

"Haven't you gone to bed yet?"

"No. I'm—uh—waiting for Dad. Is he here?"

"I don't know. I've been in my room. I haven't heard him." She glanced back toward Jessica's room. "I don't understand that. I'm going to have to talk to Dad, too, to see if I can't change his mind about a psychologist for Jessica. She can't go on having such nightmares. She never wakes up, though. At least not for long. Is a person harmed by something they can't remember?"

"You're asking me?"

"Does the subconscious harbor things the conscious mind isn't aware of? What kind of damage is done by things of that nature? Well, goodnight, Robert. I had just gone to sleep. I'd like to get back where I was. Maybe it's just anxiety. Having her mother leave, and then having her gone forever. I'm sure that's what Dad thinks it is. An anxiety that she'll grow out of. If she were an adult she'd be given tranquilizers of some sort, but what do they do for children? It isn't as though she can't sleep. She seems to sleep deeply. Goodnight."

She went on, her arms folded across the front of her body. She turned the corner and was out of sight.

While he still stood there, in the dimly lighted hall, he heard the soft sounds of a car engine and tires on the pavement of the driveway. He ran back to his window to check it out, and saw his dad's sedan pulling into the garage. The door opened automatically, and lights came on, spilling out onto the black shadows beneath the pine trees. Robert turned and ran.

He met his dad at the door to the breezeway, and he saw immediately that he was as sober as he ever got. He also looked exhausted. The lines in his face hung heavily downward, and his jowls drooped. His eyes were bloodshot.

He was still dressed in the black suit he had worn to the funeral.

He blinked at Robert. "What are you doing up? It's past midnight."

"I've got to talk to you, Pop."

Paul walked past Robert and began removing his tie as he went toward the hall to the library. "Not tonight, Robert. It's late."

"Pop, please, it's important!"

Paul shook his head. He dropped into his chair in the library. The leather made faint creaking sounds. Robert stationed himself near Paul's stretched-out feet pleadingly.

"Pop, it's about Jessica. And her robots."

Paul looked directly at Robert for the first time. "And her what?"

"Did you get her some robots, Pop? Because, because—"

Paul had begun to frown. "Explain yourself better, Robert, and slow down or you'll be stuttering. What are you talking about?"

"Big dolls that move around, like robots. Pop, the night Diane died, I saw her drive into the driveway. And in her headlights I saw these old-fashioned robots. Four of them. At first I thought they might be little people. That's what I thought they were. And the two in men's clothes, a boy with a deformed neck, he holds his head sideways, like this, and the other man, a bigger one, who was wearing an old-fashioned top hat kind of thing, they jumped on the car when Diane stopped. She backed out, fast, and I couldn't see anymore. I think she was trying to get away from them, Pop. But I saw in the lights that they weren't real people after all. They looked like big dolls. Two male dolls and two female, a woman and a girl. Robots. I saw them again, Pop, today. And they were with Jessica. So, she had to get them somewhere. The only thing is, it was in the old mansion where I saw them."

Paul's face had gone from one change to another, and now was settled back into a frown. Robert grabbed up one of his hands and held it in the vice of both his own.

"You got them for her, didn't you, Pop?" His voice was pleading, *say yes, Pop, say yes.*

"You know I never got her anything like that. I don't know what you saw, but you must be wrong about it. If she did drive in before she left again, it must have been for some reason that—uh—we just don't know about yet."

"It's true, Pop—Dad, what I saw. And I saw them again today. And Jessica, do you know where she was, Dad? In the old mansion." He repeated it all without stuttering, waiting for his dad to hear.

"*What old man*—? You don't mean the Blahough place!"

"Yes, Dad. And those dolls were there. Come with me, and I'll show you." He tugged on his Dad's hand, but Paul didn't move.

"How in the hell did she get there?" he asked, trying to puzzle it out. "There are fences between here and there. It's halfway across the meadow."

"She climbed over the fence."

"*What fence?*"

"Our big chain link at the rear of the grounds, Dad. I saw her."

"That fence is made so it can't be climbed."

"She did."

Paul seemed to relent a bit, though he still looked as if he had been slapped with ice. "It's six or seven feet high," he said. "The wires at the top are left sharp to prevent anyone from climbing over."

"She did."

Paul sat forward and shook his head. "You saw her? Why didn't you make her get down? What if she had fallen? What if she cut herself on those jagged wires at the top?"

Robert listened with his mouth open. It hadn't occurred to him to call her back, but he hadn't been telling the whole truth. "I didn't really see her climb the fence, Dad, but that was the only way she could have gotten over it to the meadow. I was following her, and I saw her cross the meadow."

Paul sagged back into his chair. "Oh well, maybe there's a hole under the fence. Made by a wild animal. I'll have it checked out."

"But Pop, listen, she went over to the old mansion."

Paul shrugged. "I explored that old place a couple of times myself. It's not a good idea that she go there alone, but I can see why it might be an attraction. I'll talk to her about it." He stood up and began loosening his clothes, as if he were going up to bed.

Robert followed him as he crossed the room, grabbing his big, thick hand again.

"Dad, it's those robots that she found! Did they have robots in those days?"

"Of course not."

"Dad, please. Come with me." He felt the hot pain of tears suddenly, abruptly, too late to try to disguise them, too late to brush them away. Paul, seeing them glisten in the light, hesitated. Robert took advantage of the hesitation by telling rapidly all he could in a moment's time. "I followed her to the old mansion, Dad, and I found her upstairs in a bedroom where there's a great big doll house. And there they were — the very same things I saw in Diane's lights. Big dolls. Robots. Come with me, Dad. See for yourself."

Instead of going toward the stairs, Paul turned

232

toward the utility room, shaking his head. "I don't know what's happening to my family. All right, Robert, I'll come with you. But we have to have flashlights."

From the utility room Paul took the electric Spot-liter, and they went out through the breezeway. Robert, silent now, hurried on ahead with his own smaller battery-operated flashlight, though he kept it shut off until they rounded the end of the brick wall and were in the woods. He turned it on to find the faint trail of the road, and the wire gate into the meadow. Without talking they crossed the meadow and Robert led the way again to the gate into the yard of the mansion. He heard his dad muttering a cuss word under his breath as they pushed through the hanging, shredded moss.

The front door was still open, though not as far as he had left it. Paul's strong light swept past Robert's head and examined the stairs, the doors off the foyer, the hall going back into the house. There was absolute silence in the house. Beyond the open door behind them the frogs shrilled and boomed madly, filling the outdoors with sound. The thick walls of the house seemed to absorb most of it, so that only the open door allowed them connection with the world.

"Dad," Robert whispered, unable to raise his voice in this tomblike place. "That stairway's got a big hole in it, but you can walk around it if you walk close to the banister."

Paul's light pointed toward the hall going deeper into the first floor. "There's another stairs back there.

233

We'll try it."

Robert followed his father, secure in his size, his authority. His father walked with sure steps down the old hall, shining his light ahead. They went through a door and turned left down a narrow hallway then turned right again and through another door. A long flight of steps rose, pinched in between the walls. Paul hesitated on the bottom step, flashlight pointed upwards, the beam filtered by spider webs that filled the stairwell.

Paul backed up and shined his light around the narrow hall. At the end there was a closed door, and against the wall beside it a tall piece of old furniture with a small, framed mirror at the top, a couple of wooden arms on which a shapeless draping of material hung, something that could have been a coat once upon a time, and beneath it, in a kind of open hamper, three sticks with curved handles. Paul grunted an "Ah!" and pulled one of the sticks out. Robert saw that it was a cane.

Using the cane to clear away the webs, Paul led the way up the stairs, testing each step with his weight gingerly before going on. The boards creaked ominously. Paul muttered something about the wood rotting, but Robert knew that no answer was expected. He followed behind his dad, aware of the terrible darkness behind. Occasionally he turned his own light back down the stairs, but the steepness made him feel a bit dizzy. The stairway seemed to fall back into a bottomless hole of darkness. He'd rather take the front stairs, even with the hole in it.

They reached an upper floor, a hallway that did not

look familiar to Robert. Paul shined the bright light in both directions, finding an end to the hall with a reflecting window glass, and an open area the other way, where it joined a larger passage.

"Where now?" Paul asked, his voice seeming to boom and echo in the half-empty house. "Where is this bedroom? And these—robots."

Robert resisted the urge to shush him. He didn't know which way, but made a silent gamble that it was somewhere in the wider hallway. There had been some furniture there, he remembered, and the big ruined painting hanging on the wall above a table. He went ahead, toward the wide passageway, as if he knew where he was going.

In the wide hall he saw the head of the stairs to his right, and in the opposite direction the table against the wall and the painting above it. Now he knew where the bedroom was. Near the end of the hall, he remembered. And a door on the right. But now that he was within yards of it, he felt too terrified to move. He could only shine his feeble light toward the door.

"T-there," he whispered loudly.

Paul passed him by and went on. The floor seemed to shake with each step, and boards creaked under his father's weight. Robert hurried to catch up.

"Is this it?" Paul said, turning to the threshold of an open doorway.

"Y-yes sir."

Robert peeked around him into the room the Spotliter illuminated. He saw the broken window and felt the fresh air that flowed through, and smelled it, and found it a needed change from the stale, musty air in the rest of the house. There, too, was the doll house, looking more monstrous at night than it had during the day. But there were no dolls. It was strangely, frighteningly empty of dolls.

Paul went about in the room shining his light, examining closely the doll house, the corners in the bedroom, the furniture. His light drew to Robert's attention the narrow white-painted wrought iron bed in the corner that still had a patchwork quilt on it, the pattern so old and dusty it was colorless. There was a small braided rug on the floor beside the bed.

"A little girl's room," Paul said, as if to himself.

"This is where Jessica was. But the dolls are gone. Dad, where—"

But his dad was testing the floor, half jumping. "Seems solid," he said. "Did she break that window?"

"I don't know."

"She seems to have found herself a kind of big playhouse here. No harm done, but the broken window. I'll have it replaced."

"But Dad—where are the dolls?"

Paul shrugged. "We'd better get back, Robert. It's late. I have to be up early tomorrow morning." He directed the light to his watch. "This morning."

"Dad, the robots—the dolls—"

Paul went to the doll house and shined his light into the cradle on the second floor, and lifted out a small doll about ten inches long. It wore a long white gown of some sort and had a china head, like the big ones, though much smaller and with cottony hair and eyes that opened and closed.

"Here's your doll, Robert," Paul said, and put the

236

doll back into the cradle. "Now let's get out of here."

Robert followed in silence, humiliated, stung to the core of his being with the knowledge his dad did not believe him. There were no dolls, no robots, just a little girl's bedroom in an old abandoned house, and a playhouse, a doll house, with one little doll.

But Robert knew, and he followed his dad with a terrible fear growing, his ears alert to every sound, every creak of wood, every heavy step that his father made. They were down the stairs again and going toward the front of the house when a sound upstairs caused his father to falter and turn slightly, as if to check to make sure Robert was still behind.

Something had struck a wall, or a floor, so hard the house seemed to tremble, and then began a steady thud, growing softer and softer, as if it were rocking to silence. The sound sent chills up and down Robert's spine and into the back of his hair. It was as if something had been pulled out from the wall and left to fall back, and to bounce to stillness.

Paul shined the light briefly up the stairs, a quick flooding of light that threw long shadows against the wall that looked like teeth, the balusters along the stairs. Robert glimpsed a pale flash of white at the top of the stairs, on the wide landing, that he couldn't remember seeing before, but the light was suddenly gone and only the palest light was left, like an afterglow. Paul was going quickly on toward the front door, the light angled in front of him. Robert forgot that he had his own flashlight, and stood gaping upward, trying to put a definite shape to the faint glow there. Cold air bathed his cheeks and chilled his

237

arms. A board creaked on the first floor back in the house, where they had just come from, and Robert hurried away from it, to catch up with his dad just as he was going out the front door.

He was glad to get out of the house, but he faced the darkness outdoors with dread. When he had seen the dolls today, up by the doll house, they were just sitting there in old clothes. Weird, but not animated. But the other night when he had seen them in the driveway they were walking, moving, jumping onto the car. And they might be here, too, somewhere, tonight. In the trees. Hiding. Waiting.

He kept close to his father's heels, torn with the humiliation of not being believed, and the fear of the shadows. But he'd never let his father know how scared he was. Not now.

Being back in his own house didn't help a whole lot. He was beginning to feel confused, as if maybe he didn't know his own mind. He was relieved to say goodnight to his dad. He couldn't look him in the eyes. At least his dad didn't eye him in any peculiar way, as if to say, here's my son, the genetic degenerate, the ding-ding. Paul just simply said goodnight and went on to his rooms, and Robert felt relieved to be alone.

In his own room he went to the window again and stood looking down into the shadows of the driveway. Light from the lanterns spaced along the outer drive ended several yards from the garage doors, but enough of it invaded the darkness for the shadows beneath the pines to be edged with a lighter darkness, and Robert stared into it. Was there a shrub growing near the corner of the garage? He didn't think so. He couldn't remember one there. The pines had been planted in a long, neat row, with no shrubbery. Yet something stood there now, at the edge of the garage. Something short and dark. A shadow within a shadow.

Robert reached for his flashlight. He had stuck it into his pocket instead of putting it away. He struggled to remove it, and for one short movement he turned away from the window. When he finally had the flashlight out of his hip pocket and shined it down toward the garage, nothing was there.

He turned the light off and waited until his eyes adjusted to the darkness again.

The skin on his cheeks pulled taut. There was nothing there now, which meant there had been something just a minute ago.

He ran, as silently as he could, leaving his door open. He hurried to the service stairs down the side hall and from there to the utility room and out the door into the breezeway. He stopped, listening, the door to the house open behind him. There were no unusual sounds. Only the frogs, with their steady, comforting calls.

He reached behind automatically and pulled shut the door to the house.

With his light out, but the flashlight gripped tightly in his right hand and held against his thigh, he went out the gate into the back yard. Here there were several clumps of shrubs, all of them black lumps in the moonless night. Faint starlight showed him the hulks of the trees and the smaller trees and shrubs.

He could see the edge of the back gallery, the posts white, ghostly pale, in the dark night.

There was a yard light, attached to the rear of the garage, and another on a post at the other end of the back gallery, but the light switch was in the kitchen. He thought of returning there, of having the nearer portion of the back yard flooded with bright light. He made a move to turn back, to go for the light switch. But then he heard the movement of something over to the left side of the yard, a rustling among the branches and leaves. He stood still, holding his breath, listening so hard his head began to feel as if it would burst from the pressure. Ducks, he told himself. The peacocks. The ducks would be close to the pond, sleeping there on the ground, near the small poultry houses back in the bushes where their feed was. But the peacocks roosted in the trees. It was the peacocks he heard. Moving. Stirring.

But he knew it was not peacocks.

It was something else, something moving stealthily in the shrubbery beyond the garage.

With his flashlight off, he slipped quietly along in the deepest shadows cast by the long garage, toward the shrubbery and the rustlings of movement.

When he had reached the end of the garage, he paused, listening, and he knew they were aware of his presence for the rustlings stopped, as if they were listening too, or watching. If they were electronic, and they must be, they could be sensitive to sound, to heat, as from the heat of an animal's body. Or, of course, human, which was also animal. Even though they might not consciously see him, or hear him, their sensors would be aware of him, and could measure the distance.

They weren't consciously aware of anything, because they were man-made. And that very fact made them all the more terrifying. After what he had seen the night Diane died.

He wished he hadn't come out. Now that he was here, so close to them, he saw how foolish he had been. He turned his head slowly, looking back toward the house. The corner post on the back porch was a pale and ghostly streak in the darkness. The gate into the breezeway was ten to fifteen feet this side of the post. He pressed back against the garage, flat against it, as if that would help conceal him.

No sound. The night was still, except for the natural sounds of frogs singing in the swamp and other ponds and pools of standing water.

Maybe, he thought hopefully, it had been the peacocks after all. The peacocks stirring in the trees, settling again. Perhaps they had been disturbed by something that had moved about and settled down once more.

Courage returning, he edged away from the garage and moved a few feet nearer to the line of dark shrubbery beneath the overhanging branches of the trees. He pointed the flashlight and snapped it on.

The face seemed to leap out at him, unveiled by the light, small, pink-cheeked, white china. The painted eyes gazed at him, round and blue. It was one of the girl dolls, half-hidden by the shrubbery, as if she had been left there by someone, by Jessica. It didn't move. After a moment of pure terror, in which

Robert could not have moved if he had tried, his heart calmed a bit and he began to shine the light around, looking farther into the shrubbery. After a few pokes into the darker places, he located another doll, the largest of the girl dolls. The lady doll. Unlike the smaller doll, which was leaning as if only the bush behind her held her up, the lady doll stood unsupported, like a statue. Now, Robert was beginning to be very sure that Jessica had brought these dolls here. And further, he was thinking that he knew now it took Jessica to activate them. And Jessica was asleep.

But where were the other two?

The sound came from behind him, and he whirled, his light tracing an arc through the dark night. The doll with the deformed neck stood almost where he had stood a few minutes ago, at the end of the garage. The light fell like a blaze on the doll's neck, and Robert could see torn fabric beneath the edge of the china neck, and, to his amazement, *straw*. Ends of straw sticking out of the torn place. He stared at it in bewilderment. He had glimpsed that once before and thought it was tiny electric wires. But now he could see the straw.

He began to edge away from something he couldn't understand. What kind of electronic dolls were these with straw-stuffed bodies? A bitterness filled his mouth and brought bile up from his stomach. The terror that was filling him was worse than anything he had ever felt. He didn't care anymore what they were or who they belonged to, he wanted only to get away from them.

But when he moved, the doll with the broken neck moved also, sideways, keeping pace with him. Robert stopped, and the doll stopped. But there was the rustling again, behind him, and Robert whirled, shining his light toward the lady dolls. Both of them had moved in toward him, as if they were helping the other doll, as if they were closing upon him.

Then he had a glimpse of movement to his left, from out of the shrubbery farther away, a kind of leaping, a flash of white china face and white china fingers curved and dangerous and stained with something dark. It was the largest of the dolls, his top hat now gone. Robert swung the flashlight at him, and missed, and something hit him in the middle of the back, knocking him forward onto the ground. He felt the hands, cold, unyielding. He tried to scream, but a rough and scratchy loop was put over his head and tightened on his neck, and it was too late to scream.

CHAPTER FOURTEEN

The scratching sound woke Brenda, and she lay without opening her eyes, feeling drugged by her need for sleep. There had been so many interruptions, it seemed. She turned over and tried to get comfortable on her other side, with her face toward the window, but still she did not open her eyes. To open her eyes would be to court wakefulness, and damn it, she wanted to sleep. In sleep she found sweet dreams, adventuresome dreams, dreams of Rick. In sleep she escaped for a while from the dread that was beginning to get to her. A dread she couldn't quite define. It had to do with Diane's death, she knew, and the change in Jessica.

She took a deep breath and tried to sink back into oblivion. Scratchings on the wall outside came through to her again. The wind must be blowing, she thought, and brushing a tree limb against her window. There was the nerve-wracking sound then of a nail across a blackboard, faint, but irritatingly real. No, not blackboard, glass. Window glass.

She became suddenly more alert, thinking. There was no tree close to the house on this side, and her window was covered by screen wire. *Yet something was scraping the window glass.*

Her eyes popped open, and in the rectangle of light that was the window closest to her bed she saw a small, paper-white face. She sat up abruptly, staring, blinking in disbelief. The face dropped slowly out of sight.

Now she was looking at the rectangle of her window, veiled by the thin curtains that hung over it, and trying to remember just what she had seen. A face in her window? On a sheer wall nearly twenty feet from the ground? Impossible.

Yet there had been the sounds, too. Distinctive enough to awaken her.

She looked at her clock, and its bright little numbers informed her it was three-fifty. Almost four A.M.

She got out of bed and went to the window. She had not raised the glass in either of the two windows since her arrival. The light blue sheer curtain hung undisturbed. She pushed it aside and felt for the lock on the window. It was in place. She turned it, and eased the window up in order to check the screen. There seemed to be something in the wire, pale, light, the barest change in light and dark. She touched it, and to her surprise found the jagged edges of the cut screen. It seemed to be a clean rip about seven inches long.

Some object must have fallen against the screen and ripped it. That had to be the scratching sound that woke her. And the screech across the window glass must have come from the sharp edges of the same thing. But a face? That was ridiculous.

A round, white object with a cutting edge.

She unhooked the screen and leaned out, looking down. The wall dropped straight to the ground. She looked up. The roof was not far away, a few feet, but its edge was sharp against the starry sky. There was nothing up there now. And nothing, so far as she could see, on the ground below. But it was a dark night, and the clumps of shrubbery were black blobs that could have hidden whatever it was that fell.

Tomorrow she'd take a look, but not tonight. Tomorrow too, she'd have the handyman, Jake, repair the screen. Tonight she was damn well going to sleep, if she could.

She couldn't.

Wide awake now, she stared at the ceiling. She felt heavy-brained with depression, or dread, as if something worse, even worse than Diane's death, was going to happen, or was happening.

After an hour, when the sky began to lighten in the east, she gave it up and got wearily out of bed.

By the time her dad came down for breakfast she had spent almost an hour cooking. When Della had come in at six, Brenda had sent her on to do housework, telling her, "When I feel like I do this morning, I like to cook. I'm going to make muffins and scrambled eggs, and I might even start some cinnamon rolls." So she had been left alone in the kitchen, and she had cinnamon rolls set to rise when Paul came in, as well as freshly baked muffins waiting in their little wicker basket. The eggs were ready, too. She hadn't cooked bacon. Like the rest of her artist best friends, she was a vegetarian. A lacto-vegetarian, at least. She didn't actively disapprove of other's eating the flesh of animals that had to be killed, but she was not going to be a party to it.

Paul did not look appreciative. He looked at the table with a faint frown. "So much food?"

"Only muffins and jam on the table, Dad," Brenda said with an edge of criticism in her own voice. "The eggs and coffee are on the stove."

"I'll just take a cup of coffee. I always take a cup along with me." Instead of using the cup set for him on the table, he went to the cupboard and took a ceramic mug.

Brenda watched him pour it full of steaming coffee, a disapproving frown beginning to show on her face.

"Dad! You need something more than that. Just caffeine? You'll feel worse than ever. You don't have to eat eggs, but at least take a muffin."

He glanced around the kitchen, and especially at the sink of dirty dishes, of mixing bowls, measuring spoons and what-not, and at the flour on the cook table. He smiled faintly. "You're just like your mother, Brenda. She used to like to dig in with her hands in flour when things weren't going just right. She'd bake cakes, cookies, and muffins, too. All right. I'll take one of your muffins. Are they as good as your mother's were?"

The frown left Brenda's face. "Not as good, probably, even though I used her recipe. Would you like butter and jam?"

"Just butter, please."

Brenda split a muffin and buttered it. Paul stood waiting with the cup of steaming coffee in his right hand. Brenda closed the muffin and put it on a napkin.

He went out through the hall toward the breezeway, coffee in one hand, muffin in the other. Brenda watched him go, then hurried out to open and close the breezeway door for him. For Paul, work was a comfort. At his various offices he would escape, in his own way.

She went back to the kitchen and sat at the table with a serving of eggs. She'd just begun to butter her own muffin when suddenly her dad reappeared in the doorway. He looked as if he had been drained of all blood, and he staggered against the door facing and hung there, head down. The muffin was still in his left hand, crushed. Crumbs from it fell to the floor.

"Dad!" Brenda cried, jumping up from the table and running to him. "Dad, what's wrong?" A heart attack, she thought. *He's having a heart attack*. And she had never felt so helpless in her life.

"Robert—" His voice croaked out the name, and Brenda thought he wanted her to go after Robert, but she couldn't leave him. And then he said, as he put his hand against her and pushed her away, "The telephone. Call—Dr. Dramine. The police. Call somebody."

She was totally confused. She still was thinking, *heart attack, heart attack, get him to sit down*. And then, of course, *Dr. Dramine*.

"Sit, Dad, sit down. I'll call the doctor."

He came with her obediently, but instead of sitting down he pulled away again. "No, my God no, I've got to get him down."

He began to run, staggering, toward the doorway, and Brenda followed him.

"Where are you going?"

"I've got to get Robert down."

He was out of the house and in the breezeway, and Brenda still followed him. She was behind him when he went into the garage, and she stood on the step in the twilight of the unlighted garage and stared in shock at the figure hanging by the neck.

Robert.

Sometime in the night, Robert had hanged himself.

For the next few hours Brenda stood around, in the kitchen, the garage, the library, dazed, in shock. Paul had almost collapsed in his office, his head on his arms. The doctor and the police had come, had asked questions, and blessedly taken Robert's body out of the garage where Paul had gently laid it.

Jessica had come downstairs, silent and wide-eyed. But Brenda had not tried to explain this time about Robert's death. It seemed too unreal. Robert couldn't be dead. Why would he kill himself?

He must have stood on the car, the police said, and then jumped off. He was close enough to the car that he could have reached out and put a foot there and saved himself, but he hadn't. So he must have wanted to die.

Everything was going wrong.

Della had gone to work quietly as a mouse and cleaned up the mess Brenda had made in the kitchen, and then had put the cinnamon rolls into the freezer for a future, happier time. Those were Brenda's stray thoughts as she watched Della wrap them in freezer paper and put them in a plastic bag, but then Brenda wondered if there would ever be a happier time.

The shock of death. How devastating it could be.

It would be several days before Robert's funeral. Because he had not died naturally, or accidentally, his body would be autopsied, examined by the state medical examiner.

Early in the afternoon, Brenda went to the telephone in the library and dialed Rick's number. She had made a vow that she would not call him. But this was a day that did not reckon with former vows. She sat with the cold phone in her hand, against her cheek, and prayed for Rick to answer.

But the voice that answered was one she did not recognize. It was neither Dale nor Stewart, his roommates, but roommates were like seasons on Mercury, they passed rapidly.

"I'd like to speak to Rick, please."

"Oh, hey, I don't know, it may be too late. He's just moved out. Took his last things down just minutes ago. Want me to go see if I can catch him?"

"Yes, please." She clutched the phone desperately. Where was he going? Back to a former girlfriend? Or north, as he had mentioned? In that event she'd never find him again, for she had no home address where he might go. The minutes passed slowly before the phone was lifted from a table at the other end of the connection.

"Hey, listen, I'm sure sorry. He's gone. Moved out. You just missed him. Who is this? If I see him again I can give him a message."

"Do you know where he went? Where he moved?" Brenda cried with sinking hopes, and then added, "This is Brenda Norris."

"Oh! Yeah, I've heard of you. Look, Brenda, maybe he'll get in touch with you. He's left here, going rural to do some work. Up north, I think he mentioned. Just around."

"He didn't leave a forwarding address?"

"No. Said he'd let us know in a couple of weeks maybe. Said he wasn't expecting any mail, anyway."

"Thanks. Uh—thanks." She didn't know his name and there was nothing more to say. She put down the phone with a greater sense of dejection than she'd ever felt in her life.

In the afternoon she looked for Jessica, and couldn't find her. Anxiety began building almost to depression again, until she finally forced herself to sit quietly on one of the benches at the pond and be comforted by the peaceful activities of the ducks. She had thought of going in to sit with her dad, but when she went into the library where he sat at his desk with his head in his hands, she felt like a trespasser.

Why, she wondered for the thousandth time, why had Robert hanged himself?

Jessica came upon the papa doll in the path halfway between the gate and the castle. He was standing beside the trunk of a tree, as still as the tree itself, his arms down at his sides. And she was startled by the sight of him. She had thought there was nothing along the path but the trees, and the bushes and the growing things, but suddenly there he was.

"Oh!" She pressed her hands to her mouth briefly, and then began giving him strict orders. "Oh, no, you

251

mustn't come out here when it's daytime. Someone might see you. Why did you come outside? Come now with me."

She took him by the arm and pulled him toward her and he started to fall forward, as if he were nothing now but a regular doll. She put her arms around him and began carrying him back toward the house, his feet dragging on the ground. She felt him stiffen suddenly and begin moving on his own, as if the nearness of the house, or the circle of her arms, had brought him to life again.

Annabelle. Annabelle.

It was a sad but eager cry, as if Annabelle had been found after a long and fruitless search. Jessica heard it in her head, but she wasn't sure if it came from the papa doll or some of the others.

We've looked for you, Annabelle. We've destroyed your enemies. Annabelle. Annabelle.

"You mustn't go out of the house anymore! You mustn't! Never in the daytime. Never, never."

She found Victor on the gallery, near the end where the upper gallery had fallen, and she found the mama doll stuck in the briars on the other side of the house. But she looked and looked for Vesta. She left the three dolls on the gallery near the door and told them to stay, and they stayed, obediently, three unmoving statues grouped together, their doll faces staring pleasantly in different directions. Victor stared at the floor, his head hanging to his body by even less material today.

When Jessica was ready to give up, ready to sit down among the briars and cry her heart out for her missing doll, she came upon Vesta, her long, beautiful old skirt caught on a barbed wire of the fence.

"Oh Vesta, Vesta, why have you been so naughty?"

She untangled the skirt, but could not repair the rip. With Vesta under her arm, she went back to the others, and entered the castle, the cool darkness. She was home. Her dolls had misbehaved, but she would be careful to close the door after this, and she would be sure to close the bedroom door, too.

There was no need, now, to leave the doors and gate open.

Vesta began to struggle when they reached the upper landing on the stairs, and Jessica released her. She stopped in the middle of the landing and pointed her finger in their faces. "You stay in the doll house, you naughty dolls. If you run out a wolf might get you and tear you all to pieces. I'm telling you, you must stay."

She led them on. When they reached the upper hall they surrounded her, and began the fine-voiced chanting, or chattering, that they sometimes did. It reminded her of the sounds of chicks, or chipmunks, yet it was different, harsher, rasping. And now, finally, she knew what the sound meant, and she stopped, uneasy, bewildered.

They were warning her.

But of what?

She moved on, more cautiously, along the wide central hall toward the light at the end where her bedroom door stood open. Their movements around her began to be jerky and agitated, almost as if they were dancing, or trying to dance. But they were warning her. There was a danger near, but Jessica could not see it.

She stopped with her hand on the table where she had arranged the jewelry, and her fingers found and toyed with the end of a necklace. She looked up and saw the face of her mother looking down. The large, heavy frame wavered unsteadily out from the wall an inch, fractions of an inch. The dolls' cries became high-pitched, their dancing movements more agitated. They seemed to have lost their ability to speak to her, they could only cry in their strange way.

Suddenly there were footsteps in the hall behind Jessica and she whirled, her heart racing. Had someone followed her? She stared into the darkness there toward the stairway, toward the branching place of the other two halls, and could see nothing at first, even though the footsteps were approaching faster and faster. The dolls' cries were so shrill they hurt her head and she hunched her shoulders toward her ears, her face twisted with the discomfort. She stared so hard toward the sound of the footsteps her eyes watered.

Waveringly, just as the sound of the footsteps stopped abruptly, as if she were looking through rain, Jessica saw the figure begin to take form. A streak of white at first, it grew, widening, and became a long, flowing gown. A pale face appeared, and long pale hair, and then two hands beneath the sleeves of the robe reached out toward her. They beckoned for her to follow.

Jessica cried out, "Mother!"

She rushed forward, but the dolls leaped in front of her, their chatters filling her head. She fell, flat, sprawling lengthwise on the floor, the heels of her hands sliding and catching splinters from the rotting wood. The dolls had tripped her! She sat up crying loudly in pain, in anger, in frustration. She blinked through her tears at the lady in the hall, but she was gone.

Jessica sat leaning against the wall weeping, her head on her lifted and bent knees. The dolls were quiet now, though they still surrounded her.

After a long while, Jessica got up and began looking through the house for her mother, for the lady who had come to her, the lady in the painting. Her real mother. But she was gone. She could find her nowhere, not even up in the tower where she could hear the chair rocking. When she climbed the stairs and looked, the chair stopped rocking, and no one was there.

The shadows were growing long in the meadow when she looked out the broken bedroom window, and it was time to go home. She tried to make the dolls stay in the bedroom, but they followed her, part of them staying in the hall so that she couldn't shut the door with part of them out of the room and part in. But when she reached the big front door downstairs she slipped though before they knew what she was doing, and so she shut the door in their faces.

She could hear them scratching at the door, but she turned and ran, leaving them safely shut inside.

"Good Lord, Jessica, where have you been?" Brenda looked at the little girl in astonishment. Her clothes had been snagged, threads pulled in her knit shirt. Her legs were scratched, with thin lines of blood dried like broken veins. Her hair was carrying something that might have been cobwebs. Her hands and arms and face looked like she'd be in an old attic gathering dust centuries old. She repeated, "Where have you been?"

"Playing."

Jessica wouldn't look at her. The small mouth looked pouty and rebellious. Brenda wondered if her own demands had sounded cross. But she had worried all afternoon, since she had discovered she didn't know where Jessica was.

"Okay," she said in softer tones, "upstairs for a bath before supper."

Tomorrow, she promised herself silently, she would watch Jessica more closely.

Dinner was very quiet, and little was eaten. Paul joined them, but said almost nothing until the meal was finished.

"Brenda," he said, "when you've put Jessica to bed, come into the library."

She nodded.

For an hour after dinner she sat with Jessica in the TV room watching the Walt Disney channel, but she saw only color and movements. Nothing that happened was absorbed by her, and the minute the television was turned off she couldn't have told what had been on.

Jessica went to bed without a word, as seemed to be normal for her lately. When Brenda asked her if she'd like a story read, Jessica only shrugged.

"Well, then . . ." Brenda tucked the blanket around Jessica, thinking of their dad. He was waiting for her. "Goodnight, Jessica." She gave the little girl a hug and a kiss, but got no response.

Brenda went downstairs and into the library. Paul was sitting by his desk with a glass of something amber. Brenda could smell the faint odor of alcohol. Whiskey, probably, she thought. She sat down on the sofa.

"I've been thinking, Brenda, about the rope."

Brenda's cheeks turned suddenly icy. The word brought the image sharply into her mind. A heavy, dark rope, stiff with age. He had tied it around a rafter above Paul's sedan. And he had made a loop at the other end and slipped it over his head. And then he had stepped off the car. Brenda would remember that rope as long as she lived, and the lifeless body it held.

"That rope," Paul said, "I don't know where he got it. I was thinking of that. And the more I thought of it, the more I know that something about it is very odd. I own only one rope. Well, two, actually. One is a thin nylon rope. The other is an older rope, of hemp, but it's still hanging out there on the wall. The rope that—killed Robert, was a much older rope. And it bothers me. He didn't get it here. Brenda, I don't think Robert killed himself."

She was stunned. She stared at her father, but she saw he was serious. And somehow relieved by his decision. But it was only wishful thinking, and might lead to even more problems. He needed to face the truth and accept it.

She said gently, "Dad, no one knows why there is such an epidemic of teenage suicides. It's something that doesn't seem to give any warning in lots of cases, so I've read. I guess they try to solve a problem, and they don't seem to realize how permanent suicide is."

Yet her convictions wavered as she talked. Robert hadn't seemed to be having problems of such terrible proportions. He was friendly and talkative, much more so than Jessica.

Paul leaned forward and motioned with one hand to get her attention. "Listen. There were no footprints on the hood of the car. And that rope—where did it come from?"

"Dad, if he didn't do it himself, who would have done it? And why? I know how you feel, Daddy. I can hardly believe it myself. I don't want to believe it. But think of the other facts. The garage doors were locked. No one could have entered from the outside."

"The back door wasn't locked."

"But that door leads into the yard. The gate into the breezeway from the front was locked and if anyone had come into the yard, they would have had to climb the fence or the wall."

"That's certainly possible."

"But not likely. Who would do that to—to kill Robert? And why? Dad, there's just no other answer. Robert did it himself. Maybe it was an accident. Kids do dumb things sometimes. He might have seen something on television, and was just—just trying it out."

Paul had sat back into his chair. The hope that had been on his face was dwindling away, as though he realized that even if he were right, Robert was still gone, forever. "The rope," he said again. "Where did he get the rope?"

Brenda had no satisfactory answer for him. And knew that nothing she could say would really be a comfort. "Maybe he found it, Dad. Kids collect things. Maybe a truck dropped it out on the road, and Robert brought it in."

"I suppose that could be it. But—"

The telephone rang, and Paul reached forward to get it. He said, "Yes," into it, and then, "Yes, she is." He handed it to Brenda.

Brenda took the phone and said Hello, wondering who would be calling at this hour, which wasn't really late, but too late for a call of sympathy. When the man spoke and she recognized Rick's voice, her heart almost stopped beating before it did a double-take and almost smothered her with its rapidity.

"Rick! Did you get my message?"

"What message?"

He sounded a long way off, the connection between them not the greatest.

"I called your old apartment, and a strange guy said you'd just left, but that if he heard from you he'd tell you I'd called." She paused, breathless, wondering if she had made any kind of sense at all.

"No. I'm in New Mexico. Tentatively headed your way, if it's all right. I talked to Rachel a few days ago and she gave me your address. I didn't even know where you lived. Only the state. Then I got your number from information. Fortunately, you're the only Norris in that area, did you know that? If there had been more, I'd been busy placing calls. How are you, Brenda?"

"I don't know what kind of answer is appropriate, Rick. We've had nothing but tragedies here. First my dad's wife, Diane, was killed in a car wreck, and then my little brother, Robert hanged himself."

"*God.* That's terrible, Brenda. I'm sorry. I guess I

called at a bad time. You won't be wanting company now."

"Oh, yes, Rick," she said quickly, tears stinging her eyes. "I do, please. I tried to reach you in Venice to ask if you'd come and—be with me. I really need you."

There was a silence, then Rick said softly, "I'm on my way. Can you give me directions?"

She told him the shortest distance from the nearest major east-west highway. "I'll be watching for you, Rick. I'm so glad you called. I was afraid you'd gone north, and I'd never see you again."

"I couldn't do that. I had to follow you, wherever you went. I don't know for sure how long it will take me to get there. I have to cross Texas. I hope to reach your place sometime tomorrow night. But I'll stay somewhere else and come on in the daytime."

"No, don't. Just come here. It doesn't matter what time it is."

When Brenda hung up the phone she saw that Paul was pouring himself a drink. His face was sagging again in depair.

"That was a friend of mine, Dad. Rick Holland. He's going to be a houseguest for a while. I hope you don't mind?"

"He's someone special, I gather."

"Very special. I love him."

Paul nodded. "Good. I hope he's worthy of your love."

"He's great, Dad, he really is."

"Is he an artist, too?"

"Yes. A very talented artist. He paints wildlife and landscapes. Mostly wildlife. Some domestic animals

260

in country landscapes."

Paul went toward the hallway carrying his drink. "I'm going upstairs now, Brenda." He paused, turned back and patted her shoulder. "I'm glad you've found someone, kitten. I hope you'll find happiness. Goodnight."

Brenda stayed in the library for several minutes after Paul was gone, standing, staring at the closed draperies that covered the window. Her mind drifting from Rick to Robert again, and to the rope. She began to realize that she was acting rather oddly, standing in the middle of a room, alone, staring. She left the library and went out into the hall, but instead of going upstairs, she went back to the small hall that connected the kitchen, utility room, and breezeway. She pushed the switch that lighted the breezeway, and went along its fifteen feet of length.

Soft, warm air stirred through. Frogs in the swamp serenaded the darkness. Their songs seemed almost deafening after the silence in the house.

She tested the wrought iron gate that led out into the front and the driveway. It was locked, as it always was at night. But the gate into the back yard was unlocked. So was the small door into the garage, as was the door that led from the garage into the back yard.

She turned on the garage lights. The cars parked within the garage glinted beneath the lights. There was her dad's blue Mercedes sedan, and her own VW Rabbit, and farther on, another car that was seldom used.

She walked slowly and quietly to the front of the Mercedes, and stopped beneath the rafter where

Robert had hanged himself. The rope had been rolled into a loop and placed against the garage wall, but it was gone now. She looked for it. Pegs on the end of the garage wall held the other ropes that her dad had mentioned, the nylon, and the hemp. That rope was much thinner than the rope Robert had used.

But where was it now?

She didn't think the police had taken it, but Dad might have. He probably had thrown it into the trash can in the corner of the garage. She lifted the lid and looked in. A couple of waste baskets had been emptied into the large plastic can, and something in a black plastic bag, but the rope was not there.

She replaced the lid of the trash can and went over to look at the hood of her dad's Mercedes. It was sleek and polished, as always. Paul disliked a dirty car. And he was right, there were no footprints on the hood. No spot of dust, no scratch.

CHAPTER FIFTEEN

Brenda was determined to keep Jessica close this morning, and when Jessica finished her breakfast and went toward the door, Brenda called her back.

"Come with me, Jessica. I'd like to spend the morning with you." She took Jessica's hand and led her back toward the TV room where a little desk in the corner held coloring books and crayons, a few games, story books, scissors, paste, and just about everything needed for quiet entertainment. Much of it overflowed onto the floor, and Della had put it into a neat stack beside the desk.

"Would you like to show me what you're working on these days?" Brenda asked, wondering why Jessica never asked where Robert was. Did she know Robert was dead? Should she tell her or try to protect her from it? She was too young to realize what death meant, probably. But still it seemed strange that she hadn't asked about Robert.

"I'm not working on anything," Jessica said. She stood with her hands behind her, as if she did not plan to cooperate.

Brenda sat down on the floor beside the desk.

"Then let's work on something together."

After a hesitation Jessica sat down too, and Brenda spread open between them a large coloring book.

It was a slow morning. Paul looked in once, said good morning, and disappeared again. The phone rang several times, part of the calls from friends offering sympathy. Brenda took the calls as quickly as she could, not wishing to leave Jessica alone.

After lunch the awkwardness of the morning burst into open friction.

"Can I go now?" Jessica asked, edging toward the door.

"I'll go with you," Brenda said. "We can feed the ducks."

Jessica suddenly wailed, "No! I don't want you to go with me!"

Brenda followed her out onto the back porch, feeling oddly hurt by the rejection. Her morning attempt at making friends hadn't worked. Jessica's face had a mixture of expressions, part of which was pouting, but another emotion that Brenda couldn't be sure of. There seemed to be a sadness in the clear sky-blue eyes that contrasted with her ordinary stoical behavior. Desperation, too, and fear.

"Where are you going, Jessica, that you don't want me to go along? I would like to be with you, I really would."

"No, I don't want you with me! Go away! Go back in the house!"

Jessica was backing away. She stumbled on the steps, and Brenda rushed forward and grabbed her arm to keep her from falling backwards down the stone steps and onto the stone path. As if Jessica thought Brenda was trying to stop her, she began suddenly to fight, scratching at Brenda's hand with her nails, screaming, tears flowing fast, wetting her cheeks and running through the edges of her mouth onto her chin. She was still pulling backwards with all her strength, and Brenda was afraid to let her go for fear the sudden release would tumble her head first onto the stones.

"Jessica! Jessica, don't—"

"Let me go! I want my mother! I want my mother! *Let me go to my mother!*"

She twisted her arm out of Brenda's hand and though she fell, she went down sideways, and caught herself with her hand. She scampered up immediately and ran without looking back, toward the tree-shrouded rear of the grounds. Brenda stood watching her, one hand cupped over the stinging back of the other where Jessica's sharp little fingernails had dug into the skin. Her heart was aching for the child. She had thought Jessica was feeling no loss. She had scarcely flinched when she was told about Diane's accident and death.

Brenda felt the presence of someone behind and glanced back to see Della standing on the porch. Della's brown eyes were quietly sympathetic, and met Brenda's in silence.

"I don't know what to do for her," Brenda said. "I can't bring her mother back." She wished for Mrs. Archer, the only mother figure that might be able to soothe Jessica, but she was still missing.

"I'd just leave her alone if it was me," Della said softly. "Grief fades."

Brenda nodded. Della went back into the house,

and Brenda went down the steps and into the back lawn. She stood in the sunshine staring at the cool shadows of the shrubbery and the tall trees toward the back of the yard. Jessica had not gone to her old playground, the swing sets, slides, sandboxes. They were visible from the porch. Sprigs of grass were growing where before Jessica had kept the ground bare. Grass was beginning to grow beneath the swings where little grooves were dug in the soil from the child's feet. Did she go to the duck pond? Perhaps there was something at the pond that drew her. The ducks and peacocks. The water itself, which could have a soothing effect.

Brenda had to know where she went. She had an uneasy feeling, increased now, a terrible feeling of foreboding, as if the worst had not yet happened in their family. The lilies growing near the edge of the pond did not comfort her. She looked at the beauty of their flowers and was blind to them, feeling her blindness and longing to see again. She wished the hours would hurry and pass, so that Rick would be with her. But still, that left Jessica, searching for her mother. Passing hours would bring her scarce comfort.

Jessica was not near the pond that she saw. She was aware that the child might be hiding back beneath some particular group of shrubs, just to be alone, to get away from her. She would not bother her again, Brenda decided as she strolled from the pond toward the back fence. She would be there if Jessica wanted her, but otherwise, it might be better if she didn't try to be a companion.

But where was the child spending her time? It

seemed very strange that she could disappear for hours, and then show up dirty and cobwebby—

She stopped at the back fence staring across the meadow, and suddenly she knew. She felt her face blanch, for in her own childhood she had wanted to go to the old mansion and had been warned away from it. "Certainly not," her own mother had said. 'That belongs to someone else. No one lives there, but it belongs to the Blahough sisters." And Mrs. Archer had said, "It's dangerous. It's falling down." And Brenda knew that was right, because she had gone green-gathering with Mrs. Archer many times in her childhood, and had gathered poke salat by the fence that surrounded the old mansion. Through the fence she had caught glimpses of the large house, and had seen that one end of the front gallery had fallen.

But where else would Jessica find webs and that kind of dust, old and dark, that had been on her clothes?

Even as Brenda stared toward the cluster of trees within the confines of the fence there, Jessica came into view more than halfway across the meadow. She was running through the tall grass and shorter stands of clover, her bright head bobbing, pure gold in the sunlight.

Brenda watched her, saw her slow down when she reached the overhang of the trees, and then go along the fence to the corner where she appeared to be opening a gate. She went through, and instantly disappeared in the green wilderness.

So that was it, after all. Jessica spent all her spare time over there, in, or nearby, the old Blahough mansion. If she went in, how had she gotten in?

Wouldn't the doors be locked?

What, she wondered, should she do? Just turn back and leave her alone, as Della had suggested? But if the old mansion were dangerous, wouldn't she be negligent by allowing Jessica to play there? Of course, she might only play on the porches, but if they were falling down, they could hardly be considered safe.

She didn't know what to do, but felt she should at least check it out. She'd try to stay out of Jessica's sight, so the child wouldn't feel she'd been deliberately followed. Later, when Paul was not so torn by the loss of Robert, she could talk to him about it.

Jessica simply might have found herself a playhouse, that was all. Something new to explore. Brenda could remember how she had wanted to explore the house. But no kids that she ever knew of had gone back there, protected as it was by the surrounding fenced land, even though they had talked of it. No Halloween had passed in her youth but that a group of kids would consider the old Blahough mansion as a good place for ghost hunting. If anyone had ever broken in, she'd never heard of it.

She looked for a way over the back fence, but there was no way except to climb, and she eyed its height and decided against it. She chose to go around the wall instead. She had to pass through the gates in the breezeway. There was a larger gate where Jake drove his truck in on those occasions when he needed to for some reason, but it was padlocked. Once through the breezeway she walked down the drive to the end of the brick wall, no longer strolling. It was very quiet on the road. No cars passed. She saw no one, and hoped

268

she drew no attention to herself. She rounded the end of the brick wall and found herself in the heavy shade of the forest that led, within yards, to the mushy ground that edged the swamp. She kept close to the wall, her white sandals staining with the moisture among the leaves.

When she reached the meadow fence she carefully climbed over, but even so snagged a thread in her jeans on the top barbed wire.

In the meadow she looked for the cows, but they were grouped at the far end, paying her no attention. She cut through the sweet-smelling meadow, angling across it to the corner gate where Jessica had disappeared.

She stood for a minute looking in. The gate was made of wood and wire, and had a heavy wire loop at the top that fit down over the post of the fence. Jessica had not put the wire over the post and the gate hung inward. Brenda stood with one hand on it and contemplated the wilderness beyond. A nearly invisible path led into it. The huge trees had limbs that hung horizontal with the ground, and long streamers of moss hung from those. There were webs among it all. A perfect place for spiders and snakes. Brenda shuddered.

The house was not visible within the green jungle from this point. If a stranger walked by here he would never know a house was buried there in the green coffin.

She pushed the gate aside and went through, then leaned it against the post again and slipped the wire loop in place. The gate now was upright, and looked a part of the fence. That stranger, passing here, would never notice there was a gate at all, unless he was looking for a gate.

She concentrated on the path, afraid of losing it. But it kept opening up, a few feet at a time, in front of her. She moved along it as quietly as she could, listening for any sound that Jessica might make, but hearing only the frogs. There must be stands of water among the trees, Brenda thought, for there to be so many frogs. It was almost like walking into the swamp.

The path seemed to go on forever. There was nothing but a greenish, shadowy light, and the moist smell of swampland.

Then suddenly she was against the stone of the lower gallery, and the gray stone seemed to be a great wall, reaching out of sight in all directions. She stepped gingerly up onto the stone floor. The gallery ceiling overhead seemed to be sturdy enough, even though the far end was the one that had fallen. The posts that stretched up two stories had lost their white paint, except for a few flakes here and there. The wood shutters that were closed over the windows were gray with age also, all paint gone.

She walked along the gallery, thankful that her sandals had rubber soles. She felt nervous being here, as if something beyond those closed shutters could nevertheless look out and see her if she made a sound.

She came to a large door deeply inset. It was closed. She stood looking at the door knocker. The hideous devillike iron mask leered down at her and she wanted nothing more than simply to take its warning and back away, and follow the path out to the sunshine again.

Instead, she reached out for the doorknob and turned, expecting to find it locked. To her surprise the door opened. She held on to the knob for a while, carefully not looking at the metal face on the door.

She was hesitant to open the door, for it would squeak, she knew. Old doors always squeaked. She edged it gingerly inward, and it moved silently, and at last with the barest groan of rusted metal. The hall inside was almost totally dark, and she pushed the door wide open, to receive as much light as possible. The greenish glow drifted in like a fog, lighting a large entry hall that was more like a living room than a hall. There were old pieces of upholstered furniture, she saw, a settee and chairs, and tables that had lost their polish a century ago, gray now with dust and thick with webs beneath. Toward the rear of the hall was a stairway, not wide and shallow like the front stairs in her family house, but narrower and steeper, clinging to one wall, then crossing over and disappearing into a lighter area above. A chandelier that had once held candles still hung from the high ceiling.

She moved to her left and looked through a door there and saw a few gray lumps that meant covered furniture. The smell was heavily musty. There was nowhere there that Jessica might be. The dust on the floor was undisturbed.

But through the central part of the hall, faint but visible, there were signs of footsteps. Or at least there was disturbed dust. It was almost a pathway to the stairs. So that was where Jessica went — somewhere upstairs. It was lighter there. Brenda stood at the foot of the stairs looking up. At first the house was as silent as a tomb, but then, somewhere deep within it, on the second floor, there was the sound of footsteps.

Jessica, she thought, and revised the thought immediately. The steps were a bit heavier than a child's, with a sharper sound, as if they were made with a woman's higher heels. They were coming along an uncarpeted hall, faster and louder, as if whoever it was came toward the front of the house, toward the head of the stairs. They carried a strangely threatening sound.

The hair rose suddenly on Brenda's arms as she stood with one hand on the newel post looking up, expecting any instant to see someone come into view. Yet a dark force tugged at her memory. She had heard those steps before, as if they were as distinctive as fingerprints. Then suddenly she remembered. In her own house, that first night she was home. The footsteps had awakened her.

Now, as then, they ended abruptly, leaving only the memory of their sound.

But leaving Brenda with a cold and unreasonable fear.

Whoever it was had gone into a room overhead and to the left. She gave a quick glance around. It wasn't possible that someone was living here. At least not legally. *Surely.* Yet there was at least one owner of this place, a Miss Vivian Blahough, who must be at least eighty-five years old now. There was another sister, but it seemed to Brenda that she recalled hearing of a death there. Whoever it was upstairs . . . she couldn't finish the thought in the most logical part of her mind. The footsteps had come to her in the other house, too, where there were no bare wood floors.

She began to climb the stairs. Near the bend she came to a treacherous-looking hole where two complete steps had fallen and were hanging as if hinged on the inside wall. In the darkness below she caught a glimpse of something pale and ghostly, like a child's face looking up at her. But it disappeared, and she was left wondering if she had seen anything at all.

She looked up. The stairs above were lighted better from the source of light that came from somewhere in the upper hall, and she could see the continuing disturbance of dust that meant someone, probably Jessica, had been going up and down these stairs regularly.

She edged past the hole and went on up, keeping to the outer edge near the banister, where it seemed more solid. Each time the stairs creaked under her weight she cringed, but the sound did not bring anyone to meet her.

At the top of the stairs she stood looking down a long, wide hall. She hadn't appreciated the size of the house from below. Doors were closed all along the hall, except at the far end where light spilled out from an open door and into the dust and cobwebs of the hall. An adjacent hall branched off part way down, but darkness was there, filtered by the many years of unuse. She turned to the left and went around the banister to the room where she had heard the footsteps. Something occurred to her. Perhaps it was Jessica playing grownup. She might have found a pair of old high-heeled shoes. That didn't explain the steps she had heard at home. She stopped, remembering the woman she had seen bending over Jessica.

Nothing was right. She was seeing and hearing things that weren't there. She brushed it aside, put it out of her mind, and went on toward the partly open door where the footsteps had gone.

She put her hand against the door and pushed it lightly, afraid it would make noises that would give away her presence. At first it moved silently, and then it began a rusty squeak. She took her hand swiftly away. Through the opening she could see a lighter, large room, that still had furniture uncovered. There was a canopied bed, so high it had a small step stool at its side. On it was a colorless, dusty something that might have been a soft mattress, or a feather bed. A dusty lace spread hung in strings around it. The same lace had decorated the canopy, and now hung in dusty ancient gray, like the moss on the trees.

The windows beyond had lost part of their shutters, letting in a filtered light. There was a door, closed, that led out onto the gallery. But in the corner was a round area about ten feet across, surrounded by windows that were shuttered, and in it was a narrow, winding stairway. Until then Brenda had forgotten about the tower.

She moved silently through the wide archway that connected bedroom to tower and stood listening. Large, bulky furniture that might have been modern a century ago made the room seem crowded. But she only glanced at it. She was positive now, with a suddenly reinforced uneasiness, that she was not alone. Whoever it was had gone up into the tower, she was sure. There were movements there, subtle, almost soundless, like the soft stirring of clothing. Jessica? She probably had found a treasure of old clothes there. Yet—if it were Jessica, why was she feeling this strange tightness in her skin, the cold, crawling fear? She opened her mouth to call out to Jessica, and couldn't make a sound. A warning bell began tapping away in the back of her brain, urging her to turn and run instead, to put the house and all it contained behind her. Even the walls of the room, and the door behind her, seemed inundated with something dangerous, as if it had taken on a life of its own in all these empty years.

She went forward instead, driven by her need to find Jessica, and to take her out of this house.

When she reached the tower room she paused at the foot of the steps. She could see through the opening above, and she saw sunlight streaked by dust motes, and above that the peaked roof of the tower. As she stood there a rocking chair began to rock, squeaking forward and backwards. The floorboards beneath the chair groaned faintly.

The sound urged Brenda to movement, and she began to climb. She came up into the opening of the tower. Sunlight spilled across the opening, into her eyes, blinding her temporarily. She stopped climbing and blinked into the shadows beyond the sun-streaks. A window high in the tower wall, unshuttered, was letting in the light, but it was behind her, in another corner, that the rocking chair moved, vigorously. She turned toward it and opened her mouth in a croaking, nearly soundless scream. She closed it off with one hand, staring.

It was not Jessica in the chair, but a woman, an apparition, only partly formed, a thing formed partly of solids and of a diaphanous substance, which she could see through. It sat in the chair, rocking, the skirt white and flowing, the hair pale and long, the head outlined only against the wall beyond. As Brenda stood there, paralyzed, the figure rose from the chair, and the footsteps she had heard twice before were coming toward her. Sunlight poured through the creature as she moved toward the stairs where Brenda stood.

As if released suddenly from a vice of iron, Brenda half fell down the steps. She ran toward the door and pulled it wide open, no longer concerned with the rusty squeak. She glanced behind her once, and saw nothing. The apparition had not come on down the stairs.

In the outer hall she leaned weakly against the wall. She felt like giggling insanely as she went over and over what she had seen. A ghost. A God-damned-for-real ghost. And never in her life since she had gotten past her fourth birthday had she believed such a thing could exist.

Still, in this house, why should she be surprised?

But ghosts were, had to be, nothing but mental impressions of some kind. Nothing more. It was without substance. It was of no danger to her.

She went on down the hall with more courage, with courage returning, though she still shook as if she were losing control of every nerve in her body. She paused and took a deep breath and some of the trembling stopped. Jessica was somewhere here in this house, probably daily, yet physically unharmed. Still, she remembered the same woman had gone into Jessica's bedroom at home, and her face had been very clear that night, as if she were real, and the look that had been on her face made Brenda shudder to remember it. And those hands—

Her courage was leaving again. The darkness in the hall seemed to be increasing. She could see an occasional heavy piece of furniture against the wall, old secretaries or bookcases of some kind whose glass fronts glinted dully in what little light they gathered.

Nearby to her left was a small table pushed against the wall, and on it, arranged carefully in circles and semicircles, was something that appeared to be jewelry. She went closer to peer down at it, but her attention was drawn upward to a large painting that seemed to be attached to the wall right where it joined the ceiling.

It was the same woman she had seen in Jessica's room, but the canvas looked as if it had been ripped and stuck back crookedly. The woman's once beautiful face was distorted and sinister.

And on her lap she was holding a blond baby.

The painting was framed in a heavy, ornately carved metal that could have been gold. As she looked at it, the painting began to move, bumping lightly against the wall, and then harder and harder, wavering out into the air, coming entirely away from the wall, hanging unsupported in the air a foot from the wall, edging along the ceiling toward her, threateningly.

Brenda at first only pushed backwards against the opposite wall, staring as if hypnotized, then by a stupendous strength of will she pulled away and ran back toward the stairs. The sounds in the hall grew and vibrated in her brain. The bedroom door began to jerk open and slam shut, repeatedly, moved by a strong and growing force. The thumping of the painting grew louder and louder and was following her along the hall. The footsteps ran out again, as shrill as the call of madness in a dungeon. Ahead of her the apparition materialized again, a tall woman in a white robe, with the same coldly beautiful face as in the painting. Brenda plunged past her, telling herself, *it's not real, none of it is real*. Yet she was in a nightmare, a horrible world that she had not known existed.

She felt it, against her back, as she reached the top of the stairs. Something solid and firm, about the size of a hand, touched her back and gave her a hard shove, and Brenda plunged forward into darkness.

CHAPTER SIXTEEN

She was still alive. But she didn't know where she was. Darkness surrounded her, but so did sound — another kind of sound. Frogs, all pitches of voices, singing near her. And there was a smell of greenness and dampness. . . .

She sat up. Her body ached as if it were bruised and broken, at the least as if she had been lying in one position for many hours.

She looked around, searching for a gleam of light, but the darkness was complete. But sensation was coming back to her, and she felt beneath her hands the cool dampness of vegetation. She was outside, somewhere. In the swamp? No, there was no water. She felt out around her, and her hands tangled in vines, and suddenly she knew where she was. In the wilderness that surrounded the old Blahough mansion. Somehow, she had gotten out of the house and into the grounds before she lost total mobility. But to think that she was still here, this close to that house, terrified her. She pushed herself to her feet and began to grope her way through the tangle of growth, hoping, praying, that she wasn't going back toward the house.

Suddenly, after yards and long minutes of searching for a way out, the light she had looked for was there, through the trees. Starlight. The lesser darkness of the meadow. She came up against the fence abruptly, was stopped by it for a moment. Then she separated the barbed wire from the three-foot-high hog wire beneath it, and squeezed through, hearing her clothing tear on the barbs. She pushed on, wanting only to be away from the grounds of the Blahough place. The clothing didn't matter.

In the freedom of the meadow she ran.

When she reached the house she saw lights in the TV room, and knew it was still quite early. She thought of going through the washroom and taking a look at herself in the mirror, but didn't. She went on into the hall and to the TV room, and looked in from the threshold.

Jessica was on the floor in front of the television, absorbed in the show. Della, sitting in a chair nearby, looked up and saw Brenda. She stared.

"Where have you been?" she asked bluntly. Jessica glanced up only briefly.

"I—uh—went out for a walk."

"Musta been a long one."

"Where's Dad?"

"Went upstairs early, I guess."

"Will you help Jessica to bed tonight, Della?"

Della nodded, still looking curiously at Brenda,

making Brenda wonder what she looked like. She drew away and hurried on up to her room and into the privacy of the bath. She was surprised to see that outside of a rip in her shirt she wasn't so unpresentable. There was nothing in her appearance to even remotely suggest her experiences of today.

She showered, dressed in a fresh summer cotton, and went downstairs to wait for Rick, praying that he would arrive sometime this evening. She stopped by her dad's room on the way down to check on him. She was worried about him, though she knew it would take months of grief before he would be himself again—if ever.

"Dad?" She knocked lightly on the door, and it moved inward, unlatched. His lights were on. Through the crack in the door she saw him sitting at his desk, and opened the door wider. He looked over his shoulder.

"Where've you been?"

His face was flushed and heavy, sagging, lined. It hurt her to see how rapidly he had aged in these past days. And it hurt her to see how he was turning to alcohol. She couldn't burden him with her own fears and the truth about today.

"I walked farther than I thought. I'm sorry I missed dinner. Hope you weren't worried, Dad."

"I'm glad you're back. After this, when you plan to be out, I wish you'd let someone know."

"Yes. I'm sorry. Why don't you go to bed, Dad, and try to sleep? I'm going down to wait for Rick. I hope he'll get here soon."

Paul nodded and turned away from her. She closed

the door, hearing the latch click.

She made a plate of sandwiches and a pitcher of lemonade and took it on a tray into the library where the windows looked out upon the driveway. She had covered the tray with a cloth, and she set it on a library table to wait for Rick. She wasn't really hungry, but there was an emptiness in her that might be helped by food, and certainly would be helped by Rick's arrival.

Headlights appeared beyond the trees on the highway, and went on by the driveway, time after time. At ten the traffic dwindled to a car passing not more than one every twenty minutes or so, and the lights that came along at ten-thirty seemed sure to be just one more disappointment. But at the driveway the car slowed, then made a turn inward, and the lights swept across the edge of the lawn and for a moment blinded Brenda at the library windows. She ran.

He had gotten out of the car by the time she reached him, and was waiting. Without a word being exchanged she ran into his arms. For a long, encapsulated moment she was lost in him, all thoughts and experiences beyond him cut off. But eventually she had to move away, take him into the house, show him to his room, and bring him downstairs again where they sat at the library windows and ate sandwiches and drank lemonade.

She told him, in broken and confused sentences that revealed her deepest feelings, about the old house and what she had seen. She drew a deep breath, having finished. Rick was staring steadily at her as she talked, without interruption. She said, "I know no one believes in that kind of thing, Rick. But I wasn't dreaming. It happened."

"If you say so I believe it. But you say the little girl spends her time there, and she isn't hurt. So whatever it is that's manifesting itself in the house, isn't harming her. Maybe it would be better just to leave her alone for the time being."

"I was going to, but now I don't see how I can. I think she is being hurt, psychologically. She's so apart from the family, too. I don't think she even knows that Robert is dead."

"How old did you say she is? Four?"

"Five. Barely. Her birthday was in May."

"She's too young to understand death. I wouldn't worry about that part of it. When she notices that he's gone, then you can tell her. When is the funeral?"

"I don't know yet. His body hasn't been released from the coroner's office. But, it probably will be tomorrow. And Rick, another thing . . . the ghosts of that old house are here too, sometimes. Or were a couple of times. The same woman was bending over Jessica one night. She straightened and disappeared when I came to the room. I saw her very clearly. Afterwards I couldn't believe what I had seen."

Rick's warm hands closed over Brenda's. "I'll help you figure it out, Brenda." He pulled her to him, and the rest of the world was set aside.

She had a new doll, a beautiful life-sized doll with golden curls like her own and real glass eyes, as blue as heaven, and real eyelashes that raised and lowered. She was even more beautiful than her other dolls,

283

and her papa had brought it to her just yesterday. He had bought it in New Orleans. She wished he wouldn't go away again, but he had. There was business he must take care of, he had said, and so she was in her room alone with her dolls, while somewhere in the house below Zachary was crying, crying. When he screamed she shuddered, and tried to shut out the sounds of it. She arranged the lace on her new doll's dress and whispered to her. "I shall name you Magnolia, or something equally beautiful. Would you prefer to be named—um—Chrysanthemum? Flowers' names are very beautiful, just like the flowers. There are others, you know. I must teach you all about them. I'll take you out into the yard and show them to you, soon. And you can choose one for your name. There is Lily, and Jonquil, and Rose. Rose is a very nice name, don't you think? But not as nice perhaps as Magnolia. I—" The screams had reached the upper story, and the baby was crying now. She could hear the bump, bump of Zachary being dragged up the stairs, and his tortured screams echoed through the long hall outside her door. The baby cried and cried in fear.

Stop crying, baby sister, stop. Quickly stop. Before she reaches you.

And then came the silence, when both voices were still.

And the footsteps, angry, sharp, in the long hall, coming nearer, nearer, louder, terrible footsteps approaching her door.

"Annabelle. Annabelle, answer me!"

She left her doll safely at the side of the doll house

284

and crept in to sit with her other dolls, the papa doll, the mama doll, Vesta, and Victor with his poor broken neck. They knew that her mama was coming, and they would protect her. "Papa," she whispered.

The long-fingered hand reached in to get her, and she saw the blood on the hand, embedded beneath the long fingernails, and in the creases of the knuckles, and dripping from the palm. She never screamed like Zachary did, yet she heard someone screaming, and it must be herself for the dolls were mute. The bloody hand tangled in her long hair and pulled her from the doll house.

"Papa! Papa!"

Behind her the papa doll stared, and began to stir, but there was no need. She threw her arms out for the new doll, and reached her, and was absorbed by her, and the scream that she heard from the safety of her new body was not her own, but the wild and insane scream of frustration coming from her mother.

Jessica pretended to be asleep, and they went away. Her daddy, Brenda, and the strange man who had stood there with Brenda when she woke from the bad dream. She heard them go away, talking in tones so low she didn't hear what they were saying. She didn't want to know what they were saying, she only wanted to know what she had dreamed. She frowned at the wall, trying to remember. She felt torn, divided, as if she lived in two worlds, and she felt scared that she couldn't remember her dream. At first, when her own screams woke her, she was still in the dream, a part of it, but as she came back into this world the other world faded away, and she was left wondering, grasping for something that wasn't there.

She was no longer sleepy. She wished the day would come, so that she could go home to her mother. Maybe it was already day outside, and was dark only in here where light in the hall made it seem like night. She'd see. She would get up and look out the window and see.

There were two windows in her room, and one of them looked out toward her castle. Now that she knew where it was, she could go to her window and look at the tower above the trees and be comforted by it. But now as she looked out she saw it was still dark. The trees were black, outlined against a sky sprinkled with tiny, tiny lights of stars. The tower was lost in the darkness.

But in the yard below someone moved. She caught a glimpse, a glimmer, of white. Someone's skirt. She pressed her face to the screen and looked hard, and now she could see the round, white faces, like balls there floating in the darkness. *Her dolls!* They had followed her. They had disobeyed her and come out of the castle where they belonged. They must not, must not come here. She didn't know what bad things would happen to them, but something, *something.* . . .

She hurried out and along the carpeted hall, her steps silent. She hurried down the stairs, holding to the banister. She went through the hall, and the kitchen, unafraid of the dark in the kitchen. She heard voices in the library, but didn't pause. From the kitchen she went out onto the back porch, and then to the lawn where her dolls had gathered.

Paul followed her, puzzled. He had come out of the library just in time to see the small pajama-clad figure disappear around the corner.

For a moment he stood wondering. Jessica? They had left her asleep, with her face to the wall, after what seemed to be one of her worse nightmares. He had tried to wake her himself, lifting her up, shaking her, talking to her, and still she had screamed, her eyes wild and unfocused. Then Brenda and Rick had come into the bedroom, and Brenda had taken her, and at last Jessica had quieted and gone almost instantly back to a sound, but seemingly restful sleep.

And so it didn't seem right that it was she he had glimpsed at the end of the hall. But who else could it be?

He followed her. He reached the inner kitchen door just as she opened the screen on the other side and went out. Instead of calling to her, he only followed in her footsteps, puzzled. Where was she going? Was she even awake? Was somnambulism to be added to her night terrors?

He stopped on the porch, squinting in the dark of the back lawn. He could see the darker bulk of her small figure, and something else — white faces, as pale and ghostly as ghost lights. She wasn't alone. What had she walked into?

He stepped back into the kitchen and switched on the yard lights. He went through the door again, and stopped, staring.

Jessica stood in the midst of a group of small people dressed in nineteenth-century clothing, and as he stared at them they turned toward him, four white, doll-like faces. *Dolls. The robots Robert had seen.*

"Jessica!"

Where had they come from? He knew nothing of this kind of thing. He was not surprised to see them moving toward him as he bounded down the steps to the back yard. Robert had told him. And now he knew it all. He knew who had killed Robert, and who would kill Jessica if he didn't get her away from them.

"Jessica, quickly, run!"

He grabbed her arm and jerked her toward the house, and heard her cry out. Afraid he had hurt her, he paused, released her, and reached down to pick her up. But she was not there. Her arm had slipped from his hand, had been pulled away. The two female dolls seemed to be pushing or pulling her away from the house, deeper into the back yard, away from him, and the male dolls were coming toward him, white, curved hands out threateningly. The one with the hideously broken neck seemed to have its eyes trained permanently toward the ground, but it was dancing before him, like a boxer, in short sideways jerks. When he moved, it moved, in some terrible way knowing his direction.

He made a dash to pass them, to get to Jessica; and he glanced up to see where she was and to his astonishment he saw that she was standing well away, facing toward them all, and the two female dolls were coming back in long lopes, their skirts brushing the grass. Their faces were white and pink, rosebud mouths as innocent looking as the mouths of small children, their cheeks plumped and rouged, but their

288

eyes were flat, painted, with paint chipping. He could see those things as they bounded upon him and crashed him back onto the ground. Screams invaded the air, Jessica's and his own, hoarse and filled with incredible fear.

CHAPTER SEVENTEEN

The night had grown silent, as it often does in rural areas after one or two in the morning, and Brenda was sitting with her head on Rick's shoulder. They weren't talking much now. She was still unnerved by this latest nightmare of Jessica's, in which it had seemed for a while as if she would never come out of it. Afterward she and Rick had gone into her room and sat down on the bed. They were still sitting there when the strange mixture of cries and hoarse shouts started, dimmed by the distance of many rooms and the insulation of many more walls. His arm tightened spasmodically around her as she jerked up. For another instant they sat there, stunned. Then Rick muttered something about, "What the . . . ?" And they both were running.

Brenda reached the hall first, but Rick passed her and ran down the wide front stairs and back through the hall toward the rear of the house. By the time they reached the kitchen they could see the blaze of the yard lights, and the scuffling of many bodies on the grass beyond the porch.

Several small people—children?—had someone

down and were battering him. As Brenda went out the door at Rick's heels she saw it all in one confused picture: Jessica standing not ten feet away from the pile of bodies, her face strained, her mouth open in a perpetual scream. The other voice, the hoarse crying, shouting voice, was still now. And she saw beneath the strange, small, oddly dressed people the sprawled length of a man, but she did not recognize him immediately, for his head was covered in blood.

Rick had reached the pile of bodies, and began kicking at them. His foot struck the lopsided head of one in a powerful kick, and the head tore loose from the body and rolled across the grass toward Brenda. It was white and staring, a perfect little face that didn't change its expression as it stopped rolling near her feet, eyes up toward her. And now she saw it was not human. It was the head of a doll. Her own startled, terrified cry was added to the raucous sounds that filled the air, the continued scream of Jessica, her *"No, No, No,"* and the incredulous shouts from Rick.

She was paralyzed, stupefied, staring down at the white, pleasant-looking little face at her feet. She couldn't move. Couldn't take her eyes from it. But she began to realize that Rick was shouting orders at her.

"Get something! An axe! A hoe! These little cock-suckers are killing your dad!"

She ran toward the garden shed, going around the headless body that was floundering drunkenly as if the head had been important to it after all, in some way. She stumbled over something on the ground and fell to her knees, and saw it was the rope that had hanged Robert. She pushed herself up and ran on to the garden shed and fumbled around in the dark for the tools hanging on the wall. Her hands brushed the sharp edges of something, a hoe, and she grabbed it down. Something fell behind it, and she picked that up too, feeling a pair of wooden handles, realizing she had gotten tree pruners, with sharp cutting edges. She ran back to Rick. The three other dolls had attacked him, climbing his body as if they were animals going up a tree, and he was fighting in a silence that intensified the horror, and she saw that one sharp-fingered white hand had reached his face. She dropped the hoe, and went in with the pruners, open, after the hand on Rick's face, praying desperately and silently that she would not cut him, too.

She felt the teeth close on the arm of the hand, and snapped down on it. The hand fell, striking the cement walk with a clunk. White fingers broke off, scattering over the walk like porcelain worms. Rick whirled in a circle, and by some miracle dislodged them all but one. And Brenda went in after him, a doll dressed in a black suit, and jabbed the pruners into the face. The doll fell back, the face cracked and shattered.

Freed, Rick picked up the hoe and began chopping at them. They fell, ripped and torn, the straw of their bodies scattering on the grass and on the walk, their doll heads shattered to pieces of china that lay on the grass like white snowflakes; and the night grew still again except for Jessica's cries, waning to sobs now as she came in among the straw and bits of glass and bent to pick them up and hold them in her hands.

"My dolls. My dolls. Oh, my dolls.

Brenda stared at her, disbelieving. Jessica seemed unaware that her dad lay on the ground in a bloody sprawl, still as death, perhaps dead.

Rick was leaning on the hoe handle, breathing heavily. One side of his face had been scratched by the four pointed fingers of the hand Brenda had cut away, and blood welled.

"Call an ambulance," he said.

Brenda ran into the kitchen and to the phone on the wall and began to leaf through the telephone book that hung on a cord beneath it, then she realized that the only light came in through the windows and door from the yard lights. She reached for the wall switch. Then she called an ambulance service.

Before she had finished, Rick came in with Jessica in his arms. She was limp against him, her face still wet, but her sobbing stopped. He gave her to Brenda.

"Can you carry her upstairs?"

"Yes."

"I'll stay with your dad."

He started back out, but Brenda said quickly. Rick. What about the police?"

Rick stopped, one hand on the screen door. "What about them?"

"Won't we have to call them?"

"What for? All we have to show is pieces of something as brittle as glass, some shreds of old clothes, and straw. What are they going to believe? Let's just handle it the best we can. Your dad is still alive. He's unconscious, but as far as I can tell the wounds aren't deep enough to kill him. Take the little girl to bed. I'll handle this."

"What about your face, Rick?"

He pulled out a handkerchief and wiped at it. The blood was drying rapidly and looked on his face like exposed veins. He shrugged and put the handkerchief back into his pocket.

"I'll wash it later and put some iodine or something on it. It's all right." He looked at Jessica. "I wonder if there are any more of those little bastards around somewhere?"

"I don't know. *I don't know*. What *were* they, Rick?"

"Damned if I know. Dolls. Hers. Jessica's. She called them her dolls. Didn't you hear her?"

"But —"

"It must be tied in with the rest, somehow. We may never understand it. I've got to get this mess cleaned up."

He went on out onto the porch, and Brenda carried Jessica toward the front of the house. She met Della on the stairs. The young girl's face was pale, her eyes large and staring.

"What — what's going on?"

Della's room was in a wing of the house that had two bedrooms, a service stairs, and was otherwise isolated from the main part. Brenda had even forgotten she was there.

Instead of answering her question, Brenda asked, "Could you stay with Jessica, Della?"

"Sure. Give her to me. She's too much of a load for you."

Della took Jessica, and Brenda realized her arms

294

were trembling weakly. "Thank you, Della. Put her back to bed and sit with her. There's been an accident. The ambulance will be coming for my dad, so don't let it disturb you."

She left Della standing there with Jessica cradled in her arms, staring after her. When she reached the foot of the stairs she looked back, and Della, prodded on, moved out of sight.

In the utility room Brenda got a small plastic tub, filled it with warm water, took a couple of washcloths and went out to kneel beside her father. Rick had turned him onto his back. Her throat contracted with rising nausea as she looked at him, but she swallowed and it eased. She began to bathe the blood from Paul's face.

Rick came, bringing a rake from the garden shed, and began raking the debris from the dolls into a pile.

By the time the ambulance arrived, the yard was neat again, the straw and china bits raked up and dumped into the big plastic trash can.

Brenda had bathed most of the blood from Paul's face, and saw that the lacerations were deep, and many stitches would be required. He had begun to stir, and to groan, but then he seemed to fall asleep.

When the ambulance drivers came they looked suspiciously at Rick. But only said, "let's get this guy moving."

Brenda and Rick stood by the gates that opened in the breezeway and watched the ambulance pull away. A few minutes later they followed in Rick's car.

It was midmorning before they returned home. The

last few hours of the night had been spent in the hospital waiting room. Paul regained consciousness at dawn, but only for a few minutes before a sedative put him to sleep. The police had come, and Rick and Brenda were questioned. But there was nothing they could say, except, "We found him in the yard, like this."

"What happened to your face?"

"Just an accident," Rick said. "Look, I'd like to take Miss Norris home now."

"Go ahead. We'll ask Mr. Norris about this. Meantime, stay around."

"I intend to."

Brenda felt dizzy with exhaustion and the confusion caused by the clash with a reality foreign to the world she knew. In the car she leaned her head back and rested with her eyes closed, but her mind worked furiously. She reached for Rick's hand, and felt it close tightly over hers.

"Rick, it's got something to do with that old house. When you cross the threshold of that house you can feel its—its evilness. Things are different in that house. Those dolls came out of the house. They fit the era. They were old dolls, antique dolls, made with china heads and hands, with bodies stuffed with straw. They were dressed in clothing made before the nineteen hundreds. Those dolls belonged to some little girl who lived then. It all ties in, Rick. The ghost I saw, and heard, and the manifestations in that house. Jessica has, somehow, released those forces. We haven't seen it all, Rick, and I'm terrified. What can we do?"

His hand gave hers a squeeze that was briefly painful. "Go home and sleep. That's the first thing."

Yes, she thought, with her head spinning inwardly with its mixture of exhaustion and confusion. First, sleep, and maybe they would wake to find it had all been a nightmare of their own creation.

Jessica had been watching for a chance to slip away, but Della wouldn't let her go. Brenda and the strange man had come home, and gone upstairs, but before she went up, Brenda had stood in the doorway looking at her, and said to Della, "Keep an eye on her, will you, please, Della?"

"Yes. She's been wanting to go out into the yard and play."

No, Jessica thought, as she pretended to get interested in her colors, her books, her art supplies. She hadn't said she wanted to go out into the yard to play. Grownups didn't listen. She had only said she wanted to go. They were trapping her. She wanted to go to her mother, to tell her that these people had killed her dolls. She wanted her mother.

She looked up to find she was alone. Brenda had gone, and so had Della. Jessica kept her hands busy, in case they came back, but she listened for sounds in the hall.

A few minutes more she stayed at her desk. The television droned a cartoon, but Jessica didn't know what it was.

She got up, brushed her hands together to rid them of chalk, and went to the doorway into the hall to make sure no one was hiding there just around the corner. The hallway was empty.

She went to the window that looked out over the corner of the back yard. Della, or someone, had raised the window, and soft air pushed in the draperies that hung over the edges of the sill. Jessica leaned into the window and unhooked the screen. A moment later she was dropping into the grass.

She carefully kept out of sight. She had made a private path around the edge of the yard, behind tall shrubs, around the pond, and to the corner of the yard where the wire fence met the brick wall. Climbing over there was easy and fast. She hurried, anxiety pushing her, afraid she might have been followed by the man who had chopped her dolls to pieces.

In the meadow her spirits soared with freedom. She was safe. She had escaped. The tall grass of the meadow brushed her face as she ran through it. The lower stands of clover tickled her knees and thighs. She ran joyously, calling softly, "I'm coming, Mother. I'm coming. Mother. Mother."

The word *mother* was soft on her lips, a lovely word that she repeated and repeated as she hurried to her castle.

She slowed at the threshold, blinking at the cold darkness inside. The loneliness of being without her dolls came down over her like a dark cloud. She had to tell her mother what had happened.

She went toward the stairway, the cold washing over her and bringing little ripples of goose bumps along the backs of her arms. "Mother," she said as she climbed the stairs, and carefully turned her back to the dungeon drop in the stairway as she had

298

learned to do so she wouldn't be afraid. *Don't look down*, something told her each time, speaking within her head almost like her dolls had done. *Don't look down*. So she didn't. She looked out over the hall below instead, and today it seemed like looking off a great, high cliff. A mist was swirling there, near the floor, like the mists that rose out of the swamp, only thicker, and swirling faster and faster. She stood still, looking down into it, but she began to be afraid, and she shut her eyes tightly and edged on past the hole, and kept edging on, walking with her toes on the bottom board of the railing, her hands gripping the top. When she reached the landing she opened her eyes and looked down over the railing to the hall below. There were only deep shadows there now. The swirling mist had gone.

But something drew her eyes back to the stairway below, and she saw that the mist was coming along the stairs after her, rising slowly, forming into a tall figure of white.

Jessica walked backwards along the landing, stumbling at last against a riser where the stairs started again going on to the hall above. The figure of mist was becoming plainer the nearer it came, and was turning to the lady with the long white gown, the lady with hair flowing down her back. She could see her face now, a pale oval, with dark holes where the eyes should be, and a mouth that was smiling. . . .

Smiling.

The lady floated up the stairs, her long white gown brushing the steps, the golden hair trailing over her shoulders, the eyes taking shape and looking at her.

"Mother!" Jessica's voice trembled. She shook with excitement. This was her mother, the lady in the portrait, but her face was beautiful, not ragged and torn like the painting was now. Her mother was coming to be with her, and Jessica cried out again, "*Mother*."

The lips were smiling . . . no, no.

Not smiling.

The hands were reaching out toward her, but Jessica drew in her own hands and arms and skin, afraid, somehow, even in her happiness. Her mother was reaching for her, but the long, long hands seemed to be poised in the air, above Jessica, arching down, like a hawk going after its prey.

The pain started at her shoulders and ripped down over her arms, and Jessica cried out and looked down, and saw red streaks of blood appear. Her eyes sought the face of her mother again, and saw the lady towering above her, and beginning to bend, as if she would smother Jessica with her flowing gown and her hanging hair, and the mouth was drawing back and becoming an open gash, silent but threatening.

"No, Mama, no!" Jessica heard the scream, *no, Mama, no*, and it sounded familiar, vaguely, like something she had heard once, long, long ago. Her memory struggled to place it. It was herself crying out, and yet it was someone else.

Her mother was angry with her today. She was going to hurt her. This was one of her mother's bad days.

"I didn't do it, Mama, I didn't!" Whatever it was she had done wrong. What had she done? Something

300

began switching her, hard, across her back, her arms, her legs. She saw only a blur of something thin and wild as it rose and fell in her mother's hand.

Run, run, the voice told her, the one that spoke within her head. And she obeyed it and ran up the stairs and down the hall toward her room, toward her dolls. They would help her. They always had. They would help her and keep her from her mother while she was so angry.

Behind her the footsteps came, sharp heels hurrying, snapping against the wood floor, and another voice whispered along the hall like breaking ice, *"Annabelle, how dare you run from me. Annabelle."*

Jessica slammed the bedroom door and paused, looking into the room that seemed bare and empty now without the big dolls. Sunshine through the window had dust motes floating in the air, and the house shook with the sounds of the footsteps, hurrying, hurrying, and the voice that seemed to come from all around her.

"Annabelle. Annabelle—"

Not the dolls this time, but her mother.

Sobbing, blinded by her tears, Jessica ran to the open window and climbed through, dropping down onto the roof of the porch below. She crept to the edge of the rotting shingles, and reached for the limb of a tree whose branches brushed the top of the porch. She grasped the branch and slipped off the roof. She felt a jarring of her body as she struck the ground, and a blackness swept through her head, rocking her softly away from her pain and her fear and that other thing that was worse than all—the crushing hurt of her mother's anger.

The next thing she knew she was in the meadow, stumbling along, weeping, going toward the corner of the brick wall and the wire fence.

She would wait, wait until her mother felt better. Maybe tomorrow would be a better day. The tears began to tickle her cheeks, and she wiped them away. At the fence she rested awhile, then she climbed over and went to a bench by the pond. She stretched out there, her face on the cool wood slats. Several minutes later she got up and slipped back into the house.

CHAPTER EIGHTEEN

Brenda woke, feeling an urgency, an anxiety that was overpowering. She got up and dressed quickly. A glance at the clock told her she'd been asleep most of the day. She made a hurried phone call to the hospital before she went downstairs, and was told that her dad was stable. He had awakened and asked for her, but had been given another sedative by his doctor, and was asleep again.

"Please give him a message for me. It's important that he get it as soon as he wakes up. Tell him Jessica is fine. I'll be in to see him this evening."

But as she hung up the phone she wondered about Jessica, and recognized the source of her anxiety. She hurried downstairs in search of her.

Before she reached the TV room she could hear the sounds of a children's show in progress and she sighed in relief. Jessica was still in the house. She looked in to see the little girl curled into a big leather chair, her head on the chair arm, her eyes staring in total absorption.

Brenda breathed a sigh of relief, part of her anxiety lessening. At least Jessica was safe.

She went on into the kitchen to find Della at the sink washing salad material for dinner.

"Has Jessica been watching television all day?"

Della nodded. "She wouldn't even come out for lunch, so I took her in a tray."

"I'll go in and stay with her. I didn't check Rick's room. Has he been down?"

"No, not that I've seen. Will you want dinner at the regular time?"

"Earlier, if you can. I'll need to go see Dad, so maybe you can put Jessica to bed again?"

"Yes."

Brenda went into the silence of the inner hall and to the TV room. Jessica didn't look as if she had moved a muscle. Brenda bent over her and lightly kissed her forehead.

"Hi, Jessica, how are you?"

Jessica didn't answer, but Brenda hadn't really expected an answer. She tried to keep her voice light and cheerful when she spoke.

"It's getting dark in here, don't you want a light on?" She turned on a table lamp as she talked, adding, "And the air is cool." She didn't want to completely close the window, shutting out all fresh air, but the darkness growing outside unnerved her. She could see again the small, unreal figures moving about on the lawn, and hear Rick's strained question again: "I wonder if there are any more of those little bastards around somewhere?" She changed her mind about the cool outside air, and pulled the window shut and locked it. Then drew the draperies.

"Jessica, I want to talk to you."

No answer. Brenda picked up the remote control

304

device and shut off the television. She heard Jessica draw a long breath, but the child didn't move. Brenda sat on the ottoman in front of her and took Jessica's chin in her hands, forcing the blue eyes to hers. She saw listlessness and sadness. Jessica moved, rising to a position on her elbow, and twisted her chin out of Brenda's hand. The blue eyes looked downward, no longer meeting Brenda's gaze.

"Jessica, where did you get the dolls?"

Jessica's mouth twitched, and she glanced into Brenda's eyes and quickly away again.

"Jessica, please talk to me. It's very important. Did you get—did you find those dolls in the old house in the meadow?"

Jessica's chin puckered, as if she were getting ready to cry. But instead she said faintly, accusingly, "That strange man ruined my dolls. He chopped them up."

"That strange man, Jessica, is my friend. His name is Rick. The dolls were killing our daddy, didn't you know that?"

Jessica covered her face with her hands, now sobbing, her body jerking with each sob. "But they were my dolls, and now they're gone. They're *my* friends."

Brenda pulled Jessica out of the chair and onto her lap, and the light from the lamp fell upon the child's arms now that she was no longer in the deep shadows of the wing chair. Brenda saw long, bloody scratches down both arms. She made a sound of surprise and horror in her throat.

"Jessica! When did this happen?"

She tried to remember—but the night before, with the nightmarish struggle with the dolls, was only a blur. It could have been easy to put it aside, as a dream is put aside and forgotten, knowing that it could not possibly be real. But she had carried Jessica into the house last night, and her arms had not been scratched and bloody then.

"Jessica, tell me."

Jessica shook her head, her hands still covering her face. The sobs ended on a long sigh. She was trembling now as if she had a chill. Brenda folded her arms around the small body, feeling a new thinness.

"Jessica, are there other dolls? Did they cut your arms?"

"No."

"Then . . ."

Brenda moved Jessica out onto her knees and lifted her shirt, not really knowing what she was looking for. But when she saw it, she was not surprised, only more horrified. Jessica's back was crossed with red welts, as if she had been severely beaten.

"Jessica, my God. This happened today, didn't it?"

Jessica nodded.

"Who? Not Della!"

Jessica shook her head, and whispered, "Mother was mad at me."

"Mother?"

Jessica nodded.

"What mother, Jessica. Tell me about her."

"My real mother. She lives in the castle."

"Is she a tall, blond lady who wears a white gown?"

Jessica nodded her head. Her lips pressed firmly together, and she was avoiding Brenda's eyes again.

"Did the lady come here today, Jessica?"

"No."

"Then you went there."

"Yes."

Brenda was silent, her own body on the verge of a chill. "Jessica, listen to me. You must never go there again. Never."

Jessica's head turned slowly until her face was away from Brenda. But Brenda could see the stubbornness there, the determination to ignore the command. Something else had to be done. But what? It was all too overwhelming. Diane's death, and Robert's, and probably Mrs. Archer's, too. Then her dad's injuries, and now Jessica's. She couldn't handle it alone. Thank God Rick was here. Later, when he was awake maybe he could help her find an answer to this. Jessica didn't realize what was happening, obviously, and Brenda was quite sure that she didn't know, either.

Meantime, until some solution could be found, Jessica must be watched constantly. If she had slipped past Della today, she could do it again unless Della, or someone, was with her night and day.

She took Jessica upstairs, bathed her, put Mercurochrome on the wounds and put her to bed, then plugged in a small television in the bedroom, hoping that Jessica would be mesmerized by it as she seemed to be at times.

"Della is going to be up to sit with you, Jessica. I don't want you to leave this room except to go to the bathroom. Della will bring up your dinner. I'm going to the hospital to see Dad this evening."

Jessica seemed not to hear her, but Brenda kissed her and hugged her, holding her a moment longer. She whispered, "I'll see you later."

On her way back downstairs, Brenda stopped at Rick's bedroom door and knocked. There was no answer. He must have been exhausted, she thought as she stood indecisively in the hallway. She needed to see him, to be reassured by his presence. She knew he was there, but she was lonely for him. Should she wake him? It would be dinnertime shortly.

She decided to wake him, and opened the door. The light from the hall illuminated the room enough for her to see that he was not there. His bed was neatly made. She closed the door and hurried downstairs. But he was not in the kitchen, or the TV room, the only two rooms that were lighted. Della was moving about in the fragrance of cooked food, setting out dishes from a cupboard.

"Della, have you seen Rick?"

"No, I haven't."

At that moment Brenda heard a door open and close, and Rick's footsteps coming across the utility room into the kitchen. She rushed to him, to feel his arms around her comfortingly close, even so briefly.

"Sorry I got back so late," he said softly, privately. "I'll tell you about it when we're alone."

Brenda released herself from him and went to help Della.

"We'll eat here in the kitchen, Della. Jessica won't be down. Would you mind taking a tray upstairs for you and her? And I'd like you to sit by her bed until I get back from the hospital. It's very important that you don't leave her."

A few minutes later when they were alone Brenda told Rick about the signs of physical abuse on Jessica's body.

308

"The manifestations have become physical, Rick, and she has to be kept away from the old house. She slipped out today, somehow, without Della seeing her, and went there. She's calling someone there her mother, and by the description, it's the same — apparition I saw bending over her here. If the woman came here once, she can come again. What are we going to do?"

"We're going to confront it — everything there."

"What?"

"Today I went to the library and read a few old, old articles on ghosts. The serious kind that was written back when people didn't doubt the existence of such things. I came away with a little bit of ammunition about how to protect yourself from such things. And, I also went to the City Hall for information about the place, and there seems to be a mystery surrounding the people who last lived there. The man, the owner, Thomas Blahough, lived there in the late eighteen hundreds with his wife, Dorabelle. They had three children, a boy, Zachary, a girl, Annabelle, and a third girl, Mary Ann. There is only one recorded death. Thomas Blahough — " He took a piece of note paper from his pocket and read from it, "was thirty-seven when he died by his own hand on December twelve, eighteen-ninety-nine. That was all the information I could get from the old records, but a woman in the office told me to go see Vivian Blahough, a niece of Thomas's, and his only known surviving relative. She's a marvelous old lady. About ninety, I'd say. Fragile, delicate, but with a mind as sharp as a blade. She talked and talked. I wished you could have been along to meet her — but maybe you already have?"

"I've seen her at church, but that was years ago. There were two of them, two sisters who never married. I thought I had heard the other had died."

"She did, Miss Vivian told me, last year. She lives alone in a big house on the other side of town—but I guess you know where she lives, too. Except for a combination companion-housekeeper. She showed me a photograph of the Thomas Blahough family. The man was bearded, the woman beautiful. Nobody smiled. The kids were cute. The youngest hadn't been born when the picture was taken. The boy and girl were about four and five years old then. Anyway, Miss Blahough told me she couldn't remember her uncle, but that his suicide had caused quite a scandal in the family. After that his house was just closed and left as it was, because his wife, Dorabelle, and the children would probably be back to claim it in time, it was figured."

"What happened to them?"

"She didn't know. They simply disappeared. It was assumed in the family that for some reason Dorabelle took her children and left."

"Why didn't you wake me up when you left today, Rick?"

"I looked in on you, and you were sleeping so soundly I didn't have the heart. You were up all last night. You'd only been asleep a couple of hours. I just couldn't wake you. And I didn't feel like I could wait. There's an answer to this somewhere, and it has to be in that old house, just as you said. I'm going over there and confront it."

"No you're not," Brenda said adamantly.

310

He blinked in surprise. "What?"

"You're not going there alone. I'm going with you."

"No, you're not —"

"I am. Rick, I insist. I won't let you go there alone."

They stared at each other, and finally Rick relented. "I would rather you didn't, Brenda," he said quietly.

"I know, but how do you think I would feel knowing you're there alone?"

"Aren't you going to see your dad tonight?"

"Yes, and you're going with me. If I have to, I won't leave your side. I'll chain myself to you, to see that you don't go alone."

"In that case, I guess we'd better wait until tomorrow morning."

"We most certainly will. Nothing could get me back into that house after dark. My experiences there were bad enough in the middle of the day."

When they had finished dinner they went to the hospital and Brenda stood by her father's side, his hand in hers. His face was bandaged loosely, the white coverings leaving only his lips and eyes exposed. The night nurse stood across the bed from Brenda and Rick.

"He's been incoherent," the nurse said, in sick-bed tones. "He's been saying something about Jessica, robots, ropes, and Robert. He gets very agitated. His doctor said to keep him sedated. He asked for you once or twice during the day, and he asked about Jessica."

"Was he given my message?"

"I'm sure he must have been. But I have it here —

311

the one about Jessica?" Brenda nodded yes. The nurse said. "I'll tell him again if he wakes. Meantime, there's no need for you to stay. He probably won't be awake again until sometime tomorrow. He's doing well. The vital signs are good."

"You will call me immediately if there are any changes?"

"Of course, Miss Norris."

Brenda wondered at times during the evening and night how it would have been if Rick had not come and was not with her now. At times when she felt it could get no worse, she reminded herself that yes it could, Rick might not have come. He might have gone on north instead, lost to her forever. She would have had to stand alone at the side of her father's bed, and later at home by Jessica's, when the true night fell with such heaviness and darkness.

He left her at midnight, at her insistence. She had slept all day; he had not. He didn't want to leave her alone, but she told him, assured him, she'd be all right. Della had been sent to her own room when they returned from the hospital. Jessica, she had said, had slept peacefully all evening. But that changed at midnight, when Rick was gone to bed too, and Brenda sat alone in the shadows of Jessica's room.

Perhaps it was her own apprehension, Brenda thought, that brought it on. But while shadows seemed to deepen and grow, changing form subtly around her, Jessica began to be restless, to stir, to turn from side to side, to toss her head back and forth on the pillow, and to whimper.

The beginnings of a nightmare, Brenda was sure,

and took Jessica's hand in hers. The child grew still for a while, with only her head turning occasionally. The small hand was ice cold, and did not warm even when Brenda cupped it protectively between her own palms. She could feel it flutter occasionally like a trapped butterfly.

Death, thought Brenda unwillingly. Not ice, *death*. Death cold.

Would she lose all her family before it was over? Before *what* was over?

It was even more terrifying to realize there was no name she could put to it. There were no explanations that would be acceptable to anyone who had not been here, and had not seen it. Antique dolls did not awaken in abandoned old plantation mansions and follow a small girl without harming her, then kill her mother, her brother, and perhaps even her father. And Mrs. Archer?

No, there were no explanations.

Thank God she had not seen it alone.

But there was more. The house still stood, and inside it the netherworld that spawned the impossible. Would burning it help, or would the fire only drive its inhabitants within other walls? Here, perhaps. To these walls, where already at least one visitation had occurred.

There was a sound in the hall, a single footstep, or the skirt of a long gown brushing against the wall. Only one sound. Brenda stared over her shoulder at the open door. Minutes passed. The sound was not repeated, but Brenda couldn't take her eyes from the doorway. She wished she had closed the door. But when Rick had kissed her goodnight there, the open door seemed to forge a link between them.

She got up, finally, and went as quietly as she could to the door and looked down the hall. It was empty. Shadows hung beside furniture and in open doorways.

She stepped back into the room and pulled the door shut, then she snapped on a small lamp in the corner, and all the shadows that remained were thrown behind and beneath the bed.

Jessica drew a long sigh and turned over, and her breathing became deep and even.

Brenda sat in the chair by the bed and finally leaned over onto the bed and slept too, too tired to realize how uncomfortable she was.

They crossed the meadow shortly after sunrise. Mists still swirled among the trees in the swamp and spread out over the meadow, untouched yet by the warmth of the sun. They walked without talking, the dew on the meadow dampening the legs of their jeans.

When they reached the fence that held in the jungle of growth around the plantation mansion, Brenda pointed at the corner and said in a very low voice, as if she dreaded awakening someone, "There's the gate."

Rick took her hand. "Let's go around. I'd like to get an idea of how big it is. How much grounds are around it."

"I don't think there's a lot. Most of it was given over to the meadow, and then the swamp starts just over there at that line of trees."

They followed the surrounding fence, and from the

side the house was clearly visible within the trees, no more than twenty feet from the fence. The back yard was broader, with less growth. At the southwest corner they came upon the cemetery. A few trees grew within it, but there seemed to be less undergrowth, and again the house was visible, the long back porch, the shuttered windows, and two doors, one closed, one open.

Rick was looking around in the meadow outside the fence, and after a few minutes he said, "Unmarked graves. Servants, do you suppose?"

Brenda peered into the grass and saw two small stones, upright in the ground, rough-edged and with only the faint scratchings of names no longer legible. "Pets maybe?" she offered.

"Could be. Whoever, or whatever, they were, they didn't deserve being buried inside the family graveyard. Think you can climb over the fence with a little help? Without ripping your clothes?"

"Yes."

"Good, let's go."

They climbed through, each holding the barbed wires up for the other.

The ground in the family cemetery seemed mushy, almost swamplike. Vines grew thickly, a good solid cover that possibly concealed snakes, Brenda thought as she followed behind Rick. He brushed vines back that had grown over taller stones, gravestones that had angels at the top, or praying hands or crosses. The names and dates beneath were crusted with moss, but still readable.

"Blahoughs," Rick said. "This must be the grandfather and the grandmother, died in eighteen ninety-five

315

and eighteen eighty-one. Grandmother lived longer. She was . . . um . . . seventy-eight."

He was talking aloud to himself, it seemed, and Brenda went along beside him from tombstone to tombstone without comment. They came to the last elaborate stone.

"Here he is," Rick said. "Thomas Blahough, *May God Forgive*, eighteen sixty-two to eighteen ninety-nine."

Brenda saw the gate in the iron fence, but Rick didn't go to it. He began to kick the vines aside in the inner corner of the plot where no tombstones stood. Finally he grunted and stooped, digging aside the vines with his hands.

"See? Some more unmarked graves. Two of them. Whoever buried these people for some reason wanted the graves marked but unidentified." He sat on his heels, looking out over the small graveyard at the other stones. "They're family, or they wouldn't be here, right? And why do they have only this kind of stone? And why are there only two? You see . . ." He stood up and hooked his thumb in his pockets. "It didn't seem logical to me that a woman would take her three kids, one of them a baby, and leave. Just disappear and never be heard from again. My thought is that some kind of tragedy occurred here, before Thomas Blahough killed himself. What do you think it was?"

Brenda stared at him. "Of course," she said. "That's why there's the materialization of a woman. The one Jessica has started calling Mother. It's his wife. She wouldn't be haunting this place if she hadn't died here, would she?"

"Not according to all literature on the subject. Hauntings occur where the death occurred, and within walking distance of it, you might say. It's as though the people are trapped. But there should be four graves, not two. If the man's wife is buried in one, which of the children is in the other? And Tom himself must have buried them, and then turned right around and killed himself. He didn't take the time to have tombstones brought in. But what happened to the other two children?"

Something drew Brenda's gaze toward the house, the crumbling back porch, and the open door at the far end. She gasped audibly, startled, her heart jumping into a smothering beat. A man, dressed in black, with a black beard obscuring most of his face, stood in the deep shadows of the doorway.

"Rick!" she hissed, clutching his arm.

Rick turned and looked, and a second later the man in black withdrew into the house, but the door remained standing open.

"Rick," she whispered, "Was he *real*?"

"Sure looks like it." He led the way toward the narrow gate, then paused and looked at the fence. A portion of it was leaning, and the iron pickets had come loose at the bottom. They were spiked, sharp as lances at the top. Rick took hold of one and wrenched it free. "Just in case he wasn't," he said, "iron is supposed to be one of the protections against ghosts."

The gate had to be opened. The fence was five feet high, and the iron pickets were spaced no farther than eight inches apart. They were topped too with the sharp, spearlike headings. The only way out of the cemetery was to go through the gate, or go back the way they had come. Rick opened the gate. It let out a long, rusty squeal.

The nearer they came to the house the colder Brenda became. *I don't want to go in there,* she thought frantically and in silence. But she stayed close beside Rick, because she knew he would go without her, and she didn't want that, either.

However, when they reached the porch and were crossing it to the open door, she grabbed his arm and stopped him. "Rick," she whispered. "Maybe we shouldn't. He was no ghost, Rick, he was real."

Rick paused and looked at her thoughtfully. "Isn't that better?" he finally said. "Would you like to wait out here?"

She didn't bother with an answer, and went into the kitchen right behind him.

It was dark, the windows letting in only enough light to allow them to see the tables, the benches, the ancient black stove that was brown with rust in places as if a blight had been inflicted upon it. Across the room another doorway led into an even deeper darkness.

"Hello," Rick said aloud, unexpectedly, causing Brenda to jump. His hand gripped hers and squeezed it reassuringly. In a much lower voice he said, "If he's real, he'll answer. If he's not he'll show up again, because I think he wanted us to follow him."

They waited. The silence in the house seemed so intense that it had sounds of its own, a throbbing, like the beating of a dozen hearts, or the memory of those beats.

Brenda became aware that someone stood, motionless, in the darkness of the hall.

She whispered urgently, "*Rick.*"

He saw it too, she could tell by the sudden tense-ness of his arm against hers. They started forward, Rick slightly in the lead. When they reached the hall they could see the man in black, no more than fifteen feet away. He was waiting for them, still and dark and in shadows, his face obscured even more. He turned when they came into the hall and went ahead of them. He went though open double doors and disap-peared.

When they came to the doors Brenda saw they were in the front hall, the large room where the staircase rose. Rick stopped, pulling her up against his side. A jerk of his arm drew her attention to the right. The man was standing there, facing away from them. As if he had been waiting for them to catch up, he disappeared again, and this time through a closed door. It was as if he had stepped into the wood. It was a small, narrow door beneath the staircase, Brenda saw.

Rick went to the door and tried the knob, but the door didn't open. "Locked," he murmured, and stooped to look at the metal plate, bringing out a small object from his pocket. He leaned the iron picket against the wall. "It's got the regular old-fashioned lock. Fairly easy to open. I thought there might be some locks we'd have to open, so I asked Miss Blahough if she had any old skeleton keys, and she gave me one." He glanced over his shoulder at Brenda. "I also asked her if we could look around this old house, and she said yes, but she said be careful, because it's probably falling down by now. It looks in better shape than I thought it would. You okay?"

Brenda nodded.

The door opened, and Rick slipped the key back into his pocket and drew out two tiny flashlights. He gave one to Brenda. "Brought a couple of these, too." He picked up the iron picket and pushed the door inward slowly.

The room beyond was small and dark, without other doors, without windows. It was no more than ten feet square, with a sloping ceiling, and furnished with one high-backed desk and one chair.

Rick's light suddenly fell upon a white face, back in the corner of the room. When Brenda glimpsed it her heart threatened to stop again, and then pounded with such force she felt faint. A child stood in the corner. A child in a long, elaborate dress, and long curls. Its lovely face stared out into the darkness of the room, as if the thin beam of light directed upon her did not exist. Then Rick spoke, his voice startling in the silence.

"Another doll." He paused. "A beauty. Life-sized, wouldn't you say?"

Brenda felt a terrible fear move over her, but Rick was going toward the doll, touching it, raising its arm, letting it fall again.

"Rick . . ."

"It's okay," he said. "This doll has been stored here. It's just a doll."

So there were others, she thought, but at that moment Rick shined his light upward, and Brenda saw the hole in the stairs above, the end of two risers hanging down, almost brushing the top of Rick's head.

He moved away from the doll and began looking around the room. "For some reason he wanted us to come in here. Was this his private hideaway? An office of some kind?" He began looking through papers in the cubbyholes of the desk. He opened drawers, and closed them.

Brenda turned her own light on the doll, suspicious of it, terrified of it, though it looked as if it had not moved, or been moved, in a century.

"Here," Rick said suddenly. "Look, Brenda."

She went to his side. He was holding a small, jeweled box. When he opened it a tinny little tune began to play. Inside the box was a yellowed sheet of paper, with an ink-scrawled writing on it.

Rick poised his light beam on the paper and read aloud, "I, Thomas Blahough, am now alone. I came back from a business trip to find that all the servants had been dismissed, and many rooms of the house stained with the blood of two of my children. The baby, dead in her cradle, and my son on the floor beside her. And my wife, with blood on her hands. Annabelle, my dear daughter Annabelle, is gone. I pray she has escaped to safety. And now I, too, have killed. I could not let her live, not after she had killed so brutally her own children, our own children. I would go to my own grave in silence, except that I cannot but leave behind an explanation of why I must end my life with another gun blast. I came home to find my wife had killed two of our children, and so I shot her, and I buried her in a grave in the graveyard with the baby she hated in her arms. In a grave beside her, I buried Zachary. Poor Zachary, only nine years old, and there is no way I can put that information on his stone. Annabelle, my sweet daughter, if ever you return, and if ever you find this note, please know that I love you and hope you have found happiness. You have gone away without your lovely new doll, so I have brought her here with me. When I have finished my message to you, I will go onto the back porch, and there I will end my life. Good-bye, Annabelle."

The door slammed shut.

Brenda screamed and whirled. Rick threw the narrow beam of his small light toward the corner, and Brenda saw what he was looking for.

The doll was gone.

CHAPTER NINETEEN

Della had chosen to read to Jessica. It was the only way she could keep the child under her eye without feeling useless. Just sitting in front of the television seemed to her a wanton waste of time. Her own mama had used the television as a reward for work well done. They had never been allowed to watch it more than two hours a day, and they chose those two hours from time left over after all the homework and chores were done. So to sit with Jessica in front of the television made her feel sinful. It was better to read. And she did so almost frantically, aware of Jessica's wish to leave the house. But Brenda had left very strict orders: get the child up, dress her, feed her, stay with her. *Don't let her out of sight.* That was important. Strange things were going on, and Della didn't know what they were, but she was beginning to feel very nervous. A job that at first had seemed ideal, was becoming a job she wished she hadn't taken.

Della yawned. Jessica didn't seem to like "Goldilocks" any better than she had "The Red Shoes."

Della chose another story in the fat book, one she couldn't remember: "The Snow Queen."

"Sounds good, huh?" Della offered conversationally, yawning again. Jessica was sitting on the footstool in front of her, staring, her eyes hypnotic in their steadiness. Della yawned again, and lay her head back just for a second.

Jessica watched her, scarcely breathing. *Sleep, Della. Sleep.*

Della began to snore softly, her mouth falling open, her head edging sideways to rest on her shoulder.

Jessica moved stealthily, slipping without sound off the stool, tiptoeing to the door, and then running. She didn't want to be in this house with these people. She wanted to go home to her castle, to her mother.

"It isn't working," Rick said, turning the key in the lock. The sound of the tumbler clanked mechanically each time Rick turned the key, yet the door remained shut. The knob turned, without result. "It's no use," Rick said, and put the key back into his pocket.

"Someone's holding it from the outside?"

"I don't know." Rick put his shoulder against the door and shoved. The door was like part of the wall. "Not someone," he added, breathlessly. "Something. Did you notice if there was a bolt on the outside?"

"Why would there be?"

Rick shrugged. "Just trying to think of something." He stood looking at the thick wood of the door, as if he might be able to figure some way through it.

They had been keeping their voices very low, almost whispering, as if both of them felt other presences in the house and wanted to stay hidden from them. Yet Brenda felt that it was known where they were, by more than one. As if the house were filled, or was filling, with things unknown. Their small lights were beginning to seem like little more than matches. The room, though small, was filled with darkness hardly touched by the lights.

There was a sound beyond the door suddenly, that made Rick stare briefly at Brenda. A door opened, and closed, and was followed by quick little steps. Brenda held her breath. *It couldn't be. . . .* She whispered, "Not Jessica! Rick, that's Jessica out there. How did she get away from—" She stopped, her voice frozen.

The other footsteps were overhead, the sharp, threatening steps of a woman wearing heels. They were coming along a wood floor overhead, and then dropping hastily, down the stairs, right above their heads.

Jessica cried out, "Mother!" A joyous sound. The footsteps kept coming, farther down, into the lower hall.

They stopped approximately where Jessica's steps had, and Jessica cried out again, tearfully, *"Mother! Mother! No!"*

Brenda pushed against the door, screaming as loudly as she could. "Jessica! Get away from her! She's not your mother! Run, Jessica!"

Jessica's scream drowned out the last of her words,

and Brenda looked at Rick helplessly. "Oh my God, Rick. We've got to get out of here."

His eyes found the fence picket, leaning in the corner. He grabbed it and aimed the pointed end at the door. "Move back. We'll break it down."

Jessica stumbled backwards away from the cruel reach of the hand. Blood dripped from the fingers, and the face was one she had seen before but hadn't remembered until now. This was the face in her dreams, the one Annabelle was so afraid of. The blood on her hands was Zachary's blood. She had just killed him, and she saw him standing on the stairs, his face torn and bleeding, mutilated so that she didn't know what he looked like anymore. He was dead, but he was standing on the stairs. Just standing, blood running from his torn mouth. The darkness lowered and swirled around him, obscuring him. But it didn't matter. She had seen him only because he was on the stairs behind Mother. It was Mother whose face terrified her, because this was the mother in her nightmares. When she became Annabelle. And Mother was going to kill her, too.

"No! No, Mother!" She screamed, feeling the hands lifting her from the floor. The walls were turning, falling it seemed, speeding past. Terrible noises were all around. Upstairs the painting was thumping furiously against the wall, shaking the house. The doors slammed and slammed. And somewhere down here there was a crashing of wood. A vague memory tugged at her mind. Brenda . . .

Brenda? Hadn't she heard Brenda's voice calling to her? Still calling to her? To someone named Jessica? Run, she was saying, run, Jessica. But she didn't know . . . how helpless she was in her mother's hands.

She felt herself being thrown against a wall, and she glimpsed something—someone—coming behind Mother. A girl. Like her. With long golden curls, wearing a dress of lace and ruffles. No, not a girl. But another doll. Annabelle's new doll. The back of Jessica's head crashed against the wall, and pain shot through her eyes, in colors like a rainbow, and she felt herself lying crumpled on the floor, unable to move.

Brenda dropped her tiny flashlight when she began tearing at the splintered wood of the door. While Rick continued to batter the breaking wood farther down, Brenda pulled aside the needlelike shards above. As soon as it looked large enough she pushed her body in and forced herself through. Rick followed. They emerged from darkness to the pale gloom of the spacious entry hall.

The sounds in the house deafened Brenda. Something was thundering through the walls somewhere on the second floor. But the sight in the hall stopped her. Jessica was crumpled on the floor against the wall, her body twisted as if broken. Standing not far from her was the woman she had seen in Jessica's bedroom. Tall, blond, with a face not beautiful now, but turned ugly with the madness in the eyes. Her mouth was open, and Brenda felt surprised that she could even see the woman's teeth. She was as real at this time as Brenda was real. And she was turning toward them, and Brenda sensed that Rick's feeble iron picket would have no power against her.

As the thought grazed her mind Rick rushed past her, like a lancer facing his enemy, the iron picket raised and aimed at the woman's breast. She raised her hand against him, reaching out to meet the point of the picket, and her long fingers closed around it and jerked it with such force that Rick was thrown across the room. She tossed the picket aside, and it rolled to the foot of the stairs and stopped.

The woman turned and stared at something on the stairs.

The house grew silent suddenly, as if it were preparing for a confrontation long in coming.

Brenda saw Rick rise to his feet and stare too, and Brenda slipped past him and gathered Jessica up into her arms. She was limp, but still breathing. There was a laceration on her head where her hair was matted with blood. Brenda turned with her, prepared to run for the door. But then she saw what had stopped the woman and drawn her attention away.

The doll was coming down the stairs. Only she seemed now to be a little girl, real in the dim light of the hall. She moved effortlessly and without fear toward the tall, blond woman.

The thumping in the walls began again, a terrible, angry sound, as if it were the only voice the materialized ghost of the woman could command. She moved toward the little girl threateningly, swiftly, her hands

328

out, reaching her hair, jerking her. But the face of the girl remained unchanged, without fear. She fell. She seemed to fall, and rose again almost immediately, and with the iron picket in her hand.

The sounds in the house screamed through the air, so that Brenda felt her head would burst. The fury of movements was like animals in combat, so that only part could be separated visually from the rest. Brenda saw the lance rise in the hand of the girl and plunge through the body of the woman, and there came a final, terrible scream, and Brenda heard the words, "*I told you I'd kill you, Mother.*" And yet she wasn't sure she had heard anything at all.

She stared, watching immobilized as the woman stood with the lance through her body, the bloody end protruding from her back. She watched as the woman turned slowly diaphanous, her gown becoming misty, and then no more than fog dispersing. The face faded. The fog swirled slowly near the foot of the stairs, as if attempting to rise, and then was gone.

Somewhere upstairs a heavy object fell to the floor and was still.

Silence hung like a weight over the house, and the atmosphere changed subtly until it was nothing but a shell of what had once been a home, and then had become a tomb for tortured souls.

Rick went to the foot of the stairs and looked down at the thing fallen there.

The gloom in the hall was lessening, Brenda saw. The front door had opened, and the filtered green light from the outdoors was pushing away the darkness in the hall. Brenda saw it now, a beautiful doll, the doll they had seen in the windowless room. It was lying at the foot of the stairs, torn and broken, its blue glass eyes staring sightlessly upward.

A purpose had been fulfilled. The doll would not rise. The house had been exorcised by the battle between the child and the woman.

In her way, Annabelle had come home.

Jessica stirred in Brenda's arms.

EPILOGUE

Summer was peaceful, though quieter than it should have been. Brenda stayed close to Jessica, to be sure that she was safe. There was still the residue of all that had happened, though it had receded to the dwindling realm of nightmares. If Robert had been there, and Diane, and Mrs. Archer, it would have been easy to forget the few days of manifestations and terror. But they weren't there. And so the silence seemed less peaceful sometimes than just empty.

When one thing is taken away another is added. She didn't remember the exact quotation, but she agreed that Emerson was right. Rick was here. They were going to be married at the end of summer, and go their own way. By then Dad would be fully recovered, they hoped. And Jessica would be busy with school.

Brenda watched Jessica, yet there seemed to be no need. The night terrors had stopped. Abruptly. There had been nothing since that last day in the old mansion. She played, she sang, she talked more, she even laughed at times. It did something great to

Brenda's heart to hear Jessica laugh.

She was playing now, with something she was bending over, as if to hide it.

"What do you have?" Brenda asked, and looked to see a small, antique doll, dressed in a long, ragged yellow gown that once had been white. It had a china head, and tiny glass eyes that moved as Jessica rocked it. Brenda asked in astonishment, afraid it had come from the old house, yet knowing of no time when Jessica had been there again, "Where did you get it, Jessica?"

The little girl lifted her head, but she did not look at the lady bending over her. "My papa gave it to me," she said.

Why does she call me Jessica, she wondered. *My name is Annabelle.*

THRILLERS & CHILLERS
from Zebra Books

DADDY'S LITTLE GIRL   (1606, $3.50)
by Daniel Ransom

Sweet, innocent Deirde was missing. But no one in the small quiet town of Burton wanted to find her. They had waited a long time for the perfect sacrifice. And now they had found it . . .

THE CHILDREN'S WARD   (1585, $3.50)
by Patricia Wallace

Abigail felt a sense of terror form the moment she was admitted to the hospital. And as her eyes took on the glow of those possessed and her frail body strengthened with the powers of evil, little Abigail—so sweet, so pure, so innocent—was ready to wreak a bloody revenge in the sterile corridors of THE CHILDREN'S WARD.

SWEET DREAMS   (1553, $3.50)
by William W. Johnstone

Innocent ten-year-old Heather sensed the chill of darkness in her schoolmates' vacant stares, the evil festering in their hearts. But no one listened to Heather's terrified screams as it was her turn to feed the hungry spirit—with her very soul!

THE NURSERY   (1566, $3.50)
by William W. Johnstone

Their fate had been planned, their master chosen. Sixty-six infants awaited birth to live forever under the rule of darkness—if all went according to plan in THE NURSERY.

NIGHT STONE   (1843, $3.95)
by Rick Hautala

Their new house was a place of darkness and shadows, but with her secret doll, Beth was no longer afraid. For as she stared into the eyes of the wooden doll, she heard it call to her and felt the force of its evil power. And she knew it would tell her what she had to do . . .

Available wherever paperbacks are sold, or order direct from the Publisher. Send cover price plus 50¢ per copy for mailing and handling to Zebra Books, Dept. 2011, 475 Park Avenue South, New York, N.Y. 10016. Residents of New York, New Jersey and Pennsylvania must include sales tax. DO NOT SEND CASH.